ALSO BY ELSIE CHAPMAN
Dualed

DIVIDED

ELSIE CHAPMAN

WITHDRAWN

EMBER

Text copyright © 2014 by Elsie Chapman
Cover art copyright © 2014 by Michael Heath

All rights reserved. Published in the United States by Ember,
an imprint of Random House Children's Books, a division of Random House LLC,
a Penguin Random House Company, New York. Originally published in hardcover
in the United States by Random House Children's Books, New York, in 2014.

Ember and the E colophon are registered trademarks of Random House LLC.

Visit us on the Web! randomhouseteens.com

Educators and librarians, for a variety of teaching tools, visit us at
RHTeachersLibrarians.com

The Library of Congress has cataloged the hardcover edition of this work as follows:
Chapman, Elsie.
Divided / Elsie Chapman.—First edition.
p. cm.
Sequel to: Dualed.
Summary: When the Board goes after West Grayer for refusing to kill her next target,
West must uncover the truth of the past to survive.
ISBN 978-0-449-81295-2 (trade) — ISBN 978-0-449-81297-6 (ebook)
[1. Assassins—Fiction. 2. Survival—Fiction. 3. Science fiction.] I. Title.
PZ7.C36665Di 2014 [Fic]—dc23 2013045377

ISBN 978-0-449-81298-3 (pbk.)

Printed in the United States of America
10 9 8 7 6 5 4 3 2 1
First Ember Edition 2015

FOR JESSE, MATTHEW, AND GILLIAN. AGAIN.

CHAPTER 1

"If you don't watch my every move, you're going to die," I say to the girl at the end of my sword.

Naya's eyes—clenched shut as she flinches away from the swing of my arm—flash open at my words. Dark gray, and not nearly determined enough. She wavers, slashes back at me, but it's too late. Her balance is off, and it's easy for me to sidestep her sword.

She swears under her breath and tucks her hair behind an ear. "I was only . . . squinting."

I shake my head. There's less than a minute until the bell, so I let my arm drop to my side. End of weaponry class for the day.

"Sure," I say. "But remember, no matter how skilled you are in hand-to-hand combat, what good is that if you keep backing away from blades?"

"I know, but I can't seem to stop myself from doing it."

I look at her more closely. She's my last student of the day, and the one who never fails to frustrate me—which she knows. Naya's seventeen. Three years and counting until her assignment goes active, and like most Alts from Jethro Ward, she has no training outside of the Alt Skills program offered through the public school system. But she moves as fast as one who has, born with reflexes others spend years developing. This would make her one very lucky Alt—except for the fact that she's afraid.

"Naya, if you just quit worrying about getting hurt, then the motions will come more naturally and you *won't* get hurt."

"I can't help it if I pass out at the sight of blood."

"Does anyone else in your family faint?" I ask. "Could you maybe ask them how they deal with it?"

"Not anyone I know." Naya shrugs, a touch of coldness in her voice. "Not someone from *my* family, anyway."

So perhaps someone from her Alt's side, then. "What does the school counselor say? If the regular sessions aren't helping, you might want to consider exposure therapy."

"No, the talks are helping. They *are,* I swear." Distaste at the thought of sitting through hours of bloody images on a screen has her making a face. "Just not as quickly as I was hoping, I guess."

For a second I almost slip and say, *You too?* I thought maybe it was just me who was taking so long to get better. That maybe there was something wrong with me, when my counselor's words don't stop my nightmares.

"Well, how much time are you going to give it before moving on?" I wonder if I'm asking for her sake or for mine.

Another shrug, this one a touch more defiant. "I still have lots of practical instruction time with you."

"*I'm* not the one who wants to kill you."

She gives a narrowed glance at the sword in her hand. "So when are we going to be done with these things, anyhow?"

I pick up the two sheaths I left on the floor nearby and pass one to her. "Curriculum calls. Besides, as quick as a gun is, it's bloody, too." I know she understands this. But not in the same way I do. In the deepest recesses of sleep, images still surface in my dreams—my brother Luc's gun, painted with swirls of his blood and all our fingerprints, the faces of the Alts I killed so I could learn how to stay alive. My Alt.

Naya sheathes her sword. "If there has to be blood, I hope it's at least painless, if she really is going to be faster than me." *She.* As an idle, Naya's got her own shadow lurking in the corners, her Alt getting ready to come out and play when the time comes. When their assignments go active.

"Don't do that," I say to her, sounding more anxious than I mean to be.

"Do what?"

"Talk as though you've already lost." There's a ring of familiarity to what I'm saying, and it takes me a few seconds to realize where I've heard those words before. Chord said them to me right before I faced my Alt, and I wonder what he would say if he were to hear me now. Gloat, probably, but in a playful way. "You don't know what *she's* going to be like, right?" I continue. "What if actually believing you're the worthy one is the only difference between winning and losing?"

"Mind over matter." Naya nods, looking far from convinced.

"Completions can be just as much a mental game as a physical one."

"Okay, Grayer," she says, calling me by my last name as all the students under my instruction have taken to doing. "You've said that before. I haven't forgotten."

"You should really consider exposure therapy if the regular counseling's not getting you anywhere."

She exhales heavily. "Fine, I'll look into it."

Her agreement is exactly what I was hoping to hear, and it makes me glad for her. But, really, our situations aren't that much alike. And just because counseling hasn't worked for her doesn't mean it still won't work for me. Nightmares are intangible, far from real, nothing like blood. They should be easy to conquer. I just need to try harder.

The bell rings, and Baer calls for class weapons to be collected at the front. All around me students break form as they start leaving the skill stations arranged throughout the room. Each station is set up for a different kind of weapon. The area should be bigger than it is, considering that the number of accidents goes up when training space is tight, but that's a luxury not easily found in Jethro Ward.

The three students assigned to floor duty this week start sliding apart the dividers between stations and wheeling them to the walls on one side of the room; three more on setup start carting desks back to the center of the room. The fading echo of steel clanging against steel dissolves into the softer rhythms of human sounds, ones far less urgent—conversations injected with laughter, the rustle of backpacks being thrown on.

Naya gives me a quick nod before returning her sword to the cabinet. Soon enough the classroom's empty except for Baer and me.

At his desk, the school's weaponry teacher is carefully inspecting a sword that's been set aside. Probably looking for signs that repairs are needed. Since we're in Jethro Ward, we're expected to milk as many uses out of as many weaponry pieces as we can, for as long as we can, before submitting them for overhaul. His posture is at ease and close to a slouch, making him appear small. But Baer's strength isn't in bulk or stature, anyway. The guy moves as fast as a whip, his power the lean, wiry kind. He reminds me of a cat that pounces only after much planning—quick and efficient.

I sheathe my own sword. I don't doubt its beauty or its lethalness—only the class time spent on it. In a world where stealth is everything, swords are far from practical.

"I know what you're thinking, Grayer," Baer says to me as I put my sword away and shut the cabinet. "And I've already explained why I've included swords on the curriculum this year."

"What?" I protest. I grab my bag and jacket off the top of my desk and turn to face him. Beneath the overhead lighting, the scars on his skin stand out more than ever, stripes of pale silver. Baer's gaze is a cool, flat blue. I do my best to hide the smile wanting to peek out. "I didn't even say it. You heard me back you up."

"As well you should. A sword might not be Naya's weapon of choice—"

"Or any Alt's, maybe?" Nearly three months of having Baer for a boss means not having to tread so carefully around him anymore. I can annoy him and know he sees the gesture for what it is—cautious affection, trust, respect.

"—but it's sharpening her skills for whatever she does end up using when she goes active, whether she knows it or not," he finishes smoothly.

"You don't have to convince me, Baer. I might not spend as much time on it as you're obviously going to, but I get it." And I do. I remember what he said to me when I first came to this classroom. I wasn't his weaponry assistant then, only an idle, and the little sister to his dead students.

Learning how to use a weapon is never pointless. Each one of them helps with reflexes, coordination, muscle strength. At all times, you'll need the three to defeat your Alt.

"Two more days." Baer, satisfied that the sword is functional enough, opens the cabinet again to put it away before tapping in the alarm code for the cabinet lock.

"Until what?" I adjust my bag over my shoulder and double-check the clasp. The motion brings a whiff of worn leather. It's faint now, but still a reminder that it's not the canvas bag I carried all the way through my training and time as a striker. It continues to reassure me that life as an idle, a striker, is behind me, and getting farther with each passing day.

"Before we move on to something else," Baer says.

A flicker of anticipation makes me look up. "So what's next?"

"Target practice."

Finally. "And we're using . . . guns? Knives?"

Baer leans back in his chair. Crosses his arms. "You tell me."

I wonder if he's actually serious. "I get to pick for this next session?"

"You're not here for your sparkling personality, Grayer."

"So I've been told." And I already know my answer. Both guns and knives were there when I needed them, but only one saved me at the very end. "Knives, then," I say to him.

Baer nearly cracks a smile. "Why am I not surprised?"

"Well, she still manages to surprise me a lot of the time."

The familiar voice from the doorway makes me turn around. Low, husky, one I like to hear as often as I can.

I grin at Chord. "Especially if I said bows and arrows."

"Especially then, West," he says with a laugh. He nods at

Baer and asks, "How's the class so far?" Chord's not talking about levels of attendance, but expected survival rates. They're what matter around here.

"Better than last year's." As always, Baer doesn't say more than he needs to. This is his way of telling me he's happy with my work so far.

"I can be here for an hour in the morning, but then I have a math test," I tell him as I move closer to the door. And to Chord, who's waiting for me. "Sorry, I can't get out of it."

Baer sighs, impatient. "Jan not letting you off the hook?"

"No, and I really should just take the test. She's already let me put it off a couple of times, and it's obvious she's not happy about it." Where Baer pushes for an education that teaches survival through weapons, my math teacher's job is to see much farther down the road. As completes, if our only skills from school lie in knowing how to kill our Alt, our society will still be lost, only in a different way. Completion doesn't excuse anyone from having to earn a living after school is done or knowing how to properly read gauges and graph estimates to make sure you or your family won't run through allotted water or food too fast. I know Baer gets this, but it doesn't mean he has to like it.

"Fine, Grayer. In the morning, then." He turns his attention to the tablet in front of him and just like that, I'm dismissed. Typical Baer. I give him a half wave that he probably sees but doesn't bother to return, and walk out with Chord.

Who promptly kisses me as soon as we round the corner. Not blatantly or a mere touch of the lips, but just . . . the perfect in-between. Until we're alone, anyway. He carefully maneuvers us until we're half concealed from the passing crowd and standing by the door to his open locker, just outside of the weaponry classroom.

I circle my arms around him, lean against him. Not because I have to, but because I can. Through my thin cotton sleeves, pulled low over my wrists and over the nude-colored bandages carefully concealing my striker marks, I can feel the warmth of his skin. Seeping in, wrapping me up. Sometimes I wonder if I'm being foolish for trusting in us so much.

But then I'm with him, and I know better.

I gently break for air, say against his mouth, "Where's your bag? We're leaving, aren't we?"

Chord runs his hand across my cheek, the way he does sometimes. Along my scar, the last physical reminder of my Alt—other than the fact that we looked exactly alike. "Sorry, I meant to text you earlier," he says. "I'm going to be a bit, I think. Quinn slacked off all weekend and now we're behind on that chem demo. Which means him, Nash, and I have to stay behind and get it back on schedule."

"That's okay. I have an appointment with the counselor, anyway."

His fingers go still on my skin, and a flash of worry turns his eyes dark before he drops his hand. "I haven't forgotten. I'm supposed to drive you to Julis's office, right?"

I squeeze his arm. "I can take the train, Chord. It's fine."

"Actually, *you* take the car. I'll get one of the guys to drive me home, or I don't mind having to catch the train."

It'd be natural enough to accept—my brothers, Luc and Aave, taught me how to drive a long time ago, and I finally got around to officially getting my license just this month—but I know Chord won't ask Nash or Quinn to go out of their way. Which means he'll take the train, even though it makes a longer circular route once the postschool rush is over. He won't get home for a while.

Too long. And it'd be just as easy for me to take the train to and from the Grid now and save him the trouble. I try to inconvenience him as little as possible, as though each time I'm not a bother makes up for all the previous weeks and months when I was nothing but. Chord would hate it if he knew I felt this way, and deep down I know it's ridiculous, but still.

"No, really, I'd rather not," I say to him. "And I can think this way, just sitting on the train, instead of concentrating on driving." I really do need to organize my thoughts before seeing Julis. She's a doctor, paid to be observant, and I'm still getting used to being analyzed for my own good.

"I'm sorry, I wish I could drive you. I told you I would." Chord frowns, and I can see him beginning to think around what he has to do.

"Quit it." I laugh. "I'll probably be home before you, knowing how Quinn and Nash work. I mean, there's a reason why you're stuck here in the first place."

"Well, on the bright side, I'll be too busy to worry about Julis during your appointment."

"Ha."

"Ha. So you're not going to leave early this time, right?"

"I only did that because she said I could leave to regroup, Chord."

"West." He smiles softly. "You skipped two entire sessions afterward."

"And it's why I'm definitely going today," I say. And

whatever it is—the worry that still comes through in his voice, my conversation with Naya about having to do more if counseling doesn't work, the way it alarmed me more than reassured me—has me freshly determined to put the past behind me for good. I squeeze his arm again. *Trust me.* "So I should get going now, okay?"

"I'll finish up here as quick as I can. Do you want me to come pick you up after I'm done?"

"No, I'll just see you when I get back." It's approaching early summer, getting warmer by the day, and arriving home from the Grid on the train won't take long. I don't want to ever take it for granted or forget how hard-earned it was—this ability to move freely, going wherever I want, whenever I want, without fear of being hunted by someone who looks just like me, simply because only one of us is allowed to exist.

I tilt Chord's head down until our lips meet again. This time I let the kiss go on, and only the mild jeers from a handful of students walking by has the two of us breaking free.

"If you change your mind about the train," Chord says into my ear, "call my cell. Even if I'm not done here, I'll come get you."

I sink my hands into his hair, a brown so deep it's only shades removed from the dark depths of my own, before starting to ease myself loose. Easier to think when we're not touching. "Go. And don't do *all* the work."

Instead of letting me go, he tightens his grip, his hands around my waist. "Quinn is going to owe me big-time," he says, sounding resigned.

"Come by later. If you want to, I mean. Tonight." My words are still clumsy in moments like these. When I feel stripped to the bone, asking for more.

"Okay." Chord's eyes roam my face, hotter on me than even his skin felt. "I want to."

A voice from down the hall makes me jump. It's Quinn, his head peering out of a classroom. Wavy brown hair that goes down to his chin, eyes a light gray. He's registered for Baer's weaponry class but is often so behind in his other classes that he misses as many sessions as he makes. "Hey, Chord, we better get moving on this thing if we're going to get out of here anytime soon," he calls out to us.

Chord sighs. "Sorry, West. I should go, too."

I nod, and we separate. I turn away to leave but then stop. Look back at him. The compulsion to watch Chord until I can no longer see him, to be absolutely sure that he's safe, is as strong as it is sudden . . . and a bit unnerving.

He's fine, West. You're fine. No more Alts.

Right before he steps into the classroom and disappears from sight, he turns back, too. He smiles at me. I'm just being paranoid. I lift my hand in a slow, careful wave, and then he's gone.

A slight tingling in my marks has me curling one hand around the strap of my bag and shoving the other into my pocket. *The marks are the past. They're no longer who I am.*

But I can't shed them, either, and by default, neither can Chord.

Walking past the last clusters of students still lingering in the halls, I push open the heavy front doors of Torth Prep and step out onto the campus.

I look up at the sky and it's a perfectly clear blue. Only when I tilt my head down a bit do I see it arcing across the horizon—the slash of black as familiar to me as the sun, and as steadfast.

The barrier is what separates us—those who live here in Kersh—from the area out there known as the Surround. Erected by the Board, the huge iron wall keeps the city safe from the perpetual state of war just beyond it. Of course, the price for our safety is that we must always be ready to fight if the barrier is ever breached. Which means only the strongest soldiers are worthy of taking up some of the limited space here—of eating the hard-grown and hard-raised food, drinking the water that needs to be constantly filtered. The Board decided the best way to weed out the weak was for soldiers to have to face down their worst enemies, those who would make the ultimate challenge.

Themselves.

Or, as the Board calls them, Alts. An Alternate version of each person.

I beat mine months ago. Sometimes it feels much longer than that, those hours of hunting while being hunted almost blurred out by the hours I spend in art class or hanging out with Chord or Dess or my friends. But sometimes, when I'm distracted and catch a glimpse of myself in the mirror, the first person I think of is not always me.

Making my way across campus to the inner ward train station across the street, I tell myself I'm moving fast because of the afternoon heat that is already starting to cool, the need to get on the next train so I won't be late, to unload the weight of my bag from my shoulder. *Not* because of the feeling I still sometimes find hard to shake—that I continue to be judged by all those I killed and am found guilty of taking far too much, survival or not.

There's a car waiting up ahead, pulled over to the curb. It's a black sedan, nondescript, and too expensive-looking to be from around here. The low, persistent hum in the air—the engine is still running—surprises me. Fuel is far from plentiful in Kersh, especially in the poorer wards. Jethro isn't the poorest—that would be Gaslight—but we're not Leyton either.

Before I draw even with the car, it starts moving again, slowly steering back into its lane and continuing on until it's gone from sight.

I cross the street behind it, nearly running now as I get closer to the station; a train's just pulled up.

As I board it and find myself some standing room and watch the suburbs give way to the Grid, I don't give the car another thought.

CHAPTER 2

"West, any changes since the last time we talked?" asks Julis.

"Yes, it's—there *is* something new. And I wanted to talk to you . . ." Damn. I forgot how hard it is to actually say out loud the things I've seen in my head. It means inviting someone else in and letting them judge me, too.

"A new nightmare?" Julis asks quietly.

I nod, suddenly feeling more exposed than I have since I first started coming to Julis's office, and it's hard to not squirm in my seat. My counselor comes across as casual and nonthreatening, and combined with her actually not being ancient and her often-unorthodox, freewheeling approaches, she's pretty popular as far as Post-Completion Treatment doctors go. With her softly dyed blond hair—the color makes me think of early-spring sun—and her jeans and casual T-shirts, she's hardly intimidating. I like her enough as far as head doctors go, but she's still associated with the Board, and only the fact that she's bound by doctor-patient confidentiality is why she knows I used to be a striker.

"Go ahead, West," Julis says from where she's sitting in the chair across from me. "Start however you like."

"I saw *her* this time." My Alt.

"Ah, I see." Julis pushes her glasses up higher on the bridge of her nose. "Are you surprised?"

"No. Well, only that it's taken this long for her to show, I guess, considering how she was such a big part of everything that happened."

"Any theories on that?" Julis asks.

"*You're* the doctor."

She laughs loudly, the way she always does—for as long as I've been seeing her, Julis has never been one to hide her sense of humor. "And you're the one who's getting tired of having nightmares," she says gently after her laughter subsides.

My nightmares. Being chased. Being hunted again.

I exhale, look at my nails. After a very long minute, I speak again. "Maybe it means I had to make my way through everyone else before being ready to deal with her . . ." I trail off, unable to hide my discomfort at having to guess, at not knowing myself enough to be sure.

"Anything else?"

I scratch the palm of one hand. "Or that it means I was wrong when I thought I was okay with killing other people's Alts to learn how to kill my own," I say slowly. To go numb so I could stop thinking about what happened to Luc.

A few seconds of silence. Then Julis says, "Want to write out the nightmare? It might help you put in perspective why she's showing up."

I glance up at her. "You think her being there is more important than the others?"

"I think that's something for you to figure out, West."

"Right." I press the tip of the stylus harder against the tablet

I'm holding in my lap. A spiral of pixels unfurls across the screen—the words *Warning! You're pressing too hard!*—scroll across, and I force my hand to relax. I know Julis is waiting to see if I have something else to say, but my thoughts are muddled, still frustratingly tangled, so I stall by looking around the office like I haven't been coming here for weeks. Since midspring, when the nightmares refused to go away, and I couldn't deny them anymore.

No pretentious scholarly certificates anywhere; instead the walls are covered with prints loud with color. Thin bamboo mats cover the floor, and there are green plants placed everywhere, all of them real. PCT docs don't get rich on salaries funded by the Board—I saw some pretty sad offices when the worker from the Board's Post-Completion department took me through the building to show me my options—but Julis really does seem to like her job. And for an office in the Grid, this place is way better than the norm.

Julis reaches over and takes another tablet from her desk, synching it with mine so whatever I write on my screen will simultaneously show up on hers. "Let's make that list again, West," she says. "The names of the people you see in your nightmare. And then we'll tackle the nightmare itself."

"None of that's changed, except that I saw her this last time." But I start writing anyway. It's part of the treatment, the physical act of writing the nightmare. Not just typing it but actually making the hand write out the loops and dashes. The theory is that the exercise of writing out the nightmare means eventually coming to understand it, that it normalizes everything about it until its potential to cause fear is gone. I'm still waiting for it to kick in.

Their faces flash bright in my mind as I write out the names of those who show up in my nightmare. Chord. Luc. Dess. My parents. Ehm and Aave, though not as often as the others. The faces of those I assassinated as a striker. My Alt.

"Now write down what takes place in your dream," Julis says. "Step by step, right up until you wake up. I know it's not fun, but breaking the process down into simple actions will help take away the nightmare's ability to scare you."

I'm walking down the street, heading toward my house. It's dark out, and cold, so I know it's winter. There is a bloody knife in my hand, and I'm trying to clean it off with my shirt, kind of like the way people will use their shirts to clean their glasses. It's strange because the knife says I'm still a striker, but at the same time, I also know I'm already a complete. Which doesn't make much sense, writing it down now, but in the dream it just does.

I'm aware of Julis looking up from her screen to watch me as I write, but I don't glance up. Just keep putting the words down, keep hoping that this time they will finally seem more like someone else's story so reading the words won't be like reliving them.

There are footsteps behind me, but I keep walking. I don't know why I'm too scared to even turn to see who it is, but I am. I can tell in my dream that I don't want to know who it is. But the closer I get to home, the farther away it seems to get. Like how dreams can do that, make ordinary things weird, bending all the rules. So now I'm running, and the footsteps behind me are, too, even though I can't actually hear them.

"Details, West," Julis murmurs. "They'll help tie it all together."

The shirt I'm wearing is one I wore when I was a striker.

I remember it because it was the one where Chord I remember *throwing it away in a restaurant in Leyton because it was stained with blood. I don't know if it's stained in the dream because I'm wearing a jacket over it.*

My hands hurt from the cold, and that's why I'm having a hard time cleaning the knife.

The air smells like snow right before it falls, sharp and thin. It hurts my nose to breathe too deeply.

My heartbeat is loud in my ears, and I'm out of breath as I run. It all seems so real. It feels like I've been running for hours, which is crazy, but even when I'm asleep, I still totally believe it.

My hand is cramping around the stylus. I flex my fingers.

"Do you want to take a break?" Julis asks.

I shake my head. I want to get this out, and I'm sure Julis's even asking is a sort of test, that she's trying to decide if I've managed to take in any of this counseling at all. Because if I have, I shouldn't be willing to walk out again, to be okay with being a failure at this point.

"So what do you hear at the end?" she asks.

The words are coming more slowly now. They're always a bit harder for me to write, this part of the dream when I'm most terrified and nearly blind with panic. The worst is that the part of me that knows I'm dreaming can't do anything to wake up, either, no matter how scared I am. It's only after I turn around in the nightmare that it finally lets me go.

I force myself to turn around, and this is where the dream changed, this last time. Instead of Chord or Luc or one of the Alts I killed standing there just watching me, always so close no matter how far or fast or long I'd run for, it's her.

Julis sets her tablet back down on the desk and motions for me to pass her mine, too. "Here, let's just have you talk for a bit now."

"I don't mind writing it out, Julis." But I hand my tablet over, anyway, knowing I'm just protesting because I like talking about any of this even less than writing about it. Julis can be big for talking out new developments. *Let's shoot the shit the old-fashioned way,* she'd said once.

She tosses me a small bag of candy from the stash she keeps in a goldfish jar on her desk. My favorites, which I'm sure she knows. "So. Let's have at it, West. What happened after you turned around and saw your Alt?"

I open the bag of candy, begin to pick out the blues. "Normally that's right when I wake up. But she . . . talked to me."

Julis leans back in her chair. Waits patiently.

"She said that she'll always be with me," I say, trying to sound normal, pretending that a cold chill isn't crawling up my spine at the memory of her face and voice. So like mine, but not. "She said that she'll never leave me alone."

"And?"

I frown. "And what? Am I weird for being freaked out? Who wants to have their dead Alt talk to them in their sleep?"

"I didn't know you believed in ghosts, West."

"I don't. Just . . . sometimes."

"Like when?"

"I don't mean with her, or Luc, or Ehm, or Aave," I say carefully.

"So you mean . . . ?"

"I mean the Alts I killed, when I was a striker."

"Ah."

Not sure what to say next, I start sifting out the brown candies from the pile in my hand. Only reds left, already beginning to stain my palm.

"West, think back to a few sessions ago, what you said to me about why you see the people that you see."

"Shame. Guilt. Learning to live with both."

"Good, solid reasons for you seeing them, yes? So your Alt showing up . . ." She leaves it at that, and I know she's waiting for me to fill in the gaps.

"Maybe seeing her means I'm just working out the fear still," I finally say. "From being on the run. The more I see her, the faster the shock value goes down. Like exposure therapy."

Julis tugs a thread from her sleeve and lets it float to the ground. "What about the idea of her being an *active* participant in your healing?"

"That makes no sense."

"What she said to you is absolutely true—she won't ever leave you alone because, dead or not, she is always going to be a part of you."

I lift an eyebrow. "This is that technique, isn't it? When you tell me to reimagine the nightmare into something that can't scare me."

"No, it's not that. This isn't necessarily a new nightmare. Having your Alt appear at the end doesn't change the structure of your regular dream."

"It hasn't really worked, anyway. I've written out so many different versions—like I'm going to Chord's house instead, or going to school. It's like boring fan-fic or something."

"I think you seeing your Alt is a significant step, West," she says, leaning forward in her seat, her hands clasped in front of her. "I think you already know that, too."

I shake out more candies into my hand without eating them. "That maybe I'm finally ready to face what happened, and that's why it took her this long to show?"

"Ask yourself why you'd want your Alt to say something like that to you. What kind of response do you think she's looking for?"

"In other words, if it was the other way around and she was the one who was still alive, what would I want to hear from her?"

"Your Alt *is* dead, West. She's simply a reflection of something in your own head. Reason it out, just as you reasoned out why you were seeing Chord and your family and those Alts you killed."

For a long minute, I stay silent, letting what Julis told me roll around in my mind, trying to knock answers free. "I guess if she had won and I were the one who died, I would want her to be okay with me always being a part of her," I eventually say. "Physically, we were the same, you know? And even though she's the worthier one after all, she has to understand that I make up a part of her; however she beat me, I helped push her to do that, too, in some weird, twisted way." The words feel right as they pour out, and suddenly I don't feel nearly as lost as I did when I first stepped into this office today. "My Alt showing up in my dream means I have to accept that I owe *her* my life, too."

"No one ever said this Alt stuff was simple," Julis says. Her words are light, almost a quip, even though her tone isn't remotely so.

"It's not, at all. Sometimes it seems . . . hopeless."

"You're not hopeless, West. And I think you are really on your way. Today was a good day, remember that."

"Okay, what now?" I ask her, crumpling the empty candy wrapper in my hands, then immediately smoothing it out again. Restlessness, relief, confidence that there's an end in sight—that's what I feel now. "I'm really ready for all of this to be over."

"Again, none of this is simple." Julis leans down in her seat, picks up the garbage can from under her desk, and holds it out to me. I toss the wrapper inside. "So go home, do your writing exercises, and I'll see you Friday for our next session."

The late-afternoon crowd swarms around me as soon as I leave the office building and step onto the sidewalk. Rush hour is always chaos here in the Grid, and practice has me diving expertly into the mass of bodies and moving with the flow before I get knocked aside. Noise is constant and all around, alive in its own right—chatter, traffic, footsteps on dirty pavement. The heat of the day is giving way to the cooler temperatures of dusk.

Through the propped-open door of the restaurant across the street, the smell of fried noodles and brown house sauce wafts out. It is strong, mouth-watering, and reminds me that it'll be dinnertime when I get back. It also reminds me that I didn't go to the store like I should have this past weekend. I do a mental rundown of what food I have in the house and I come up empty. Crackers, hot sauce, a bag of fresh bell peppers in the fridge, iced tea—not much of a meal.

And Chord might be coming over.

And I want to see him.

A sudden wave of sheer giddiness ripples right through me, catching me so off guard that I almost stop walking. I'm grinning like a fool and notice people passing by turning to stare at me—an old woman who smiles in reaction, a mom with two kids in tow, irritated at having to navigate around me, a boy a bit younger than me with encoded eyes who has no expression at all. I cover my mouth with my hands, but the smile lingers behind my fingers, a new and fragile thing. I guess it's a smile that knows I'll see Chord soon and that I'll finally be able to tell him something good about counseling for once. Julis says it's a breakthrough, a corner being turned. And even though I don't know what's going to happen next, things feel like they're moving in the right direction, closer to the way they're supposed to be.

Impulse has me turning toward the restaurant instead of the way I meant to go, back toward the inner ward train station to get home. My pay credits from teaching at Torth are still in my wallet, as good as money, and the idea of surprising Chord with dinner simply because I want to and am able to seems perfect. The last time I brought him food unexpectedly . . . well, my intentions were twofold back then, considering I was doing it to drug him in order to keep him away from my Alt, safe.

You? Making me breakfast? In bed? No way this is happening, West Grayer. The way he shook his head, the way he laughed.

Shut up. My instant response, a typical one for me back then.

I stand aside as I wait for a customer to leave the restaurant— the entrance is too narrow to fit more than one person at a time. Just a guy, but one who is vaguely familiar, in that odd, warped way people tend to be when you see them out of context.

It clicks. "Kasey?" I call out to him.

He looks over at me at the sound of his name, and dawning recognition has him smiling. His hair is a mop of reddish brown curls, most of it hanging over eyes that are half squinted against the dropping sun. "Hey, Grayer! Whoa, it's been a while, hasn't it?"

"Since late fall, maybe?" I say, trying to place when I last saw him at Torth Prep. Right before I went active, I'd see him in the halls once in a while, his goofy bellow of a laugh reverberating off the walls like a low, pleasant rumble. But it was only because he used to hang out with Luc a bit that I knew him well enough to tell him apart from the other students. "I didn't even know you got your notice, Kasey. When did you complete?"

"How did you—"

I look at the thin black cuff strapped around his upper arm.

"Oh, yeah, of course." He grins. "Just over a month ago."

"Well, it's good to see you again." Acquaintance code between Alts for *I'm glad you didn't die, even if I don't know you that well.* Now I gesture more pointedly toward the cuff. "And this explains why you haven't been back, I guess."

The black cuff is required dress for completes on a tour. Monthlong stints of manning the barrier, tours are required of all completes, to be fulfilled once a year for five years. Protecting Kersh from the Surround during a tour is usually viewed as an honor because of the path it takes to get there, but it doesn't mean the completes have earned the right to coast. Sometimes the tour is standing guard along a portion of the barrier's length, watching for signs of it being breached. Sometimes it's collecting data brought back by drone scouts sent in the form of bot birds and bot snakes and any incoming audio over the airwaves that could be taken for assault codes and sending all of it off to the Board to be deciphered.

"Yeah, this thing." Kasey lifts his arm with the cuff and I can see the code BPS15J etched into the black label: *B* for Barrier, *P* for Patrol, and *S15J* for Sector 15, Jethro Ward. So he's walking the barrier for this tour, then, and I look over to see that his expression is both proud and weary. He meets my gaze, his face suddenly clearing. "So, heard you're working for Baer after you completed. Now, *that's* brave."

I have to laugh. "Some days I think I must have been crazy to accept."

"That guy had me cleaning knives every day after school for two weeks when I was in weaponry last year. Made the mistake of nodding off while he was talking. He wouldn't let anyone wake me up until the end of class, just so he could say I slept the whole time. Opened my eyes to the point of a blade an inch from my nose."

No, Baer wouldn't take Kasey's less-than-rapt attention too well, and I have to laugh again. Argue with Baer as much as you want, but never let him think you've got nothing else to learn. "How is falling asleep even possible, Kasey?"

He shrugs. "Not sure. I'm probably still the one and only, considering the punishment." He shifts the takeout container he's holding from one hand to the other. "Hey, Grayer, how about you?" It's how he used to address Luc—*Hey, Grayer, can I grab a ride? Hey, Grayer, let's go grab some food.* "You do a tour yet?"

"Not yet. Soon, I think." Once Julis signs off on me being fit, then I can look into registering. "So how is it?" I ask him. "You're happy with where they placed you?"

"Jethro, north side, Sector Fifteen." He flashes me the cuff again—BPS15J. "Not exactly scenic, but none of us are out there for the view, right?"

"At least they're not making you commute out of your ward every day."

"True, there's that. And I'm still getting paid the same as if I were putting in my part-time hours down at the plant. Even my crank of a boss won't argue with the Board about maintaining salary for employees on tour."

"It's really not that bad?" I ask him, unsure if I'm reading him properly. I don't know Kasey well enough to tell if he's just putting up a front for how he might really feel about being so close to the Surround every day. It's funny—all the way up until completion, tours are distant shadows without identifiable form, a vague and fuzzy danger compared to that which came with being active. Now that I'm a complete, I can feel it, sharper and more pressing.

"Compared to being active?" Kasey shakes his head. "They're so different, you know? Still a lot of walking around, looking for anything suspicious. But this time the enemy is the Surround and, well . . . hell, I don't know. It's crazy since the Surround is way more than just one person. I mean, it's the rest of the world out there, and we're not exactly friends with them. But the danger you feel . . . it's not the same."

I nod, knowing instantly what he means. The Surround wants everyone in Kersh dead, its goal to kill us all, focusing on no one person. But that's not true for your Alt, the person born to kill a single, lone target.

Yet, already I can tell what Baer and Dire would say if they were here, listening to Kasey right now. They'd tell him to wake the hell up if he didn't want to die on his first tour, mere weeks after surviving his Alt. Directly outside the barrier lies a strip of huge, tangled, thorny bushes and patches of wild horsetails as tall as a little kid and about as stubborn. We call it the Belt because that's exactly what it is, a no-man's-land measuring a hundred meters deep at its shallowest point as it encircles Kersh. It's ugly but invaluable and together with the barrier, it is what lies between the city and the Surround. To reach Kersh from the outside, this no-man's-land would be the first obstacle that would have to be overcome. But those thorn bushes and horsetails still just grow on hard earth . . . earth that enemy feet can walk on.

"The toughest part is all the alone time," Kasey continues, frowning now, that weariness coming through again. This time, there is no pride to soften it. So opposite of the guy I remember swaggering his way down the hall. "Other than occasionally seeing the two completes on watches for the sectors on either side of me, there's no one. So that part of it is like being an active again, if I'm going to compare. All that time just *thinking*. You know, a lot of what your brain cooks up can get pretty dark. Being out there by yourself, no one's around to remind you that you're a trained killer. If you forget for even a second, anything can happen."

An old man brushes past us on his way out of the restaurant and pauses to look back at Kasey. I watch his eyes fall on the black cuff around Kasey's arm and then back to Kasey's face. For a second, shadowed by the sheet metal overhang jutting out from the restaurant's storefront, he and Kasey look nearly alike, marked with shared understanding. Then the old man gives Kasey a slow nod, turns back around, and disappears into the crowd.

"I think the old dude approves," Kasey says, laughing his laugh that makes me think of Torth, of Luc, who is fading a bit more day by day. "Man, but I should get back to work. I only signed out for thirty minutes, just long enough to run out and grab some food." He gestures with the takeout container, and the whiff of grease and sauce has my stomach growling.

Kasey gives me a wave and then he's heading off, in the same direction that old man went. Both of them are completes, soldiers who know what it's like to be standing right at the barrier where the division between friend and enemy is most clearly drawn.

Chord would know, too, having finished his first tour only weeks ago.

But I learned more about tour duty from Kasey in just a few minutes than I have from Chord, ever.

He'd report to his sector right after school and not get back to his place until close to midnight. For that long month, our time together was threaded with odd, heavy silences, with Chord sometimes falling into quiet, thoughtful lapses that seemed to come from nowhere. When I asked him what was wrong, his answers didn't tell me much, always coming down to him just being tired.

What Kasey just said, about having too much time to think . . . I bet that was how it was for Chord, too. And now that he's done and home and acting normal again, I still can't figure out how real that normal is, or if it's something he does just for me.

I head inside the restaurant, where the sounds of people eating and drinking and laughing fill the air just as much as the thick scent of food. The front counter is lined with customers passing the time on their cells as they wait to be seated or for their takeout orders. Cooks and servers are yelling, but there is no anger in their voices, just urgency.

If there are actives or strikers hiding here, they've chosen well. And if there are, I feel sorry for them. Whether actives are running from their Alts or the assassins those Alts hire to kill them, I remember all too well how disappearing into a crowd means having to be someone else, someone not quite real, and you begin to wonder if you can ever really come back.

A baby's loud delighted laugh rings through the noise, high and without any reservation. That earlier rush of happiness I felt, the one that drew me here in the first place, comes back, and suddenly everything from a few minutes ago no longer seems so important—the barrier, tours, and the fact that it'll be my turn soon. I think of Julis back in her office telling me I'm not so hopeless after all and am actually on my way to getting better. If I can make that happen, I can be there for Chord, too.

But first things first. Food.

Making my way back to the train station, I'm still adjusting the to-go bag filled with hot noodles against the crook of my arm when I see the Board Operator standing across the street in front of Julis's office building.

I freeze, all thoughts of dinner and getting home and Chord

suddenly lost in the panic that floods my brain. *They know,* is what a cold, logical voice whispers into my ear. It sounds a lot like my Alt's voice, I realize, because it's mine but not. I shudder. *The Board knows you used to be a striker.*

Staring at the Operator, I take in all the details even while a part of me tries to push them away. He's wearing the gray suit assigned to all Board Operators, complete with tweed shoulder epaulets and polished shoes. His head is shaved smooth enough to have the late-afternoon sun glint off it. Apart from the poppy red handkerchief tucked into his chest pocket to note his rank as a Level 3, he could be mistaken for any Operator. His sheer lack of personality, an utter nothingness that's carefully maintained by the Board, is as much a part of his uniform as silk and cotton. His sleek black sedan—is it the same one I saw parked alongside the curb, back near the train station outside of Torth?—doesn't look out of place at all in this part of the Grid.

He must sense my fear. How else to explain the way the Operator's head swivels in my direction and stops when he meets my eyes?

He steps away from the building and starts heading my way and I wonder if he knows he's approaching a cornered animal. As the distance closes between us and the crowd on the sidewalk instinctively parts to make way for a member of the Board, time seems to run backward. And of all the moments I could ever want to relive over again, this would not be one of them. Not even close. I can't tell if it's the same Operator who appeared at my front door all those months ago. Maybe, maybe not; it doesn't matter. The last time I saw one, my world changed forever. He told me it was time to either kill or be killed.

As a complete, I should be free of the Board.

They know you used to be a striker.

He stops when he's a foot away. Too close.

Being noticed by a member of the Board is guaranteed to leave someone cringing. I'm no different. They breathe, they move, but any creature with a healthy brain stem would do the same. It doesn't mean they're human. More like machines, no longer knowing how to feel.

I fight the urge to check the bandages wrapped around my striker marks—I know my marks are well hidden. I'd only be drawing attention to them.

"West Grayer?" His voice is toneless, static.

The world around me is like a dying lung, expanding, shrinking, spots of dark decay dancing along my vision. From far away, I hear my voice. I sound weak again, just as I did when I first received my assignment.

"Yes. I'm her." The words burn a trail in my throat, hurting the way smoke does. I take a deep, shaky breath that does nothing to calm me. "I'm West."

He pulls out a Board-issued cell from his suit pocket, taps in something. Repockets it and says, "This way, please." He turns his back to me and heads toward the car.

He turns his back to me. An Operator, leaving himself vulnerable to a known striker?

It would never happen.

Is it possible they don't know?

And then I remember his bright red handkerchief—a Level 3 Operator and not a Level 2. How could I almost forget seeing that? The first twinges of relief let me breathe properly again.

Though the Board has Alts and completions to keep the

system running smoothly, outliers of the system who threaten the city's safety—such as strikers, such as *me*—are handled by the Board in a different manner. I'd be a black contract, officially unofficial, and it's Level 2 tactical Operators who decide which ones call for stealth . . . and which ones don't. When cells throughout the city utter a low, gentle purr, sometimes it's the vibration of an incoming news file informing the people of Kersh that someone has overstepped, not understood that the system is in place for a good reason, and met a nasty end.

It doesn't happen often, these official reports of black contracts. Five times in the last three years, and those are just the ones the Board decided they want us to know about. The last one was a woman in her late twenties, an eye surgeon who decided she would offer her skills to Alts wanting to excise their assignment number software from their eyes. She blinded more than forty desperate Alts before Level 2 tactical Operators caught her. Story was, they were aiming for stealth—she had good, if deranged, intentions, so no reason to be insensitive about it—but she ended up jumping off the Fourth Narrows Bridge that divides Calden from Gaslight. So much for stealth.

Strikers are not known for their good intentions.

"Wait," I blurt out to the Operator before I can stop myself. "Why do I have to go? What do you want from me?"

He stops, turns around. His eyes narrow just the slightest, and it's next to impossible to make anything out of their depths. Whatever *could* be there. " 'You are hereby summoned, immediately and without further delay, to report to Board headquarters in Leyton Ward to speak with Board representatives.' "

A robot, sheathed in human skin and clothes. I shudder. So

not just a strongly worded request, then. But if it's not because I'm a striker . . .

"Is this about a tour?" Even as I'm asking the question, I don't think that's it, either. Barring circumstances like illness or injury, which would weaken one's effectiveness, completes are the ones who decide when to do a tour, as long as one is done each calendar year. "I still have to be signed off. It's legit with the Board. My counselor sent in my data."

"This is not about a tour," he answers, his gaze still fixed on me. I refuse to squirm, though it's like being an insect speared to a board and trying to not flail helplessly.

"What if I say no?" I ask.

The Operator's eyes narrow even farther, his mouth tightening just a fraction, and for a second I'm sure I'm wrong about the Board not knowing about my striker past. I've simply taken too much from Kersh in exchange for survival, and this is where it ends.

"You are not given the option of refusal," he says finally.

"I know where headquarters is." Already I can see it in my head. A behemoth of a building, the brain of the filtration system is located at the heart of Leyton Ward. "I can get there myself." I'll have to. They'll only find me again if I don't. But if I can avoid getting into that soul-sucking black car, from which there's only skin-peeling, bone-crushing concrete to catch me if I feel the need to escape—

"Immediately and without further delay, and you are not given the option of refusal," the Operator repeats. "This way, please." Without waiting for me to reply, he turns away, another attempt to leave.

There's nothing left for me to counter with. So that's it. One single demand and I'm once again at the mercy of the Board.

The flash of memories, of my time on the run, of my time on the hunt. Of days both fleeting and endless. Hunger and pain, fear and hate. The Board didn't notice me then, so why now?

It's this question that nips at my heels as I slowly follow him to the car. I'm vaguely aware of the package of noodles clasped against myself, and how it's gone cold.

CHAPTER 3

Most of Kersh's general public has no reason to enter the thick glass doors of the Board's headquarters. I always thought it would be like walking into a sniper's field. Now, standing here in the main entryway, I still believe it, still half expecting not to make it out alive. It's my first time here, and already I think it's one time too many.

My initial registration for counseling meant going to one of the satellite buildings. Even people wanting babies go straight to the lab, another satellite building located directly behind this main one. So unless a person is working directly for the Board or lives here in the apartments reserved for families of Operators, headquarters isn't a place where someone would go. There's a sense that just by being here—standing in this lobby where the floor is pristine, the windows naked and pure—I'm marring its cold perfection.

Someone murmurs politely behind me, all cool and perfectly clipped syllables, and I quickly move aside for her to pass. A well-dressed lady, her navy suit perfectly tailored and shot through with cream pinstripes. Not an Operator but someone connected to the Board in some way, considering she's here. As she walks away, my eyes follow her, then catch on a man dressed just as smartly heading across the lobby in a different direction. One more person making up the quietly milling crowd in front of me. I see some Board Operators now, that shade of familiar gray flitting through like ominous clouds. The elevator opens with a soft *whoosh,* and some teenagers step out into the lobby. They are just like me, but of course, not like me at all. They are Board Alts, children and relatives of Operators, and if not already completes, they most likely will be.

I look away from them and take in the rest of the room.

The lobby is a huge expanse of wide-open space, amplified by the soaring height of the ceiling, the sheen of slick ceramic floor, and the glare of cool, clean sunlight flowing in through wide, bare windows. At the far end is the building's main tower; from here, the only part of it that can be seen is the extra-wide elevator at its base. The rest of the tower's massive height is only visible from outside, where it shoots up from the rear of the main structure toward the sky. In front of the tower, on the roof of the main structure, is the iron sculpture of the Board's symbol: the profiles of two Alts facing each other, their eyes given startling depth with a spiral of black iron numbers. It occurs to me that I must be standing directly beneath the symbol, here inside the lobby.

The central tower is where the Board's Level 1, 2, and 3 Operators and their immediate families live. Each floor contains multibedroom apartments. I bet they're larger and more spacious than most houses in the poorer, crowded wards.

The wide elevator at the tower's base anchors one end of the lobby, and the glass front doors anchor the other; the space between branches out into six separate wings—three to a side, each three levels high. Three levels of circular walkways—constructed from the same black iron as the city's huge barrier and then reinforced with glass and steel—curve along the inner walls of the lobby, connecting one wing to another on all levels.

Looking up at those walkways, with their direct lines of sight to me down on ground level, I feel like an easy target. Impossible to miss.

This place is so . . . open. *Too* open.

I can't begin to guess which floor is reserved for what, but common sense says divisions have to be organized in *some* way. Maybe it really is just the simplest, one floor for each Level and their associated duties.

One thing's for sure—somewhere in this building are the computers that randomly select and then activate assignments, setting two Alts on a course in which only one can survive.

Seeing all this, I suddenly feel alien, a fluke who shouldn't be alive. How can any Alt from outside the Board possibly compete with them?

"This way, please." The Operator's voice breaks through the low, controlled hum of the lobby.

I turn to face him. He's taking back his cell from the guard behind the entry kiosk at the door after having it scanned and verified for entry. Tucking it into his breast pocket, he motions for me to follow as he heads toward the southwest wing, clearly expecting no argument from me. We're on his turf now, not mine.

We cross the vast sheet of gray floor. There's a round brass disc in the very center, engraved with a spiral of words that I don't get quite near enough to read. But I already know what it says—the one phrase we all know by heart.

Be the one, be worthy.

Entering the wing, I feel the world shrinking, closing in. The hall is long, with both sides marked by wide closed doors made of thick etched glass lit from within—the day's lingering sunlight streaming in from the exterior windows. Even the ceiling seems lower than it should be, rushing me along. The sound of my footsteps is flat and thin. Here, I can't help but feel diminished. Not worthy, or even a complete, but the latest cog in whatever plan the Board is working on, a piece being readied to fall into place.

What could they want from me?

We stop in front of one of the doors, and the Operator slides it open. "You are asked to wait in here."

I step past him, already on my way to forgetting him, concentrating on who's going to be coming along soon enough, the one who really wants me here.

"Please take a seat," the Operator says. There are black couches against two walls of the room. I walk over to the far couch, the one that faces the door with clear sight of anyone coming in, and sit down.

"Do feel free to eat, as we've disrupted your schedule without warning," he says. I watch him as he steps back into the hall and slides the door shut behind him.

Finally alone, I pull out my cell and turn it off. I don't want Chord calling me while I'm here. Shoving it back into my pocket, I set my cold dinner on the couch next to me, slip my shoulder bag onto the ground at my feet, and look around.

It's just a meeting room, but it tells me a lot. A large window, as wide and tall as the room, originally made in Jethro Ward—only the best grade of bulletproof glass for Leyton, every square inch without flaw. The large table in the center of the room is a rectangular slab of metal and would have come from Jethro, too, fired smooth and carefully welded together before being trucked in. The two glasses sitting on its surface are filled with water dispensed from the tall column of a purifier located in one corner of the room, set to release fresh, bubbling water piped in from Gaslight. And the smell of leather is in the air; my hand runs along the couch I'm sitting on, feeling the rough yet perfectly serviceable hide delivered from Camden's farms.

Nothing here comes from Leyton itself. Of Kersh's four wards, its main good is less tangible, but far more important: power.

Too restless to stay seated, I get to my feet and sling my bag back over my shoulder. The strangeness of the situation, of actually being where I am, is like liquid adrenaline working through my veins, making my mind whir into action, making my limbs want to do *something*.

I cross the room to stand at the window, looking outside. The lines of the buildings across the street are steady and unwavering, as perfect as if nothing stood between us. I lean closer, puff out a breath to fog up the glass. The misshapen blur that forms is the truth: I really am trapped in here. A bug caught in a web, just like the small husk of the fly I see, its body lying on the sill, easy to miss by even the best of cleaning bots.

With one slow swipe of my arm, the blur on the window is gone, and I turn around.

I should leave. Just walk out. I've done everything a Kersh

Alt is expected to do, barring full-fledged war with the Surround. I fought my Alt and I won. I will be doing a tour soon enough, and now Chord is out there, waiting for me—

There are voices coming from outside the door, muffled and indecipherable. One must be the Operator, and the other . . . the other would be the one who matters.

It's ingrained instinct that renews a beat of panic I haven't experienced since seeing my Alt in my nightmare, since the last time I had to kill. My eyes scan the room in a rush, looking for something that can be used as a weapon if necessary. A drinking glass from the little collection next to the water purifier—I can shatter off the edge. The thin bamboo chopsticks the restaurant should've tossed in with the noodles—

Oh, stop it. This is no drugged-out criminal in a seedy back lot in the Grid with a knife to your throat. This is a high-level Operator from the city's most respected establishment. A different kind of danger, maybe, but the potential for witnesses is probably too much, even for the Board.

The door slides open and I stare at the Operator who enters.

He wears the same gray suit as all the ranking members of the Board. Same pants, same shoes, same shoulder epaulets. Same, same, same. Perfected to the most exacting degree, a single, unified front representing a streamlined system to keep the city safe. Except the handkerchief tucked into his chest pocket isn't the red of poppies, the color of blood that marks Level 3 Operators, or even the black assigned to Level 2. Instead it's the color of things that hurt, of blades and bullets. Silver, the signature color worn by Level 1 Operators.

And his eyes aren't blank, or even angry, so much as they're nearly . . . friendly. I say nearly because I know better than to be fooled so easily by the Board. I know what it's like to have to hide a secret. Beneath that thin veneer of warmth, it's still there, no matter how cleverly masked and disguised—infinite emptiness. It's what all Operators need to be in order to do what they do. Otherwise they could be us, or we could be them . . . and I've already done enough to blur those boundaries as a striker.

A cool sweat breaks out along my hairline as I slowly put my hands in my jacket pockets, making sure my wrapped wrists are covered. Hide the fuel from the fire and hope to walk out of here unburned.

"West, thank you so much for coming in," he says. It's curious, his voice, how very animated it is. Inviting, even. I expected a Level 1's voice to sound completely flat and robotic. This is far more unnerving.

"Why did you ask me here?" I blurt out. Fear and irritation are taking turns swinging at me. I have no grip on any of this, and the longer I'm here, the worse I'm going to slip.

He gestures to one of the couches. "Would you like to—"

"No, I'm fine. I'll just stand." He's already much taller than me with both of us standing—I don't need to feel even more diminished.

He lifts one eyebrow—barely visible, it must be very blond or perhaps shaven off just like the hair on his head—and says lightly, "If you're sure."

I say nothing in response. Just wait. And watch.

He pulls out one of the chairs from the far side of the center table. Sits down and faces me from across the span of steel. The warmth in his gaze confuses me, has me on edge.

Whoever says there's an advantage in standing while an opponent is seated is dead wrong.

The Operator speaks next. "West, can you assure me of your understanding that this discussion is of a . . . sensitive nature." It's not a question so much as a statement. Maybe a warning, too.

"You mean, I can't tell anyone," I say to him.

"Well, yes. Involving any outside parties would mean the Board having to rescind this opportunity."

An opportunity. The word has never seemed more loaded. "And if I did tell someone, what would you do?"

"That's not the question you should be asking, West." Despite his smile, I don't think I'm imagining the hint of a threat here.

"What do you mean?"

"Rather than wonder what we'd do if you slipped, perhaps you should ask yourself what you'd have turned down."

I stare at him as I struggle to think of something to say. "Then I can leave right now and you wouldn't stop me?"

His smile turns sad. "Actually, no, we wouldn't. And couldn't—even as Level One Operators, our reach only goes so far."

"Officially, anyway."

A bright glint in those knowing eyes that quickly disappears. "Yes. Officially, anyway."

It reminds me whom I'm dealing with here. The Board, who buries Alts as easily as they save them. Who could all too easily do the same to a complete, if given a reason.

I start moving toward the door. Suddenly I'm more frantic than ever to leave.

"I'm sorry, but this is not for me," I say to him, backing away all the while.

He looks perplexed, upset at the idea of my leaving. "But you don't even know why you're here, West."

My hand is on the doorknob. I turn away to face the door. "I don't want to know. I really don't."

"Even if it means saving someone's life?"

Slowly I turn back to look at him. He seems relaxed now—the opposite of me.

"What are you talking about?" I say.

"Stay, and I'll be more than happy to tell you."

This is my last chance. I only have to say no. Open the door. Walk out and don't look back.

Instead I utter a single word. "Who?"

His eyes are warm and luminous. "The child you'll choose to have one day."

My hand falls from the doorknob—clumsily, heavily, as though it's been shocked. Which is about how I feel.

"What did you say?"

The Operator gestures again toward the couch across from him. *Now sit. And listen.*

I don't take my eyes off him as I move back to the same couch I was sitting on earlier. I let myself sink into the cushion, my bag dropping to my feet once again. The scent of the couch's leather in my nose is a thick, warm wave, and it's all I can do to not shut my eyes and give in to the nausea.

"Let's start over again, shall we?" he says cheerfully, as though we were just discussing whether my ride here was pleasant. Not something that feels like a loaded bomb being dropped in my lap.

The child you'll choose to have one day.

"First of all, though I'm here alone, I'm speaking for the rest of my colleagues at Board headquarters," he says. "This offer comes from Level One as a whole."

I don't want to know.

Even if it means saving someone's life?

"Are you listening, West?"

The sound of my name on his lips wakes me up. I scowl at him. "I don't have a child," I say lamely.

"No, but you will—someday. Maybe even more than one, in which case this offer would extend to them as well."

I can feel heat flush along my cheeks—this conversation is unreal, maddening. Talking about my future with the last person I'd ever want involved. "That's not even . . . it's too far away to—"

"And if I told you the child wouldn't have an Alt to kill?" His voice is as smooth as oil now, like he's flicked an invisible switch. "That your child would never have to kill to survive?"

My mind, cartwheeling backward in time. Except it's not myself I see, not me slipping through the dark streets of the Grid, hunting even while being hunted. It's Ehm, my sister, who became an incomplete at eleven, who didn't have much of a chance at all . . . who was just a little kid.

If Chord and I ever had a daughter, would she look like—

I shake my head. "No, it's impossible."

"Why is that?"

"Because." Too many reasons. Yet why does saying them out loud somehow make them flimsy, easy to overcome? "Only the bio lab knows how to work the Alt codes, not you or any other Level One Operator. You'd have to ask them to do it for you—to *not* make an Alt. Which would be way too risky. No outside parties, right?"

"No, you are correct—the lab techs cannot get involved," he says. "A possible leak would cause doubt in the filtration system. We can't have people wondering why we'd interfere if the system is sound. But it wouldn't be unheard of for a Level One Operator to show up at the bio lab to run a routine check. Which would enable me to log in to their computer system and discreetly alter the status of one particular gene map."

The idea is like being fed salt and told it's really sugar. A total disconnect. "So you would fix the status so it would show that the Alt code's already been created, and an Alt already implanted in the other set of parents?"

"Yes."

"What about the other set of parents?"

"They would exist in name only."

"So the only real lab work would be done with me." To have a child without an Alt. Worthy from the beginning.

"And the 'Alt' of your child would be very unfortunate, getting into a fatal car accident while still an infant. You'd receive a notice about her death and would be, of course, incredibly yet tactfully grateful."

"You make it sound so simple."

"Come now, West. It's not that complicated, really. One Alt lives, the other dies. And in this case, one doesn't even have to die. It's a win-win situation, wouldn't you agree?"

"I . . . I guess so," I manage to say, thinking how he really is making the scenario sound not only tempting, but also easy. Mine for the taking. But the glimmer of satisfaction in his voice—at whatever I can't keep hidden on my face, in my eyes—has my guard up. Everything has a price; dealing with the Board, I know it won't be a small one.

"What do you want from me?" I ask.

"We need you to kill again, West." His words are clipped and precise, a staccato hammer in my head. Nails in my coffin. "Just as you've done before. For your Alt . . . and those other Alts."

I swear my wrists are burning beneath their flimsy coverings. He knows their secret.

"More precisely," the Operator continues, "Level One wants to hire you as a striker for the Alts of our children."

I can't speak. Caught between the instinctive urge to run and the urge to stay. Listen.

"There will be three Alts," the Operator continues, as though I've already agreed, "one for each of the three children of the Level One Operators. You will be given twenty-four hours for each completion."

Kill three more times. Can't. *Can't.*

"I stopped doing that," I whisper. "I'm not a striker anymore."

The Operator's mouth thins. "The marks on your wrists say otherwise."

I pull my hands from my pockets. The bandage on my left wrist is starting to loosen along one edge. There is a peep of my striker mark through the gap, a shadowed wisp of gray I can trace in my dreams. That they've been concealed for this long suddenly seems beyond belief. "How did you—how long have you known?" I ask him stiffly.

"We've been keeping track of Dire since we first got wind

of his operation. That includes his recruits and their contracts. You signed on more than a year ago."

"Why haven't you ever stopped it?"

"The Board doesn't make rash decisions. It was simply more practical to let Dire be. Give him his side project and hope he's satisfied with that. We'll continue to watch him, of course, and watch for signs of anything more significant."

I frown at the Operator, wondering how this would sit with Dire if he knew. If the discovery that he's been indulged this whole time would compel him to push the limits even further. "You're not worried it's just going to blow up in your face one day?"

"Not if we let them keep relieving some of the pressure. An animal on enough of a leash is much less prone to snapping than one on too tight of one, but in the end, both are still leashed. And if circumstances change and our system does become affected, tactical can always be sent in." He gives an elegant half shrug, clearly dismissive of what can be passed on to others for cleanup.

"Why me?" I ask. "If you know I'm not the only striker out there. I haven't killed anyone in a long time. You don't want me."

"When you signed on as an official weaponry assistant for Baer at Torth Prep, you created another entry for yourself in the Board's data. It's public knowledge that we monitor the quality of the Alt Skills program. Compiling all our information together—what we have on Dire's strikers, the program at Torth, our completes archive, those with no living relatives to reduce outsider risk—only one name showed up in each of those logs: West Grayer."

So it's what I hate the most about myself that is suddenly valuable: my ability to kill for money, my skills with weapons, and my being the last surviving member of my family. Strange to think of them as strengths.

I don't want to go back there. I might not come back whole this time.

And Chord. How much could he give this time before it's too much? Even if he would want this future for us, what this Operator is offering, would he ask me to pay this price?

"Their self-detonation switches," I say to the Operator. There's a desperate edge to my voice, the words raw. *Don't make me want to. Don't make it all seem possible.* "If you want your kids' Alts dead so badly, then you'll just have to risk getting the lab to pull them early."

"Ah, but self-detonation switches are tied to both Alt codes, remember?" he says gently, as though reminding a forgetful child. "And one switch going off automatically kills both Alts."

"You make it sound so simple," I say again, breaking the silence as soon as it creeps back in. "But it isn't. Letting someone else kill your kids' Alts goes against everything the filtration system stands for, what the city is built upon. The Board would mean nothing, no more than a cheating ring."

The look he gives me is full of surprised disappointment. "Who better to understand this request than a striker, the biggest cheater of all?"

Annoyance tinged with an all-too-familiar shame makes the top of my ears burn. "You're not exactly making me want to help you."

"Whether you *want* to do this means very little to us. In fact, you should be thankful for this opportunity, West."

"I don't think so."

"We're kindly overlooking the unnatural completions you've already committed as a striker. You see, with each one, you left the city weaker. You countered the very system that keeps you safe. So now"—the Operator holds his hands out, a grand gesture of generosity—"you can make up for those mistakes."

"How? By choosing between Alts again? What if it's the wrong choice?" I ask.

"These are not just any idles you'd be saving. They're the Board's next guard: groomed to eventually succeed as Level One Operators. Policy calls for Level Two Alts to take over if Level One Alts end up as incompletes, but the particular wave of Level Twos we have now is rather . . . unsatisfactory." A sour expression darkens his face. "In the best interests of Kersh, the Level One Operators decided not to leave any of these future Level One completions to luck."

"Your idles don't need luck. Not only are they Leyton Alts, but they're also Board ones. *Level* ones."

"Then think of these striker contracts as being no different than any of those you've already completed, West. You once had no problem killing Alts. Do it again, this time for the right reasons."

It's true. I did kill for the wrong reasons. It wasn't because I thought myself a champion of underdogs, rebelling to help the weak. I spent hours planning strikes so that I wouldn't think about Luc's death, and each downed target became a weight in my favor in the tug-of-war of skills between my Alt and me.

"Tell me about them," I say. "The Board's children."

His mouth thins a bit. "They have nothing to do with your contracts. Except that they are the worthy ones."

"How can you be so sure? Even if they *are* born for the guard, sometimes that's just not enough. Maybe you know these kids suck at fighting."

"They do not *suck,* as you so eloquently put it. They received the most advanced Alt training. They excelled in all their fields."

A part of me wonders how far I can push him. The foolish part, the part that always moves too fast, according to Luc. "Why not just let them fight, then?"

"We might be Level One Operators, but we're also parents, are we not? And if someone was absolutely sure his own child was the worthy one, and if he had the means to ensure that outcome, can you think for one second why he wouldn't?"

"So now instead of being cheaters by hiring a striker, you're just good parents? Which one is it? You can't have it both ways, you know."

"The difference between us, West, is that we're doing this for Kersh's sake as well as our own. Everything you've done so far was for no one other than yourself."

Not true, I want to yell at him. But I can't. The Operator doesn't look like my dad, but right now he makes me think of him. Of any ordinary parent in Kersh who wants to save those they love.

"There's another difference you're forgetting about," I say, standing up and clumsily kicking my feet free of my bag strap before picking it up. "The Board punishes people for doing exactly what you're doing. But who catches you?"

He takes a slow, patient drink from one of the glasses of water in front of him. Setting it back down on the desk, he asks, "Would you like to view our training facilities, West?"

"What?" I'm ready to take off, but he's caught me off guard.

"Time," he says out loud to his watch as he gets to his feet.

19:17

"A tour of the facilities," he continues. "Unfortunately, I cannot permit you to have any contact with our Alts, but perhaps seeing for yourself what they have at their constant disposal will convince you that they are worthy of being saved." His words are nonthreatening, but I feel threatened, anyway. *You will believe it, and you will do this.* "Well?"

No, I'm not interested. Let me go. "Fine."

CHAPTER 4

With the sun gone even lower, the lobby is now bathed in a new kind of light. A fuzzy, pale amber that streams down from above. I glance up at the ceiling. Sometime since my arrival, solar panels have flipped on to distribute whatever light they've managed to collect on an early-summer day in Kersh.

It should make the room seem warm but fails miserably.

It's still way too open. The fact that the workday is over and the lobby is nearly empty doesn't help, either. Footsteps echo and bounce off the distant walls, testimony to the size of the space.

The Operator comes to a stop in the middle of the lobby. His left foot is on the brass disc at the center of the spiral, obscuring more than half of the etched words. "This is, of course, your first time visiting headquarters," he says.

I give him a look to hide how strained my nerves are. "You mean because someone poor like me wouldn't have reason to be here? I don't get the feeling walk-ins are exactly welcome, anyway."

He nods at the guard behind the entry kiosk before turning to me. There's a bemused expression on his face. "Well, I have to agree that we . . . discourage casual visits. But I wouldn't go so far as to say we're not welcoming, West. We're here to assist Alts, after all."

His words bring to mind terminals, centers that also offer actives temporary refuge. They help Alts, too, but it doesn't mean it's necessarily a place someone would want to visit if they didn't have to.

I point to the row of tiny green lights above the main entrance door and windows as we walk past—cameras, I bet—and note the single, larger red light on the lock plate of the door. Locked.

"A lot of security," I say to the Operator, "even with someone at the door. Do you guys watch the lobby from the same room you watch Alt data roll in?"

A pause, and I realize he's digesting what I've said. How close was I to guessing the truth?

"Is that what you've been told?" he finally says, and his tone is still friendly. "I'm happy to let you know that that's not the case. We don't consider anyone in Kersh a threat." Now he cocks his head, offers a slight smile. "*Have* you spoken to someone who's been here before?"

"No," I mutter, still reluctant to talk too much, but his friendliness . . . I admit it's wearing me down. "But we do study the history of the Board in school."

"So you know the basics about the Founders."

I nod, my mind already recalling what we're all taught as part of the basic curriculum in school regarding Kersh's origins. "Yes, of course."

Cris, Jackson, and Tamryn. Together, the three best friends claimed a swath of land in the Pacific Northwest as their own and called it Kersh. Tired of the Surround's endless, cyclic wars, they erected a massive barrier around Kersh to keep it safe.

They formed a new governing Board inside the city. At the helm was Cris, whose political background proved invaluable in making decisions and proposing ideas. His division became known as Level 1, and over time he created additional positions for friends and citizens he thought suitable. Jackson did the same for his division, and Level 2 was trusted to handle all military matters. Tamryn was a brilliant scientist, and her very small division—originally Level 3 before it split off and became its own specialized department—was the most important. New city or not, people still wanted to have babies, and only lab technicians could make that happen.

But nothing good ever lasts.

Less than a decade later space was tight.

Resources grew dangerously low.

People still wanted families.

And the Surround continued to threaten to attack—to break down the barrier and reclaim the territory.

So Cris, Jackson, and Tamryn came up with the idea of Alternates.

Most Kersh citizens credit Cris specifically since he had a mind that could run circles around even the most unwieldy of problems; some say it was Jackson, considering the system was fundamentally a military one; and some give Tamryn the nod, since Alternates could never have come into existence in the first place without her expertise in biological sciences.

I blame them all equally.

The population would be controlled, and only the worthy would survive to use up the city's resources. This plan came with the added benefit that by separating the weak from the worthy, the slow from the fast, an army of soldiers is always maintained. The Surround would not dare attack a population made up of killers.

The citizens rebelled at first, made attempts to rush the barrier. But Cris's persuasive magic worked: it was either fight once in Kersh, live gloriously, and most likely never fight again, or fight every day in the Surround until you had no more fight left.

The city gradually came to accept this. If you're the Alt who is proven to be worthy, then life is yours to live.

And I'm that Alt—no longer an idle in limbo waiting for my assignment, no longer an active battling to outlive my Alt over the course of thirty-one days, but a complete. For months now, I've been . . . living. Doing the things I've earned the right to, like meeting up with Chord or other complete friends from school and not having to avoid talking about the future.

I should not be here. I have nothing else to give them.

"West." The Operator breaks into my thoughts. "What do you know about the Kersh bio lab eventually breaking free of the Level Three division and becoming its own department?"

He starts walking again, and I have no choice but to stay with him.

"Only that Tamryn decided to give the lab a quieter profile," I say. "After seeing Kersh's first reaction to the idea of Alts, she was probably right to be scared." We continue across the lobby, chased by our reflections in the windows.

"That is correct—but not nearly as interesting as the entire story." We're almost at the entrance to the northeast wing now, and he pulls out a cell from his pocket. When his pace slows and he turns toward me, there is a new, conspiratorial air about him and it leaves me confused. "May I speak with confidence that the privileged information I'm about to reveal remains between us?" he asks.

Another secret to keep. But he sounds so eager to share and not threatening at all and . . . "Okay."

"Tamryn was in love with Cris. Ever since they met as teenagers. She made no secret of it. But he eventually committed to someone else, despite knowing how she felt."

Surprise has me looking at him more carefully. "Is that why Level Three broke off and became an independent department? She couldn't handle being around him anymore?"

"Yes, in so many words."

"I guess she must have really loved him." Reading about the Founders is required in school, but most of the material is bare, soulless information. Cris was a born politician, Tamryn a brilliant lab scientist, Jackson a sharp strategist. That was all.

"They were very good friends," the Operator says. "I'm sure the situation was not an easy one."

"But didn't Jackson want her to stay?" It doesn't need to be pointed out to me that we've entered the training wing. No indulgent glass doors here, only slabs of Leyton-grade steel. Meant to contain bullets and blades. "He was her friend, too."

The Operator comes to a stop in front of one of the steel doors. He scans his cell across the lock. There's a soft click and he tucks his cell away before taking a second to adjust his silver handkerchief, knocked slightly askew by his hand. "Jackson was the one Cris committed to."

"Oh. That's . . . it?" I can't hide my surprise. It's odd to think of these names as having once been real people, alive, with their own wants and needs. Suddenly the Founders seem more real than they ever have before. Years of studying them are nothing compared to this one tiny glimpse, a peeling back of the veil.

"Tamryn was hotheaded and stubborn. She stopped speaking to both of them for a while, moved her lab to an outer building, and declared herself a service independent of the Board. Cris and Jackson had to resort to using go-betweens just to communicate with her. Today you know these go-betweens as Level Three Operators. And over time, other subdivisions such as legal and clearing were folded into that Level as well."

"So they were never friends again?" My heart aches for these people, who came together as friends to leave the only world they knew to create a new, more peaceful one. In many ways, they succeeded, but in the ways they didn't, would they be disappointed?

"No, they eventually reconciled. Though Tamryn never worked alongside them again on a daily basis. Particularly with Cris, since the only thing Jackson did wrong, really, was to end up with what Tamryn wanted. It wasn't until after her death that the Board was able to once again claim the bio lab as one of their official services." The Operator slides the door open, and the sound of steel brushing against steel brings me back to the present.

"After you, West," he says, and I can swear there's a smugness to his words.

At first, I see nothing. And for one very long thudding heartbeat I'm sure this is a trap. He's brought me here because of what I did and this is what they do when they find out and why not kill two birds with one stone since their idles need training and *I am their mark*—

The Operator swipes his hand along a panel on the wall and bright white light fills the room.

Empty. No one's waiting. Just him, waiting for me to react. To tell him he's right, there's no way any Alt surrounded by so much wealth and privilege and sheer advantage could ever not be worthy. Be made worthy.

I blink, adjusting to the light. Breathe out a low, shaky sigh as I look around.

It's not right for so few people to have so much. This room isn't just about survival—it's about total decimation. The Alt to any of these idles has absolutely no chance.

I step away from the door and make my way inside. The Operator stays close, watchful. I'm a striker let loose with fresh, tempting arsenal, after all. But also I suspect he doesn't want to miss my reaction. To feed off my awe at the Board's power and to gloat at my defeat.

The room has the typical setup for any Alt training facility; in this, it's not all that different from Baer's weaponry class-room or the pay-to-use ones established throughout the city.

Cordoned off into stations with fluorescent paint slung across the floor in an uneven grid pattern like a huge zipper that refuses to meet in the middle, each specializes in a single technique or skill set. There are no more than a dozen stations in the room altogether—any more than that and the risk of injury is too high.

But that's where the similarities end. Everything in this room is about taking what's typical and amplifying it.

The Operator starts the tour by leading me to the left side of the room.

"Oxygen pods," he says at the question in my eyes as we approach the station along the wall. It's a long row of round glass windows, reminding me of pictures of old ships that used to sail the oceans before all the waters of the world became clogged with warships and wreckage. "For helping speed up the healing process if there's an injury during training. They also help build an Alt's endurance and resistance to fatigue, with enough use."

I can see now that the windows are really doors with a latch along the side of the rim. An Alt would press it open, slide in, and lie down. I'm no stranger to oxygen chambers—they're old technology—and I saw some at the hospital in Jethro. But those weren't nearly as sleek as these, just bulky pods with scratched-up glass walls and waiting lists that went on forever.

The Operator has moved along, and I follow him, overwhelmed into silence. What to say when I'm envious at having never used any of this, and sad for my students who will also never use this and might even have to face an Alt trained on it?

I listen to him talk as we make our way through the room. The outlines of human figures digitally projected onto sheets of steel to mimic live fire scenarios, with dots of pulsing red to indicate shifting vital points as the outlines move. No static bull's-eyes here. The old compost bags Aave, Luc, Ehm, and I used to carefully stack together for target practice now seem silly, when before they seemed so clever and efficient.

A barrel of pure steel blades, swords so pristine they don't even seem capable of getting chipped or bent or clouded with wear. Racks of small to large knives. A shooting station with enough guns to outfit all of Torth Prep, including Ronins, the kind of gun only the privileged of Leyton can afford to have.

I must be a monster, because as angry as I am that some completions are over before they've begun, I'm also relieved. This makes it easier to do, what the Operator is asking of me. If I can figure out a way to do it so it won't hurt, maybe it's not unforgiveable to gain something from it, too. Maybe guilt won't eat me alive afterward.

I'm still wondering how a Ronin would feel in my hand when I see something I've never seen before.

A gun of another kind.

I walk past the Ronins and pick up what's suspended on the two hooks next to them.

The gun is . . . heavy. Surprisingly so, considering how small it is. It doesn't even look that different from a typical gun, if we're just talking about the most basic of components—it has a barrel, a grip, a trigger.

The details, though.

Compared to the blunt and squared-off lines of a Ronin, the gun is slim and sleek and reminds me of a slightly oversized syringe. It's matte silver in color, the hue growing lighter as it narrows from handgrip to muzzle. The trigger is a thin curve of steel against my finger as I slide it past the guard, a mockery of a ring.

"Of course a striker would find the one weapon we can't use."

I glance up at him. "What is this?"

"A gun, but one that doesn't shoot bullets."

I can tell he's waiting for some kind of reaction—maybe shock, probably admiration—before saying more. I try to remember everything I might have ever heard about such a weapon. But then I realize there's nothing to be gained from the Board knowing how much I know.

"I don't know how this works, if it's not with bullets," I finally say to him. I think it's a beautiful weapon, almost elegant, but I keep that to myself.

"This, West, is a Ronin Mark II—a Roark. Built with mercy in mind, it promises instant death."

I take a closer look at the gun in my hand, the shape of the barrel, the width of the muzzle. "Poison?"

He nods. "Instantaneous and completely painless if used properly; agony and a prolonged death if not. Unfortunately what makes it so effective—the heating of the liquid as it exits the gun—also compromises the accuracy. Which is why we can't approve it as a Board-sanctioned Alt weapon until the designer improves it. We need completions to happen, but we're not monsters."

Monsters.

I close my hand around the gun, test its weight. It's disconcertingly comfortable. If my striker marks weren't covered, they'd be right against the grip, silver against silver.

"The incompletes wouldn't feel any pain?" I ask him.

"Like dropping off to sleep."

"What do you mean when you say 'if used properly'?"

"Heart, base of the neck, temple. There are other pulse points on the human body the poison could neutralize, of course, but those three are the ones that lead to the fastest deaths."

"Built for mercy for *both,* then. Completes would know they at least did it painlessly."

"Again, only if used properly."

Carefully, I place the gun back onto its hooks. "A good enough shooter should be able to make up for the faulty accuracy."

"There are problems with the recoil. Unpredictable explosions. Chemical burns."

My hand goes to the thin scar on the side of my face. I didn't get it from poison, but still my skin was altered forever. Chemical burns would do the same.

The Operator's eyes follow the path of my fingers, and I cover up my discomfort with a flustered scowl. Avoiding his stare, I look past him, wondering what else I'm missing in this house of terrible beauty, when I spot a door.

"What's in there?" I ask.

"Surely you didn't think this room was all," he chides.

I did. How can there possibly be more? "I . . . I wasn't sure."

"Again, after you."

We enter darkness again, but now I know it won't last. When it finally lifts with a touch of the light panel, I don't know what to think.

Here's a room much like the one we just left, a concrete cell built for abuse. But instead of stations set up throughout, there are tall, hinged panels of mirrors. So many of them, all at different angles to each other, creating a maze of mirrors.

Mirrors aren't that well received in Kersh. Homes often have them, but public places usually don't. One unguarded glance and you're seeing your Alt.

I walk up to the maze's entrance and step inside.

The effect is dizzying and terrifying. There I am, pale face making my scar more vivid, eyes a touch wild. And there I am again, and over there . . . and over there. An infinite parade of Alts.

Suddenly I hear a brief, high-pitched whir in my ears. It's followed by a flash of light across my eyes so bright it leaves me blinded for a few seconds. When it clears, I see a shadow moving behind me, a girl's shadow, and it's not mine.

I whirl around. Though I know—

It's her.

—I'm simply seeing things because—

My Alt.

—she's already dead.

The girl standing in front of me can't possibly be real, despite how much we look alike. The same long black hair, the same chin and cheeks and nose. Except for her eyes, and I'm thankful when I stare into her dark, coiled pupils and see nothing of myself in there.

"She's a replication of your Alt, West," the Operator says, coming to stand next to the shape. Not girl, not human, but shape. "When you stepped into the maze, you were scanned by our mirror program in order to produce a suitable training opponent. Someone with the same build and the same way of moving. She can't read your mind, but she mirrors what she sees by feeding off your actions. Also, the more engaged you are in the training session, the faster she learns."

"Learns to what?"

"To initiate action, instead of simply reacting. To become as close to your Alt in a fighting situation as possible."

"She's just an image," I say, trying to sound normal. As

though I see my Alt come back to life on a regular basis. But standing this close, I can also see how she's made up of pixels, suspended in air. Not real in the least, but real enough to be effective. "How would she help me with training?"

"Not in combat, but in a chase-or-be-chased scenario, with the main goal to strengthen you mentally rather than physically. The chase only ends when physical contact is made. And the preferred setting, of course, is having *you* chase—knowing how to hide can also be useful, but ultimately that's not why we created this training station."

I think of running the streets and alleys of the Grid as a little girl, using them to train in much the same way as this maze of mirrors. But back then I'd only had my brothers and sisters to pretend they were my Alt. This replica is much closer to the real thing, would test me on a whole other level.

"And measuring nearly two thousand square feet in size, the station can also accommodate more than one Alt per training session," the Operator says, a proud parent, "and therefore a variety of replicas. Such scenarios won't happen in the natural environment, but it's a unique option that only our elite mirror program can offer."

"An Alt learning to chase down one that isn't their own?" I shake my head. The idea is exactly as he says—not natural. "Why?"

"I believe what the program designer had in mind was for the kids to achieve a sense of camaraderie, which is loosely connected to the release of endorphins to produce a performance 'high' that can help during completions."

My stomach is in knots. The way he talks about

completions . . . as if they are a *sport*. "How do you change the settings?" I ask, still looking at my Alt, if only so the Operator can't guess how his words unnerve me. A handful of pixels on her cheek is darker than the rest—a reflection of my scar. "To go from being the chaser to being chased?"

He points to a control panel mounted on one of the mirrors at the maze's entrance. "Stripping the code resets it. Though, again, teaching our Alts how to be the aggressor is why we designed this program. There is little room in the maze for those who hide."

If I wasn't sure before, I am now. These Board idles . . . they are the ones. They are worthy.

I poke my finger into the girl's eye and the replica of my Alt dissolves into nothing; I wish it were as easy as that to pretend she never existed in the first place.

I brush past the Operator on my way out of the maze. "I'm leaving. I don't need to hear anymore." Home calls, *Chord calls,* and I desperately want to get away from here.

Whatever he sees on my face convinces him there's no point arguing, and his expression is as pleasant as it was when he first walked into that meeting room. The same way the surface of a lake looks inviting, until you dive in and your breath is taken away at just how cold it is beneath.

He passes me a small, white, round disk. Nothing on it except for a bar code. "Scan this with your cell when you're ready to talk. You have until morning to make your decision. I hope I've managed to convince you to make the right one."

I take the disk and stuff it carelessly into my pocket. "And if I make the wrong one? Am I supposed to believe you'll be fine with that?" Because I know the dangerous truth now.

That even the Board can't guarantee that the system always works.

"If that's the case, then we'll consider the offer void and without repercussions of any sort." A chill in those hazel eyes. Then slowly, deliberately, he continues. "Of course, circumstances might change if we find that details have leaked."

My skin crawls at the meaning behind his words. They fill me with grim premonition, the sense that my life has again altered forever. I stalk past him and head for the door that connects to the training room. The way out. There's another closer door that opens to the outer hall, but it's still pulled shut.

"Wait here," the Operator says to my back. His voice isn't raised, but irritation filters through, anyway. I'm not supposed to be left alone, to navigate freely through the Board's territory. "Someone will lead—"

I yank at the closed door, suddenly not wanting to see all those stations again, and dart out into the hall. Half running down the wing, I will myself not to fall apart, not here. The sound of my footsteps is desperate, my breathing more ragged than I want to admit. I dash across the amber-lit lobby, that cavernous trap of a wide-open room, and burst through the revolving front door as though I'm being chased.

And I *am* being chased. By guilt over the ghosts of the Alts I've killed, by what I'm already starting to consider.

CHAPTER 5

Considering the Board's offer means no longer being able to see the people seated around me on the outer ward train as just people. They're now reduced to *maybe thems*. I don't know what those Alts—my potential strikes—look like. They can be anywhere, anyone.

Perhaps the girl near the front of the train, the one sleeping in her seat with her platinum hair half shielding her face. Or the boy across from me, reading on his cell while hearing nothing but the music blasting into his ears. Both would be easy to kill. Not *girl* or *boy* but each a *target*.

It's an ugly view, but a familiar one, too.

And then there's what's behind me—*who's* behind me.

Two parents with a little kid. The little girl's got a messy bob of light brown hair, eyes nearly the same shade. Her face is round and unassuming and still way too young to fully realize what's in store for her.

She doesn't look much like me when I was that young. Or like Ehm, either. Still. I'm hyperaware of her sitting in the seat behind me. When she laughs, the sound leaves me bewildered, curious . . . and thinking of Chord.

Kids. A mix of him and me, the two other parents in the Alt Code absolutely insignificant in this moment. How dominant would Chord's features be compared to mine? Where would one give and another take? Would they be stubborn, smart, skilled?

The train pulls to a stop at the station. I make my way to the door and step off onto the streets of the Grid.

It's raining and completely dark out now and I pull my hood over my head. An inner ward train blasts by without stopping, heading the same direction I need to go, and I swear under my breath. A particularly cool rivulet of rain runs down the side of my face and I decide not to wait until the next train comes. I want an end to this day.

Across the street is a café, its windows steamed from the cooking going on inside. It reminds me that I've missed dinner, the takeout container still on the couch in that meeting room. I'm no longer hungry in the least.

By the time I turn onto my street, I'm hunched over and soaked through and silently cursing the rain. Even this close to summer there's not much relief. My own fault for not carrying an umbrel—

"West."

My name comes out from the dark. He's standing in front of my house right beneath the burnt-out streetlamp.

"Chord?" I call out. "What's wrong? Are you okay?"

"Yeah, I'm fine. I was just coming over to see if you were home," he says, stepping out from the shadows and closing the distance between us. It's true; he obviously wasn't planning on going any farther—he's just as jacketless as he was when I left him back at school, despite the rain. It's thinning his T-shirt, revealing the hard planes of his chest, dampening his brown hair. He's smiling anyway, despite the question in his eyes. "You weren't answering your cell . . ."

"What?" My hand automatically goes for my jeans pocket before I remember that I turned it off earlier, when I was waiting in the meeting room. I forgot to turn it back on.

"Sorry, I guess it must have died," I lie. "But you have a house key . . ." I gave it to him for emergencies, but now that I think about it, he's never used it. Though his place is so messy with all his tech projects lying around in different stages of progress as he waits for a certain part to show up. "Did you lose it?"

"No, of course not," he says with a low laugh. "And I can tell you were just picturing my room—"

I have to smile back. "I was, yes."

"That key is one thing I'm careful to keep track of, West." His eyes gleam a bit beneath the lamplight.

"That's good," I say, my pulse taking a little leap.

"And, well, as much as I wanted to see you, it didn't feel right to call that an emergency."

"Like tempting fate, or something?"

"Something."

"But now you're all wet. You should have just waited for me to call—"

Chord comes closer, pulls me to him. "Hi," he says, interrupting me.

"Hi." So good to feel him again.

He kisses me. Rain washes over our faces, mingling with our lips, the heat from our mouths. My hands are on the back of his neck, where his skin is still warm.

Our kids could be free . . . but it's too late for me.

I shiver, and Chord feels it, wraps me up tighter. "It *is* kind of cold out here," he says, laughing. "I'm ready to head inside if you are."

I grab towels from the hall closet and bring them to the kitchen. Chord's deep in the fridge, looking for something we can eat.

"I'm sorry, Chord," I say to his back, placing the towels down on the counter. I start unwrapping the gauze from around my wrists; it got damp from the rain, the feel of it now chilly and clammy. I don't bother covering up my marks when we're alone. "I . . . you're not going to find much in the fridge."

Chord emerges, a container in his hand. He looks at me questioningly. I only shake my head. "Don't eat that," I tell him. "That's old."

"How old?"

"I can't remember what it is."

He chucks it back in the fridge, shuts the door. "You do know food's a good thing to keep in the house, right?"

I pass him a towel. Instead of using it to dry his hair, he reaches over and starts in on mine. My dark hair goes everywhere, loose and wild. It's growing back, playing catch-up after I cut and dyed it during the winter. When I needed to be someone else to kill my Alt.

"Sorry," I say again to Chord. "If it makes you feel better, I do keep my other kitchen well stocked."

"Yeah?"

"It's just five houses down from here, believe it or not."

He grins, tosses the towel on the counter behind me. "We

could go back to my place, but it's raining even harder out now. And I brought the rest of my math homework to finish for tomorrow. Ordering pizza okay with you?"

"Sure. Go crazy with the toppings." I'm hungry now; things feel almost normal, buffered by the familiarity of my surroundings. To cover for my earlier lie about my cell being dead, I wave it over the recharge on the wall before tucking it into my jeans pocket.

You have until morning to come to a decision.

"Still?" Chord takes out his cell, taps in the order.

"Still." My attempt to sound fine, to wipe away the Operator's voice continuing to sound in my head. "Humor me?" I'm not used to being a complete yet. I can't help but order as much as possible from the complete menu, with its better-quality food. Whatever I decide to eat now is only restricted by what I can afford to spend. And I still have my striker savings.

Chord's turned on the kitchen news screen, and even as I turn to see what's on, my cell thrums in my pocket. One long purr that lasts for a good ten seconds.

Chord looks down at his own cell. It's humming, too.

It's a citywide news file being released by the Board. Announcing the fulfillment of a black contract on all news screens and cells.

Rebels.

Strikers.

Like me.

We both pick up our cells, tap them awake, and read the words as they scroll by.

A complete was caught and killed while digging a tunnel underneath the barrier in Calden Ward. A small tunnel that he would cover up with plywood and a layer of fresh turf before going back to work on his farm for the rest of the day. Six years of furtive, secretive work, gone just like that.

The funny thing is, the guy wasn't trying to leave Kersh—he was building the tunnel for someone from the Surround to enter the city. He claimed that a voice in his head kept talking to him about someone preparing to come to the city, this safe haven. The voice said if he didn't help this person get in, Bad Things Would Happen.

"Something happened on my tour that I never told you about, West," Chord says quietly, startling me so I look up from the news file on my cell. "Out there along the barrier."

He's watching the news screen, where the same news file on our cells is playing out. Just words, no picture of Level 2's latest contract. My guess is the Board chose not to publish photos or videos this time because his mistake was made out of goodwill—to someone in the Surround, yes, but it's obvious there was no true intent to harm Kersh.

I move to stand next to Chord, wondering what he's reading behind the words on the screen, ones I can't see, having never gone on tour myself. His tone was uncertain, as if he wasn't sure what to say.

"No, you never mentioned that," I say.

"Usually we just walked back and forth along the Kersh side of the barrier, from one end of our sector to the next," he begins. "Just . . . walking, gun in hand, scope with the other in case we needed to take a closer look at anything in the Belt or the Surround just beyond it. Once, when I was close to finishing my tour—it must have been about three weeks in—the

Surround set off a series of flares." Chord finally looks at me. "Remember the last time we saw flares on Fireton Street?"

The name takes me back to that run-down house where Luc died. But now it's also where Chord had his first tour. East side of Jethro, just off Fireton, BPS24J.

"Fireton." I say it out loud, try to normalize it, make it nothing. Julis would be proud of me, I think. "I remember, yes."

"It was like that, but brighter, since I was so much closer this time. I pushed my way through these crazy kaiberry bushes that had grown as tall as my shoulder, and this huge tree, all silvery and really kind of beautiful—the only one I've ever seen like that, I still don't know what kind it was—to get even closer to the barrier to watch. There was a clear path through the Belt on the other side. Short, but still clear enough to pretend I wasn't staring directly into the Surround. If I blurred my eyes the right way, it was just this perfect, open path." His bemused smile makes me feel sad. "Baer would've kicked my ass if he were there, seeing how distracted I was," Chord says.

"How close did you get to the barrier? Chord, the electricity . . ."

"I didn't touch it . . . at first."

My heart leapt in fear. *"Chord."* It's not unheard of for cleaning to find the occasional body out there, sometimes actual incompletes but more often than not a careless active or idle blackened to a crisp. Get too close to the barrier and you risk getting charred to death. There're signs up along the barrier, all along its circumference—REMEMBER THE BARRIER IS CHARGED DO NOT TOUCH THANK YOU THE BOARD—but no one in Kersh needs to be reminded. It's a part of life, just like knowing that all restaurants have both a complete and an idle menu from which to order.

"Well, I got close enough that I should have smelled something burning, and I don't mean the smoke from the flares, either," Chord says. "I mean, I know how strong the barrier's currents are. But there was nothing, and that was wrong.

"Then I realized what I had in my pocket. I'd left it in there from the day before. It was a new piece I was playing with, trying for a new kind of key-code disrupter. Like the one I made for you when you were active."

I think of the cool, smooth strip, made of mesh and wire. How I'd hold it against my palm to break open locks of houses. "Why would you want to make another one?"

"Why did Luc and I ever make any of the crap we made?" He shrugs. "Just because we could."

The memory of how they'd claim victory with each new contraption, even if no one else could understand the purpose of it or showed much more than a passing interest. "Okay, that's true."

"So this new key-code disrupter was in my pocket, and I think it was reading something inside of me—*using* it—that let it temporarily neutralize the barrier's charge."

"Using something inside of you? What do you mean?"

"Whatever's left of my Alt code inside my head. The spent shell of it, I guess you could say. And the dead code would be the bullet, already shot and fired."

"I still don't understand."

"It's the same way your old disrupter used your striker marks to scramble lock systems long enough for you to get inside a house. It took a single material and used it as a conductor to make something happen, right? So this new disrupter does the same thing, except it uses whatever's left of my Alt code to *stop* something from happening."

"The barrier's charge," I say through numb lips. It's finally starting to sink in. "The new disrupter used the remnants of your Alt code to temporarily neutralize it."

"Yeah. The barrier will no longer burn us, but it won't keep us safe, either—as long as we have the disrupter on us."

"Can only completes do this?" I ask. "What about an idle or active with an Alt code that's still working? Could the disrupter use the whole thing as a conductor to neutralize the barrier's charge?" I can't help but picture that guy who was just on the news, caught trying to break through. Bad enough to imagine even one complete without Chord's sense of caution or logic somehow accessing that kind of disrupter and using it, thinking he was actually helping Kersh. The idea of the whole entire city suddenly capable of doing the same thing was bone-chilling.

Chord shakes his head. "It's not built to conduct more than one material at a time. And the Alt code and whatever gets left behind after it's used up are made up of slightly different components. Like a bullet and its shell."

At least there's that, then. "So completes will still burn up if they get too close—unless they have the disrupter to temporarily neutralize the barrier's charge."

"Exactly."

"In a way, it'll be as though *we* go neutral, too," I say slowly. "Because for those few minutes our Alt codes are probably completely neutralized. It would be as if we aren't even Alts."

Chord grabs my hand in understanding. "West, I touched the barrier."

I squeeze his hand, rub my thumb over the healthy, unburned skin. My hand is shaking. Anger at what he risked wars with relief that he's okay—relief wins. "That's one sentence no one in Kersh has ever said before, I bet." I blow out a long sigh. "Why didn't you tell me?"

"I never said anything because . . . well, at first I thought I was losing it. All that alone time on watch. Then after I was sure it really happened, I didn't say anything because I was worried what you'd do, if you knew." Chord frowns at me, touches the side of my face. "You were just starting to see Julis, and then there's Dire, you know? I know you trust him, but I don't. That disrupter puts Kersh in danger—what if the Surround learned about it and tried to use it to break in?"

"Where is the disrupter now?" It must be small to fit in his pocket. But it doesn't feel like a small thing. Not what we're talking about. Not at all.

"I took it apart. The barrier returned to normal as soon as I stepped away, already charged again and back to keeping us safe. But I still didn't want the wrong person getting ahold of it." His eyes are unsure. "Was that wrong of me? I couldn't think of what good it would do for anyone in Kersh. What would you have done, West?"

The Surround, coming through, wanting to destroy us all. I shiver. "I . . . would have done the same. And Dire would have done the same, whatever you might think of him. He might not like the Alt system, but he doesn't want the Surround to invade, either."

He sighs. "Sorry."

"Don't be. Dire's heard much worse things said about him, I'm sure."

He laughs softly. "Not for what I said about Dire. For not telling you earlier."

"Then thank you for telling me." And because I don't want to think about it—the potential of what it all could lead to, the danger and temptation if in the wrong hands—I kiss him, knowing he wants to stop thinking about it, too.

Afterward, he reaches over and swipes the news screen to sleep, news file broadcast long over.

"It's been a while since we got one of those alerts," he says distractedly against my hair. "I can't remember the last one."

I have to admit the timing of it is eerie, having just spent the afternoon at the Board. It casts more of a shadow on the Operator's warning about revealing anything.

"The last one was that lady, the eye surgeon trying to mess with the Alt codes and the assignment number software," I say to Chord. "Remember?"

Chord shudders. "I do now, thanks. I can't believe you remember that, West."

"I . . . watching that last news file just reminded me."

"Hey, where did you go after school today, anyway?" he asks. From his back pocket he pulls out a folded sheaf of paper. His math homework.

"Oh." *You know, I took a trip to Leyton, went to visit the Board.* "I forgot I needed some oils for Saturday's class, so I went to pick some up."

"You have lots of art supplies back at my place. Maybe there's something there you can use."

Good. A window out. "Are you sure? I'm surprised you can find much of anything in there at all."

We really should be living together by now, either here or

at Chord's place. It simply makes sense, considering it's just the two of us and our houses are both too empty, quiet. But Julis argued against it, focusing on my need to get better on my own. Chord never lets me forget how much he's looking forward to when that happens.

"As long as I can find what I need, I'm okay with messy," Chord says to me. His hand comes up to tangle in my still-damp hair before slowing, then runs down the length of its strands. "Your hair's nice this way."

"Messy?"

"Long," he says quietly. His face goes tight with memory. "And not dyed blond."

I catch hold of his hand with mine. "I like it better this way, too."

Chord flips my hand over and grips it with his. With a finger from his other hand, he traces my striker marks. When he does something like this, I am almost okay with what they stand for. Not with the fact that I was—*am*—a striker, but that I did what I had to do to survive.

Now they mean something else, too. What can be mine, his, ours—if I can only make myself go under again. Be numb, a striker. Not think and just . . . kill.

"You don't hate them anymore, do you?" I ask on a rush of breath. Feel red-hot heat blaze across my cheeks with the suddenness of such a loaded question.

When he doesn't say anything right away, I try to twist my hand free, but Chord won't let go. "No, I don't, West."

"You did once."

"Yeah, I did." His voice is flat. "*Once.* Not anymore."

"Chord, I . . . can I ask you a question that you might not want to answer?"

"Okay."

"When were you finally okay with me killing people for money?"

He enfolds my wrists with one of his big hands. I wonder if it's because he doesn't want to see them anymore, or if they're really as insignificant as he wants me to believe. I wonder if I'll ever really know. Slowly he pushes me back into the counter until I can't retreat any farther and he's right up against me.

"I understood why you did it as soon as you were the one who lived," he says softly. "Because if everything hadn't happened exactly the way it did—you taking on those contracts, you not wanting me there, even Luc dying the way he did, then things might not be the way they are today."

"Like I might be dead?"

He gives me a crooked smile, which doesn't go anywhere near his eyes. "Or me, don't forget."

I lift my other hand up, tug his mouth down so I can kiss him once, twice. No words could say it better—to tell him I could never forget how close we came to losing each other.

"So I don't hate your marks anymore," Chord says. His arm goes around my waist and holds me so tight that there is no space between our bodies. Nothing can get through us, separate us.

"And if I could go back and change things? *Not* become a striker before getting my assignment?"

His eyes search mine. "Would you still end up a complete? The worthy one?"

Slowly, I shake my head. "No guarantee."

"Then no." Suddenly his hands are on my face, nudging me to look up just enough to meet his eyes. His voice is low, raw. "I would want you to do it. Fair or not, I couldn't watch you live through your assignment again. Each day just another chance of you dying. That's something I wish *I* could forget."

I can't look away now. I owe us that much—to ask as well as I can, and decide once and for all. "Chord, what if I had to do it again?"

"To kill? Why?"

"I don't know." Telling him the truth—that it's the Board, asking me to be a striker again, to make up for what I've done, for a child we might or might not have—is not possible. "What if it meant . . . saving someone," I finally manage.

He looks at me as if I'm going crazy. And it *does* sound crazy. "You mean yourself?"

"I mean . . . yes, of course. Myself." In this moment, it's not the truth, but there is no other answer that makes sense without telling Chord everything.

"In the end, it's what we all do it for, right?" he says. "Completing. A life with no Alt, no self-detonation switches in our brains counting down how much time we have left. Get married, have kids, die in our sleep when we're really, really old." Chord's voice gentles, becomes his again.

"Chord . . . those kids . . . you already know you want them? Knowing what they'll have to go through?"

"It's not just up to me, you know, but . . . yeah, I think so. There's a lot of good stuff in being alive here in Kersh, too."

"You think you can handle watching them maybe becoming incompletes?"

A slow intake of breath. "No, but we'd have to find a way, wouldn't we?"

"What if you could help them? Somehow?"

"No strikers, West. We end that here. How can you even think about that? You did what you had to do, right or wrong, however that might have weakened or strengthened Kersh. But that's over now. You *don't* have to do it again."

"I don't really mean strikers. I mean something else . . ." I'm floundering. Suddenly there's no safe territory here, and that's not supposed to happen with the two of us anymore.

"Training, fine." Chord's gaze is troubled now. "We'll work our asses off and make tons of money and get them the best kind of training we can buy."

I can't do it. I can't put into words what he can't understand and what I can't seem to turn down. He can't offer me absolution this way.

If I'm going to be a monster, then it has to be my own choice.

"You know, I still think of Taje sometimes," Chord says. "How I couldn't save him, despite being his big brother and the one who was supposed to look out for him. It hurts to know that maybe he wasn't worthy, no matter how much I might have wanted it otherwise. But if I knew for sure that he was, don't you think I'd have done *anything* to change things?"

I nod, unable to speak past the ache in my throat.

"When it's our future we're talking about, the kids we might have one day . . . West, going along with the Board is one thing, but I'd be lying if I said I just want kids out of civic duty. And when I think about it, I hate myself for wanting them to know all the good parts about being alive, despite what they'll have to go through, and me being helpless to stop anything bad from happening to them."

The guilt and shame in his voice tears me up. I bring a hand to the back of his neck. As though my touch could make things better. "Chord, you shouldn't—"

"Please tell me I'm not freaking you out with all this," he says, a note of sheepishness in his voice, coupled with a low laugh. "But you *did* ask."

"I don't get freaked out easily," I say, still caught up in his words.

He leans down and presses a kiss to my neck, then my collarbone, then back up along my jaw before coming to a stop so his eyes are on mine again. Sadness lingers there, but I can tell he's making an effort to shake it off.

"So don't get me wrong, West. Talking about the impossible might depress the hell out of me, but there it is. If there's anything I could do to make sure our kids would be safe, to know for sure that their completing is *right* and not just for our sake, you know I'd do it in a heartbeat."

And with that, I make my decision. I'm split in two again. Striker—and the real me.

But not for long, I swear. I wish I could tell him this. For a second I'm terrified of what I've chosen. To go for everything and risk being left with nothing.

The doorbell rings.

"Dinner." Chord starts to move away to get the door.

My hand reaches for him. Holding him there, with me.

The doorbell rings again, held down longer this time. It's

the sound of impatience and momentum, telling me that life keeps moving, whether I like it or not.

"West? We should get that before they take off with the food." Chord kisses me fast and quick, and I can feel the smile on his lips. The warmth of it against mine, fighting the chill already settling through me.

So I let him go.

I lock the front door after Chord leaves. The click of it is undeniably . . . final. A barricade between us, like Kersh in miniature. Except whether I'm the city or the Surround, I don't know. But it has to be this way. Once I engage in a contract, I won't let myself come back until it's done—the idea of Chord seeing me kill again is something I can't let happen.

I move over to sit down on the couch in the front room and turn my hands palm-up on my lap. Stare at the thin ribbons of dark gray that are nearly elegant against the light gold undertones of my skin. When I run a finger over them, no bump gives away the tracking chips embedded in there. They healed well, I know.

Chord's able to look at them now and think *West* and not *striker.*

I see *striker.* I *feel* it sometimes still, no matter how much I want to pretend otherwise. When I'm in weaponry class showing a student how to properly brace for recoil or how to line up a target with a blade like they're threading the eye of a needle. Most of that's just me, just Baer's assistant, but not all. There's the ghost of someone else, a part of West I left behind. I needed her so badly at one point, that hardened part of me who could and did defeat my Alt. I used her and discarded her and hoped to leave her behind.

The terrible truth is this: what drives me now is not the guilt of jeopardizing Kersh with those Alts I killed or even the desire for kids without Alts, as much as I wish this could be true.

It's something much more selfish, and much uglier.

It's my desire to start over. Be clean again. Begin again.

On my lap, my striker marks glare up at me like an accusation. Smooth and unbroken and meant to be permanent.

If anyone in Kersh has the power to erase them, it's the Board.

From my jeans pocket I tug out the small, white disk the Operator gave me. Holding my cell in my other hand, I scan the bar code.

"Yes." His voice is as I remember it, gliding into my head with its too-polished smoothness.

It takes me two tries to speak past the nerves in my throat. "It's me."

A second of silence, then a cautious yet warm, "Hello, West."

"If I do this, I need to meet with you again," I say to him.

"Fine. I can send a car to your house as early as tomorrow morning."

I shake my head, then realize that he can't see me. "The morning is fine, but, no, not another car. And not at headquarters. I don't want any other Operators near me. Somewhere neutral."

"Where would you prefer?"

I don't even know, because I've moved too fast again. Didn't think things through. Still rusty. I quickly name a café in the

Grid—more my turf than neutral, but he doesn't need to know that. And maybe too close for comfort for me . . . but he doesn't need to know that, either.

He agrees, says good-bye, but I'm not done just yet.

"If I do this, there's two more things I need," I say.

"We're already offering more than enough."

I don't answer, letting the quiet speak for me. Seconds drag nearly into a minute before he finally speaks. Cooler now. "What is it, West?"

"First, I want to use a Roark gun to do this."

"You can't be serious."

"I am. I want to do this as quickly and painlessly as possible, and you yourself said it was instantaneous."

"*If* used properly."

"I know how to use a gun."

"The recoil and chance of explosion—"

"I'm willing to take that risk." I deserve to take that risk.

"Someone finding a dead striker with a weapon that would directly trace back to the Board is not something—"

"That's not my problem. You are asking me to kill innocent idles. So I will only do this with that gun. And you'll have to bring it with you for our meeting. I'm not going back to head-quarters to get it."

Heavy silence on the other end of the line, and my hand is starting to shake.

"And the second condition?" he finally asks. The chill is reined in now, carefully smoothed over.

"I'll tell you tomorrow. Oh-ten-hundred." I disconnect, feeling sick to my stomach. I'm sure he's going to dial back, demand that I tell him what else I want, that friendly-yet-not-friendly voice unsettling enough to make me cave.

But he doesn't. My cell stays quiet, and I shove it back into my pocket. I get to my feet and walk upstairs.

In my room, I step into the closet, start feeling around on the top shelf. I haven't used it since my assignment, but I know it's up there some—

My fingers touch bunched, rough canvas, brass zippers, and I pull the whole lot of it down. I'm cradling hell again. Right here, a symbol of the moments and days and weeks when I was on the run. My old bag, the color of olives and camouflage, making me feel invisible.

There are a few smudges of old bloodstains, too set and too stubborn to wash out by the time I was done. The faintest, lingering scent of gunpowder makes my eyes water.

Until now, I've never thought of using it again. Not this way, for this reason.

I toss it onto my bed. Take only vague notice of how easily it comes back to me, the narrowing down of what I can afford to bring with me. Two T-shirts, a few pairs of socks, a handful of underwear joining them. Toothbrush and toothpaste from my bathroom. The Operator said three contracts, at twenty-four hours each—this should be enough to last me until the end. I won't come back until I'm done. Letting that world touch this one is . . . not possible.

I open my bag and slowly stuff everything inside, each item like kindling for that striker part of me. The fuel? My weapons—most of which I've left in Baer's classroom at school. One more thing that's going to have to wait for tomorrow. I'll have to cut classes, but that's not what bothers me. I hate to miss weaponry with Baer. My job and responsibility, and now I'll have to think of a lie for why I can't work for three days.

Only one weapon I decided to keep.

I reach under my bed for Ehm's old jewelry box and open the lid. I take out my gun, the one Luc gave me in another lifetime, the one I haven't held since I killed my Alt.

It's full of more memories than bullets now, and I hope I won't have to use it at all. I start loading it. The act is comforting, bringing to mind my father's patience in showing all of us how a gun is put together. When I'm done, I set it aside.

I reach back into the box and pull out what I nearly forgot was still inside, placed there because I wasn't sure where else to put it. Not a weapon, but not exactly innocent, either.

The key-code disrupter that Chord made for me when I turned active. A thin black strip that used the tracking chips in my striker marks to bypass a house lock, it's no bigger than my hand. He meant for me to use it to find shelter, keeping me safe even as I pushed him away.

Using it to break into the house of a target was not what he had in mind.

I place it in my bag.

After my bed is clear again, I zip up my bag and carefully set it down on the ground, near the door. Within reach if I have reason to leave fast, in secret.

It takes hours to fall asleep. But it's not Chord's dark eyes that haunt me, but pale hazel ones instead. Flat and empty and too much like the color of false gold.

• • •

"I want you to erase my striker marks."

If I wasn't watching him so carefully, I might have missed the tiny flicker in his light eyes. A lick of flame that's gone before it's really there. Irritation, surprise, admiration—I can't tell.

"Otherwise your answer is no?" the Operator says.

"Yes. Otherwise I'm out. You'll have to find someone else."

He continues to watch me. Seems content to say nothing in response.

My foot drums rhythmically against my school bag. Not the bag I need, but I had no choice except to take it when Chord picked me up for school this morning. I left school grounds as soon as his back was turned, grabbing the first inner ward train here to this café.

The bag is not empty. It's got the homework I didn't do last night . . . and the Roark gun the Operator handed over to me as soon as he sat down. In its neat little case, it could pass for something innocent.

"You don't need any further instruction on how to use it?" the Operator asked me, watching as I'd tucked it carefully into my bag. His light tone was underscored with just enough annoyance that I could tell it was probably killing him to have to listen to my requests.

"No, I've got it" was all I said. Whatever other plans I had, they weren't for him to know.

Inside my jacket pocket is my gun. It feels awkward there, the fit not quite right—it's been a long time since I've worn a gun with my jacket, or at all.

"You know I cannot risk asking another striker," the Operator finally says.

"Then you don't have a choice, do you?" My hands clutch

at the coffee cup in front of me. It's steaming hot, even through my sleeves. I don't drink it. He hasn't sipped from his cup, either. The coffees are just props. To make us seem normal, two commuters on their way to work or school.

For the Operator, this means being forced to wear something other than the Board-issued gray suit. He's chosen a suit of a darker gray, and he's wearing a fedora to cover his bare scalp. His chest pocket has no handkerchief of any color. It feels good to know that I've made a Level 1 Operator do something out of the ordinary. Become ordinary—on the surface, anyway.

"The marks are permanent," he says. "Our lab does not—"

"Your lab can engineer two people who look identical to each other, set up a minibomb in their brain, and tattoo their eyes with a long string of numbers. If they can do all that, then they can remove striker tattoos."

His face is cold. "It doesn't change who you are or what you've done."

I can't argue with the truth. "I never said it would."

The customers at the table next to us get up to leave, and one of them—a boy a bit older than me—has to squeeze past the Operator to get to the door.

He's too close, and the Operator mutters something under his breath at the contact.

"Sorry, man," the boy says.

The Operator's only response is to tip the front of his hat down another degree, hiding his eyes that much more. His shoulders stiffen just the slightest. No doubt he's irritated. Here in the Grid there are always too many people and not enough space. Not what a Level 1 Operator is used to.

"Fine."

I'm caught off guard by the Operator's voice, lost in my thoughts. "What?"

"I said we will have your striker marks removed and your striker status erased." The Operator's words are clipped. Backed into a corner. "*After* you've completed the contracts."

I nod. Relief and dread mingle in my mouth, the bitter dregs of finality. It's done, then. And so it starts.

I take a deep breath and hold my mug even tighter. Warmth. "You said twenty-four hours for each contract?"

"That is correct."

The same as any striker contract. Blurred lines, blurred lives. I can't decide if it's fitting or morbid. "So I text in the completion for each new contract?"

"That won't be necessary. Normally Level One monitors only the active Alt log for natural completions; unnatural ones such as Peripheral, Revenge, and Assist Kills split off into their own separate logs and feed into legal for processing. Until these particular contracts are complete, we've set up shadow feeds for those logs to run on a delay. Those are what legal will be receiving while we get the originals. With each strike you complete, we'll reroute the original entry into the natural completion Alt log before it can show up in the feeds for legal."

Each piece of information he gives me is not done in the name of generosity, but as another shackle to tie me down to what I'm about to do. The more I know, the more of a danger I am—to the Board.

"Expect the first contract via cell tonight," he says. "Cover your tracks. You can't be found for seventy-two hours." For the first time, the Operator touches his coffee, pushing it away with a well-manicured hand. He stands to leave—

And suddenly I'm panicking. Not ready.

"What's your name?" I ask him.

He frowns. "You don't need to know irrelevant information."

"You know a lot about me. And you just asked me to kill your kid's Alt. I'd like to know who I'm doing this for."

An impatient hiss of breath through clenched jaw, the snap of biting teeth. "Sabian." He turns to go, more agitated than I've ever seen him.

"Good-bye, West," he says. His hand automatically goes to smooth the handkerchief in his pocket, falls down awkwardly when he finds it missing. A flash of pure fury crosses his features.

It's those kinds of fires that are the most dangerous of all. The kind that refuse to light at first before exploding in your face, the inferno of it so sudden, so huge, there's not even a chance of escaping before being enveloped.

I nod. Stare hard at my cup and will the warmth to stay. Once he is gone, it takes me a few minutes to gather my stuff to leave. I move mechanically, trying not to think too much. Safest that way.

Outside, I pull my hood over my hair. It's starting to rain.

But Dire's place isn't far. And it's where I go to find out about killing.

CHAPTER 6

I wouldn't be alive without the skills I'd gained from working as a striker. But it brought out the very worst in me, so sometimes I wish I'd never met Dire.

Being fair is not one of my strong points.

I haven't seen him in months. Ever since I stopped being a striker, when I became a complete.

Yet here I am, standing on the sidewalk in front of his store in the Grid. The familiar words *Dire Nation* printed on the front door bring a bittersweet pang to my chest. Everything about the place looks the same as the last time I stood here. Even the little blobs of old gum plastered to the window ledge are the same. Layers of old graffiti still there like permanent clouds of sad color.

I wonder what we'll have to say to each other. Apart from business, I mean. If I think of Baer as being something close to a nurturing father figure, then Dire's the surly uncle who has no problem letting his more-than-likely-unpopular opinion be heard. Never was this made clearer to me than the day I told him I was out, done.

He leaned back in his seat, making a point of looking directly at the still-fresh scar on my cheek. The lighting in the basement of the music store wasn't bright, but it was bright enough. "Why? You got scared because of something like *that*?"

"No." Sitting across the table from him, I was all too aware that I felt more like a child than an employee. I pulled my legs up and wrapped my arms around my knees so I wouldn't be tempted to shove my hair over my cheek, something I was still learning not to do. Not that it made much difference—a week after completing my assignment and both my face and hair weren't mine yet. One still healing, the other still growing back. "It's not that. I just don't need to do it anymore."

"You're good. You could get even better still. Hell, the pay would help grease your way into courses, now that you're eligible, if that's what you're thinking."

I shook my head. The thought of it made my stomach curl. As though it were a competition, with prizes at the end. I got what I wanted; there was nothing else. "I only did it as a form of training. You knew that."

"And I'm glad to see you made it." The brief warmth in his blue eyes told me he meant it. That it was more than just his being relieved at not losing a striker. "But you don't have to lie about it anymore."

"Lie about what?"

"The other part."

I frowned, looked away. The other part. How I used contracts to distract myself from the guilt over Luc's death, hold it at bay. All strikers had their own reasons for assassinating—from money to rebellion to something more personal. I'd only told Dire it was because I needed to get stronger to face my Alt. Not the rest of it. So how did he know?

"Baer texted me to see if you had come in," he said in answer to my unasked-yet-clearly-obvious question. "Told me about your brother being a fresh PK. It wasn't hard to put the pieces together, especially after meeting you, seeing you stumble around with your answers. Hey, you wouldn't be the first striker with issues I've taken on. Anything is better than that counseling crap the Board offers."

How stupid of me to think he didn't know. I was always better at running than hiding. Now I was slowly learning that just staying put could work, too. "And since I was still messing with the system, then what did it matter, right?" I said quietly.

"You help me, I help you."

I shrugged. It was over. Whatever part I had played in the fine balance of worthiness and sacrifice, I was stopping it here.

"So, did it work?" I knew he wasn't just asking for the sake of asking. He needed to be assured that he didn't make a mistake by taking me on.

Did it work? The answer wasn't simple. Dire was still down there, waiting out whatever damage he couldn't shake. Dire had no Chord to pull him free.

"It . . . helped," I managed.

"Good to hear, Grayer," he finally said, his voice gruff.

I nodded.

"Keep those marks hidden, you got me? The Board finds out, you won't be spared just because you gave it up."

"I know. I've gone this long without getting caught, haven't I?"

"And don't forget to come by this place once in a while, if only to save me from having to track you down to make sure you're not dead somewhere."

"Thanks."

"You never know—you might change your mind one day."

But I never did go by to see him after that. My marks were enough of a reminder of what I'd done. As I slowly pull open the front door to the store and step inside, I hope his being right about my changing my mind will be enough for him to forgive my avoidance.

I can never forget the face of someone who almost got me killed, but I'm still surprised to see Hestor behind the counter.

I walk past customers waiting their turn at the plug-in and downloading stations, arrive at the counter, and wait for him to look up from whatever he's doing.

"Yeah, what can I—" That's as far as Hestor gets. His eyes widen for a fraction of a second before narrowing. "What are *you* doing here?" he asks, and his voice can't hide the fear lurking behind the words. He *should* be scared, I think resentfully. He sold me out to another striker.

"Where's Dire?" I ask, adjusting my bag. Let my sleeves roll up past my wrists so he can't miss my wrapped marks.

Hestor shakes his head, glancing over my shoulder to take in the rest of the store. Leans closer so whatever he says will remain for our ears alone. "I know you're not working for him anymore. I don't have to tell you nothing."

My voice is just as low. "Why are *you* still working for him?"

"Not my problem you didn't tattle on me. I explained it was all a mistake, that striker getting ahold of your location. Besides, Dire don't have much of a choice, considering I know about what he does."

"Do you feel bad for taking money from that striker?" I hiss at him. "Because he wasn't very good."

A snort of hot breath against my face, full of indignation. "He said he wanted information! That's all he said! He—" He stops abruptly as a customer draws dangerously close.

I pull back, force my shoulders to relax, make sure my bandages are still secure around my wrists.

"Thanks, I'll just go find him myself," I say to Hestor in a voice I hope sounds close to upbeat. As the customer starts in with a question, giving him no choice but to turn away from me, I duck into the doorway behind him. I head down the dark stairway, the same one I took my first time here.

Dire's at one of his many computer workstations, maybe even tracking one of his strikers right this very minute. He speaks without turning around.

"Well, Grayer, if this isn't a hell of a surprise." His voice is a familiar rumble, more comforting than frightening, and the shock of hearing it again brings sudden tears to my eyes. Time has passed, but not really. And it *is* good to see him, whatever the reason for my return. "I knew you weren't dead, but I would have put money on never seeing you here again."

"Sorry," I say as he gets to his feet, walking over to me. I blink fast to dry my eyes. "I didn't—Hestor, he—"

"He's been dreading the day you might show up." Dire grins, his wide face showing his genuine amusement before turning annoyed. "Serves him right for letting the contract log out of his sight."

I don't correct him. It won't change what Hector's done, what I've done. "I should have called first, I guess," I finish lamely.

"Calling just to tell me you're around and you want to say hello?" Dire shoots me a look. "Or for something that needs a little more warning?"

"Something like that."

"Something like being a striker again?"

"Kind of."

"What do you mean?"

"I need some advice about a weapon."

"I'm flattered already, Grayer."

"A Roark gun."

"How did you hear about that?" Dire asks. He's guarded now, almost wary. Unless I'm working for him, I'm a danger—someone who knows too much about what he does. The last thing he needs is to give me even more ammo, in case I turn against him. Or already am turned against him by someone else.

My answer isn't going to help with that. "I can't tell you. I'm sorry."

"Well, poison being used for completions isn't exactly light, easygoing conversation, Grayer," he says slowly. "Especially coming from someone who shouldn't even know about it. The Board hasn't approved it yet—might never, in fact. I know the tests have been all over the place, down at headquarters."

"That's what I was told, too."

"Who told you?"

"I can't tell you that, either."

"You're not making it easy for me to tell you anything, you know that?"

"I could have talked about you a long time ago."

A grunt. "Okay, you got a point there. I'll answer what I can, then. And I'm holding you to that promise about not saying anything."

"I won't. You know you can trust me."

"Fine. So shoot."

"You built the Roark gun, didn't you?"

He barks out a laugh. "I'm not that smart. Or skilled. Or patient."

"Then you know who made it."

"I do. Damn, Grayer. I should be scared how fast you connected the dots."

I shrug. "No, it's not that. You're not being obvious or anything." The Operator—Sabian—never once bragged about the Board being the ones who came up with the design. And without a doubt, he would have bragged about it if he could have. "I just figured outside of the Board, you'd be one of the very few people in Kersh who could have come up with the idea of that gun."

"The person who designed the Roark is the same person who came up with that binding agent we use for making our marks, the stuff that speeds healing afterward. She makes the guns under another identity, of course. The Board thinks my bullet supplier over on the south side of the Grid came up with it."

A flash of the lady who told me not to scream as she injected the tracking chips into my wrists. "You mean the woman who gave me my marks?"

"Yes, her name is Innes. I don't have any Roark prototypes here to play around with, though—no point if the Board's willing to take the worst of the abuse. Really is a sick but genius idea, reformatting a binder agent so it combines speed with a lethal component instead of a healing one. Instant death when it hits right."

Innes. Now I know her name. A person capable of creating

something to help speed healing, and then something to help speed death.

But shouldn't the fact that she's created an absolutely painless death count for something? No other weapon can promise the same.

"Dire, would you ever consider using a Roark for a completion?"

He scratches the scruff on his chin. "Or for one of my strikers to use one?"

I nod slowly. "Yes."

"Nope. Never."

His instant answer has me blinking in surprise. "But why not? If it's supposed to be the most efficient way?"

"Too risky. The test reports from the Board don't make me feel good enough about having them around as an option. The recoil and all. And someone finding a dead striker with a Roark gun still in hand? That'd be one hell of a news day, you can bet on that."

His words are an echo of what Sabian said to me yesterday. It casts new doubt, fresh and nagging. Sabian's warning about the Roark's danger didn't register, but hearing it again from Dire does. Maybe because I have no reason to look for hidden meanings in everything he says.

"So you came here to ask me some questions about a weapon you'll never have to use?" Dire asks. "Well, I'm going to believe it's 'cause you really just missed my fantastic and witty sense of—"

I swing my bag onto my lap, unzip it, and pull out the Roark gun, still in its case. Few but Dire would guess what was inside.

"How the hell did you get your hands on one, Grayer?" he asks.

"I'm sorry, but I can't say. And don't guess, because I don't want to have to lie."

He gives me a sour look and pulls out two of the chairs from around the table in the center of the room. "You do not make things easy," he mutters. He shoves one of the chairs at me and sits down in the other. "Sit, then. I don't know *how* you got one, but I know *where* you got it."

I sit down and lay the gun on the table. "Just how bad is it for the target if the shooter misses?" I ask Dire. "I heard it's painful if the shooter isn't accurate, but is it that much worse than a regular bullet missing its mark?"

"Yeah, you bet your ass. It's poison designed to act as soon as it makes direct contact with a pulse point—some points make better targets than others, depending on location and size. If the poison doesn't immediately connect with a point to neutralize, it gets confused. It spreads out into the body, keeps searching for one. Melts you slowly from the inside out."

"Oh." One syllable, said more like a breath, and it takes with it whatever reassurance I was hoping to hear from Dire. I didn't want to know that using this gun could somehow make pain *worse.*

"And I gotta tell you, I've seen a lot of death in my lifetime," Dire says, "most of it ugly, a lot of it inhumane. But reading those reports, what happened to those test bots . . . The worst were the ones that didn't even end up killing the target, believe it or not."

"You mean there were survivors?"

"Well, *physically,* sure. Turned out that shooting a target directly in the eye led to a different kind of reaction, one that didn't kill. What the poison did instead was read a working Alt code as a pulse point and permanently and completely neutralized all parts of it. Instead of the target dying, they became a non-Alt, a non-person. Incompletes might be dead, but at least they don't have to try carving out a life without an identity, sneaking resources they aren't qualified for."

Sabian didn't mention this at all. Which makes sense. If today's prototypes of Roark guns got in the wrong hands, a whole new kind of Alt would be created. The system would go to hell. My mind is all over the place with the implications.

"But then no one would have to die," I say to Dire. "Strikers could use it and not have to kill. And the other Alt would be complete and Kersh would still get its worthy soldier."

He shakes his head. "No, that's the wrong way to look at it, Grayer. Strikers don't leave loose ends. Also, the Board would never stop hunting them because they aren't part of the system. They'd be wild cards, and wild cards are unpredictable. Difficult to control."

I stare at the gun, at a loss. Within the span of a few minutes, Dire's shoved reality down my throat—that the Roark might not be the best choice. That it might not be a choice at all.

Unless I can be better than I've ever been before.

"Still not feeling talkative, Grayer?" Dire asks, watching me closely.

I shake my head. "Thank you for answering my questions, especially considering how much I was able to tell you."

"Which was next to nothing." He reaches over and picks up the gun. He slips off the case and looks at it beneath the thin lamplight over the table.

It's exactly as I remember it from headquarters. Weird to see the same weapon in Dire's work-roughened hands and not in Sabian's well-manicured ones.

Dire removes something else from the case, a slim silver sleeve. He unfurls it onto the table, a lethal snake, and I lean over to look with him.

The poison. Three thin, transparent vials, each the width of a small straw, half the length of a cigarette. Inside each vial is a tiny dart of poison, as fine as a hair, as pale as gold. It's this dart that breaks free as soon as it's discharged from the gun, entering the body while leaving the vial behind.

"Three shots, Grayer," Dire mutters. "That many targets, eh?"

My head snaps up. "I'm . . . sorry. I can't—"

He waves away my fumbling. "What I mean is, I don't have any extra vials lying around. Is this enough?" *Will it be enough to kill who you need to kill?* "You know what you're doing?"

I don't, not at all. "Yes."

"You might not be working for me anymore, but I still don't want to see you get into any trouble out there. And I think I'd hear from my old friend Baer if he knew you came to see me and you end up in the deep end somehow."

Heat in my eyes at his caring. "I'll be fine." All I can force out.

"Don't be so stubborn, Grayer. Or stupid. Don't go into whatever you're about to go into without telling at least one person what's going on. Who knows where you might find yourself with no one to come save your butt."

"I'll be fine," I say again.

"Suit yourself, Grayer," Dire says, sounding disgruntled. I don't blame him. I show up and demand answers for half questions and now I'm insisting on doing everything the wrong way.

"Now look," he says. The gun looks ridiculously fragile in his hand, like a delicate bird cupped in an oversized palm. An optical illusion—I remember how heavy the thing is. "It works the same as your basic gun. Load the vial as you would a bullet. Aim. Fire. Complete. Strike done."

"I'm not a—this isn't a—"

"Sorry, I forgot." He places the gun back into its case, hands it to me, and gets to his feet. I stand up, too, tucking away the gun and the vials inside my school bag before slinging it over my shoulder.

"I don't need to ask you not to flash that thing around, okay?" he says, giving me a halfhearted scowl. "Don't get dead, Grayer."

He turns back to his computers. I don't bother to say anything else before I start walking upstairs. There's no point. Good-byes between killers seem like a funny idea, anyway. Our strikes don't get the chance before we take them out; who says we should?

Hestor's eyes bore a hole into my back as I leave the store, but I barely notice.

"Time," I mutter as I push the door open and dive back into the Grid. The crowd already feels different—cover rather than company.

13:15. Way past lunch, but I don't feel like eating. The need to get everything done that needs to be done before I go under tonight dulls everything else. I make myself stop at a kiosk for a sandwich that I slowly eat while waiting for the inner ward train.

Since I'm in the Grid, it's not long before an active comes by. I watch her, a girl a bit older than me, as she digs through the green bin at the train stop. Her eyes are black—with hunger and the spiral of her assignment numbers. Desperation is her perfume.

I cut through passersby—all in a hurry, desensitized by time, too fearful of the Board to even think of interfering with an assignment—and hand her the rest of my food. She takes it without a word before slipping away. Which is what I expected. I remember that feeling as an active. Pride doesn't go easily.

The train comes, and I slip into a seat near the front. I still have to explain to Baer that I won't be around for a few days, without telling him the truth.

And Chord . . . I'll have to be careful to avoid running into him. I'm not ready to see him yet. Not when I know I'll have to leave him afterward, and why.

I arrive right after the bell rings. I have ten minutes before last period starts. It's a Tuesday, so I should be heading toward math, but instead I head for Baer's classroom.

Standing in the doorway is not a good idea. Chord's locker is just outside—if he comes by to get anything or drop something off, he'll notice me. I already texted him that I won't be around after school, that I'll meet him at home later, so he won't think of looking for me.

Inside the classroom, students shuffle past me, in a hurry

to get to their next classes. A few say hello, and I smile back without seeing them.

Baer's not inside. But I recognize his jacket draped over the back of his chair. He's around somewhere.

I'm bumped as someone rushes past. One of the last students to leave, the one assigned to collect the throwing blades from the stations on the way out.

"Sorry, Grayer," he calls out as he sets the bag down on Baer's desk before taking off.

Restless and anxious, knowing the classroom is going to start filling soon and it'll only get harder for me to tell him my news, I drag the bag of blades toward me.

Flicking one open, I check the release for catches. Run my finger down the edge. I set the blade aside on the desk and move on to the next, then the next, a mindless chore that's still not mindless enough to help my nerves.

Where is Baer?

When I come across a familiar blade, I stop. It's one of Aave's. My oldest brother's. I took it after his incompletion. With my assignment over, and working for Baer at the school, I guess it was a slow, natural migration for my weapons to end up here.

Aave. Memories of him showing us how to hold a blade properly, how to let the weight of the weapon carry out its own momentum instead of relying too much on the force of our throws. It's not the only way I remember him, but they're the strongest images I have of him now. Softened and faded by time.

I set aside Aave's blade and dig through the bag until I find the one I'm looking for. The knife I took from my Alt's boyfriend when I had to kill him. The knife I used to kill my Alt.

So much hurt, all by my hand. I flick the knife open, slide the blade against my finger. Her blood's long gone. The immediate aftermath of that day is blurry, something I'll probably never remember all that well. Like the afterimage you see when your eyes have been singed with a flash of bright light.

A hiss escapes from between my teeth. I've pressed too hard. A thin line of blood stains the blade. The sight is unnerving—it's been a long time since I've seen red on steel, and I wonder if I'm as ready as I need to be. I wipe the blood off on my jacket and drop the knife next to Aave's blade on the desktop. Together, they are the bookends of my life up to this point.

I put the first blade back in the bag and shove the whole thing onto its shelf in the cabinet.

We're supposed to be starting target practice next, knives. My heart sinks. I should be here for that, to teach what I know.

"Better late than never, Grayer?"

I turn around to see Baer—and the first of the next class's students filing in behind him.

"Where were you this morning?" he asks, frowning. His gaze falls to his desk.

Crap. The blades. And I was supposed to be here this morning.

"I'm sorry, I forgot." Stumbling, already swearing silently at myself. The worst time to break routine and get Baer wondering. In all the months I've been his classroom assistant, I've never missed a class without giving warning. "Really," I add lamely.

"Well, what are you doing here now? You're not sched—"

"I won't be able to help for a few days," I say in a rush,

conscious of the steadily filling classroom. "I have to . . . There's something I need to do."

Baer's frown gets bigger and his pale eyes narrow. "Does the school admin know?"

"I was going to tell them on the way out."

He turns around, watches as more students start to settle in. Only a minute or two before the second bell rings. Baer takes another look at the blades I've left out on his desk.

"Dire?" he asks quietly.

"*No.* Not him." My face is stiff. I want to think it's like a wall rather than glass, without signs blazing everywhere revealing what I'm getting ready to do.

Baer moves closer and picks up the two blades from his desk and holds them out to me. His eyes are worried, tired, older. The same as any parent of an active. There's no way he can guess it all—the whos, whys, whens—but he's guessed enough.

"You'll want these, I think," he says. "For whatever it is you're doing."

I clutch the blades to my chest. "I—"

"Go, Grayer." With that he steps away and calls the students to attention. Starts the class.

I walk out, arms numb from holding death so tightly that none of it will fall and call further attention to myself. I am already gone, already under. The sounds of Baer's lecture follow me out, familiar words that I've heard him say hundreds of times to students.

But this time it feels like they're directed only to me: *Be careful. Use your skills. Remember that there is no bigger challenge than your Alt. You can't lose.*

There's always something to be lost.

My gun is still in my front jacket pocket, so I shove the blades in the other. Some habits just won't die.

I'm sitting on the curb of the outer school grounds, waiting for Marsden and Thora—I promised them last week I'd go shopping, which is impossible now, and I need to apologize in person for having to ditch them—when Dess's text comes through on my cell.

Hey West?

For a second, I want to just ignore it. Dess is the younger brother I never had. And at the same time, a weird blend of the siblings I did have once—Aave, Luc, and Ehm. All of them rolled into this little eleven-year-old whom I've come to love. I can't let him find out. And I don't want to lie to explain why I'll be out of reach for the next three days in case he calls. But it didn't go so great the last time I told him a hard truth.

I remember every bit of it.

"I'll wait here for the food," Chord said. He gave me a pointed look. "You guys want to grab a table?"

"C'mon, West, that one by the window is free now." Dess took off across the restaurant, weaving past crowded tables, the blue cap on his head a blur. Lunchtime meant chaos in the District Grill, his current fast-food place of choice. Who was I to argue with him when I was about to tell him I used to kill for money.

Maybe being in a public place would keep him from freaking out. Maybe. Not likely.

"Chord." I looked up at him, feeling guilty that I asked him to come and relief that he was there. "I don't know if I can do this," I muttered. My hands were shoved deep into my pockets, sleeves pulled down. Safe still. "He might never have to know, ever, if I just leave it."

"You have to, West. Dess isn't stupid. He hangs out with you for long enough, he'll figure it out himself." Chord's dark eyes go soft with sympathy. He brushed my hair—just starting to grow out—away from my face, touched my healing scar with his fingers. "Don't you think he'll take it better if you tell him first?"

I took a deep breath. "Right. Okay."

Approaching an eleven-year-old kid to tell him something he won't like is as frightening as any strike.

I wove my way through customers and tables and pulled out the chair across from Dess. Sitting down, I watched him start a collection of straw wrappers in preparation for blowing them at other customers. Or just Chord and I, more likely.

I shoved the tray out of the way. *Do it fast. Like a Band-Aid.* "Dess, I have to—"

"Man, I'm starving!" He was as excited as I've ever seen him, as excited as Ehm used to be when we took her out without our parents. Older siblings were cool. Finding out they were assassins, not so much. "My mom said I have to be home by six for dinner. The movie will be over by then, right?"

I nodded. "Yes, you'll be fine." *Please be fine.* I took my hands out of my pockets, crossed my arms in front of me. My wrists, still covered. "Dess—"

"Because she said that if I was even one minute late—"

"*Dess.*"

"Yeah, what?" His confusion was innocent. How much

easier it would have been if there was even a little bit of suspicion there.

"There's something . . . ," I began. Shook my head, started over. My hands ached, I was squeezing them so tightly. "Do you think if you're going to complete your assignment, it matters how you do it?" I finally ask him.

Dess went still. His own completion still fresh, just weeks ago. "What do you mean?"

"You know how there's extra training out there for some idles, right?"

"Yeah, if you can pay for it."

"I wasn't one of those idles who could pay, Dess."

"But you're really good with blades, West. Remember how you helped me that first time we met? I thought you must have—"

"No, I didn't. Some of it was just from practicing on my own, or with my family, but some of it . . . I chose another way. To learn how to beat her." I took a deep breath.

I couldn't miss the alarm that crossed his face. "There's no other way."

Say it. "You know about strikers." I wasn't even asking. No point. Everyone in Kersh knew.

Dess nodded. Fresh bewilderment was written all over him, and I wondered if that was how I looked when Baer first told me about Dire: soft, impossibly young. How Ehm would have looked. *They are no urban myth,* Baer had said.

"Yeah, but I don't know any for real, though. . . ." Dess trailed off.

His eyes fell to my wrists. I could see him thinking about how my wrists were always hidden from plain view. Shock and disgust, anger and betrayal. I was everything that was wrong. I killed according to who could pay me, not because of weakness or strength. If the barrier around Kersh broke, I had something to do with it.

"You know one, Dess," I said bleakly. Too late to take it back, any of it. "Me."

Dess got up. Afraid. Of me. One wordless shake of his head and he was gone.

I was still sitting there, unmoving, when Chord showed up a couple of minutes later. He simply placed our food on the table, pressed a kiss to the top of my head, and took me by the hand. We walked out. And I went home to wait.

When Dess finally texted me two days later, it was this:

Are you still striking?

No, I'm done, I texted back.

Then: *Good. It's okay, then.*

I pretended everything was fine. So did he. Eventually it was fine. It *felt* fine. And that was how we left it.

Until now.

What's up Dess? I tap onto my screen, still sitting on the curb outside of school. On impulse, I switch it to visual so we can see each other. It feels right to have this conversation face to face.

"Hey, West!" His cheerful kid face is on my screen, and in the background I can see a bunch of other boys. There is a corner of blue sky, green treetops.

I like seeing Dess like this, just hanging out with his friends—a complete, no worries about death, just living life.

But it's also sad to see his friends. Boys, all around his age. Qualifying age, but not yet active since they're on campus. If

I visit a year from now, how many of them will be left? In two years? In three? Not this many.

If I could spare any kid from facing their Alt, is it wrong to want to? What about my own? *Especially* my own?

"Hey, West!" Dess says again, his grin at seeing me contagious enough that I can smile back, even if my heart isn't in it.

"Hey, Dess. Where are you off to?"

"We're going to go check out that virtual arcade, the one they just fixed up after that fire last year."

"Sounds fun."

"Hey, so I just wanted to make sure. Are you and Chord still taking me to that sports tourney on Thursday? The one in Calden?"

I'm already letting people down, and I haven't even started yet. First Baer, now him. "Dess, I'm sorry, I can't make it. I won't be in Jethro then. There's some required upgrading for the assistants working with the skills program." Lie, lie, lie.

His face drops. "But it's opening week."

"We'll take you—Chord and I both—when I get back, all right?"

"But you promised me ages ago."

"I'm so sorry, Dess. I can't."

"Sure, West, okay." His disappointment is palpable, even through the screen.

"Dess, I'm sorry."

"I'm going to go now. My friends are waiting."

"Okay, I'll—" But the screen turns dark. He's disconnected already. And I don't blame him.

For a long minute, I just sit there, unable to move. Finally I text an apology to Marsden and Thora, blaming a bad headache and the need to get home. I get to my feet. Against the heat of the afternoon sun, my face burns, and I can swear my marks are burning, too. Home, then, and I start walking. I replay Dess's words in my head, the ones he asked me months ago to make sure he wasn't wrong to trust.

Are you still striking?

No, I'm done.

Lie, lie, lie.

CHAPTER 7

I remove all my weapons before heading over to see Chord. No guns, no blades, no poison. This is the last of my time with him, before I let myself go cold again.

He's at the door seconds after I knock. All height and wild dark hair and even darker eyes. I've never been happier to see him.

"Hey, where have you been?" he asks. He's got a tablet in one hand. I've caught him doing his homework. "Thora said you had a headache or something?"

I step up and wrap my arms around him tightly. Press my nose into his chest so I can breathe in his scent, absorb what I can of this normal after-school life. Like a safeguard until I'm done, this gleaned antidote. "Sorry, I did." Lies, once they start, take on a life of their own. "But I walked it off."

Chord holds the back of my neck with his free hand and leans down to kiss me. "That's good. You didn't want a ride?"

"No, I think I just needed some air."

He grabs my hand and squeezes. "Hey . . . listen . . . ," he starts.

His voice is not his own, full of distraction, and I'm mad

at myself for not realizing right away that something's wrong. A single curl of alarm pierces the heavy anxiety that's taken up most of my stomach, ever since the Operator showed himself. But I just talked to Dess, and Chord's right here, safe . . .

"What is it?" I ask.

Over Chord's shoulder, I can hear someone moving inside his house.

"It's Nash," Chord says quietly at my look. "We're just finishing up that chem demo I was telling you about. Cutting it close, but it should get done in time. Too late to replace Quinn with someone else."

"Where's Quinn?"

"He went active last night."

I picture the boy who spoke to Chord in the hall at school yesterday. His clear gray eyes are no longer clear. They'll be closer to black now with assignment numbers.

I follow Chord inside, and Nash is in the front room. He's gathering his stuff—tablet, papers, charts—off the coffee table and pushing it into his backpack. He looks up as we come in. A sunburst of sandy hair, eyes a light brown. In their depths, and in the sluggish movements of his hands, is dull shock, shot through with fear. And I know it's not just because he and Quinn have been good friends for years, but also because Nash is still an idle.

"Hi, West," Nash says. "How's it going?"

"Okay. You don't have to leave, though."

"Nah, me and Chord have one more day. We can meet up tomorrow."

"I'm sorry about Quinn." I want to tell Nash that everything will be okay, but I don't. Can't. I have no clue how strong

Quinn's Alt might be. It might already be over, and we simply don't know it yet.

"Yeah, thanks." Nash slowly zips up his bag. "I think . . . I think he'll be the one, though? He's always had a really good aim, you know? And he's sneaky as hell when he wants to be, don't you guys think?"

I look up at Chord, who only shakes his head at me. He looks grim, but as a complete, as the one left in the wake of the incompletions of loved ones, this is familiar ground. Terrible and ugly, but familiar. "See you tomorrow, Nash," he says. "Let me know how much I can do on my end tonight."

"Sounds good. See you at school." Nash opens the front door, is about to step out, when he stops. Looks back, his face vulnerable. "You guys are both completes. You know what it takes. And you've seen his skills. Does he even stand a chance?"

Chord looks at me, his expression torn open, apologetic. Because Nash doesn't know *how* Chord completed his assignment. Chord being the one, and worthy, never even came up. It was my brother—and Chord's best friend—who died the day we found Chord's Alt. Luc's death saved Chord.

The silence is stretching out too long, so I snap it with a half-truth: "We all stand a chance, Nash. It's how the system works. You know that."

He exhales, nods. Gives us a wave and leaves, careful to shut the front door behind him.

Chord sits down heavily on the couch. Tosses the tablet he was still holding onto the coffee table. His expression is bleak, broken.

I move closer to him, aching to do for him what he always

seems to do for me without any thought at all: make things right.

"Chord, I . . ." Stumble to a stop.

Because I'm not him, far from it, and I'm still learning and still at a loss when he's the one hurting.

Chord looks at me. And waits. He never seems to lack patience when it comes to me. I don't know how he does it, when I would have walked away from myself many times over by now. But his eyes are full of ghosts, and right or wrong it's on the tip of my thoughtless, careless tongue to tell him. About Sabian, about his offer, about *everything*—

He takes my hand and pulls me down to sit on his lap. Fits me against his chest until neither of us are going anywhere. He bends his head down and sighs against my neck.

"Tell me again that we're done," Chord says quietly. His lips brush my skin. Painting me.

I touch the side of his face. *We're done, Chord,* is what I want to say. Instead I say, "It's really sad about Quinn."

Another sigh. "Yeah, it is. What do you think? About him completing?"

I try to place him in class and come up blank. "I don't know. He might be okay, in the end. Depending . . ."

"On his Alt."

"Yes."

"Poor guy."

"Which one?" I ask him.

"Both, I guess."

I nod. It's easy to forget that both Alts are just as worthy to those who love them.

"But it doesn't change me wanting Quinn to win," Chord says. "Or feeling for his family, his friends. Like Nash."

"I know. Same for me."

Chord slowly presses his mouth against my neck. Tilts us over and slides us lower until we're both lying down on the couch. Him beneath me. Eye to eye. No hiding possible. Only because it's Chord is this bearable. To be vulnerable but not feel like I'm in danger.

I trace the lines and angles of his face with my eyes, so familiar to me now that I see them in my sleep: the ebony slashes of his eyebrows, eyes dark over high cheekbones, the overly wide mouth, the strong jaw. Skin neither light nor dark, his head full of thick brown curls.

"Hey," Chord says to me softly. We're mere inches apart. My trembling exhales are his inhales, our blood warming each other through our skin, his thudding pulse setting the pace of mine.

"Hey." Despite it all—the sorrow over Quinn, the weight of what I'm about to do pressing ever closer—I'm smiling. Right here, right now, I'm happy. "I'm glad I came by," I say to him.

"Me too." Chord's voice, huskier now, his words liquid with heat. His eyes, even darker, narrow slightly. He tugs me closer. He tastes and smells of everything that is him, everything that I love, and I wrap my hands around the sides of his face, not wanting to let him go. Not wanting to miss the feel of his body beneath me, holding me to this life, this world spun between just the two of us.

So I let myself drown. In him, in this. Chord kisses and

kisses me, devastating me and saving me, and I meet him beat for beat.

Forget everything for just a while.

Until the cell in my pocket buzzes. A text. Sabian.

Against Chord's mouth I freeze.

"West?" Chord winds his hands deeper into my hair. My name is a rough whisper on his lips. Still tangled against mine.

Slowly I break free, lean back.

I can't be here anymore.

"I should go," I say to him. I press another kiss against his mouth, slow and full, a brand and a claim, and sit up.

He looks at me. His eyes are like fire on my skin. "You're kidding, right?"

I shake my head. "No, I . . ." My pulse is heavy in my throat. "I've got so much homework to catch up on. I've been so distracted with counseling . . ." I get off him and stand up. The ground is solid, but I still feel shaky inside.

Chord sits up, swings his legs around, and stands. He catches my hand with his and tugs me closer until I'm standing right against him. Nothing to look at except his face, and no way to hide mine from his.

Never do I need to be more careful than right now.

"Hey, why the hurry?" he asks. His eyes chase mine down. "You want me to come over? I got that chem demo I can—"

I shake my head. "You know we wouldn't get anything done if you came over, Chord." I grab his hand tight. "And I really have to."

"Is it something else?"

"Like what?"

His gaze is both troubled and embarrassed. "I didn't mean to push you. Have I been pushing you lately? I thought we were okay, deciding to go ahead and—"

I kiss him. "No, it's not that. At all."

He sighs. Runs his free hand through his hair, making it even messier. "West, you're killing me."

"I'm sorry."

Chord kisses my wrist. "You sure?"

I nod, not trusting my voice.

"All right, if you say so." He wraps his arms around me so tightly I can barely breathe. But I don't fight it. I don't care that there's no air, that I can't move. It would mean having to stay. Safe with him.

He relaxes his grip, and time restarts, my decision still made.

Chord tucks my hair behind my ears. "I should feel guilty that I don't care about you getting your homework done, but I don't."

"I know you don't. I'm *glad* you don't."

Chord adjusts the neckline of my shirt, smiles, lets his lips brush against my forehead. "Can I walk you over?"

Say no. And get moving. He's *waiting.*

"No, it's fine. Stay here and get your demo done," I say.

"I'd rather spend time with—"

I stand on my tiptoes and tilt his head down and press a final kiss onto his mouth. "I love you, Chord," I whisper roughly.

He doesn't let me pull back before he's there, capturing my words with his, letting them gather and grow together. "I love you, too, West Grayer. Don't ever forget that."

Not even possible. "You don't, either, then."

"I won't," he says. A promise. I take it with me so it can lead me back.

• • •

I sit on the edge of my bed, and with the silence of the house like thunder in my ears, I tap my cell awake with a finger that's not quite steady.

And learn how to best complete my next assignment. Memorize her face and form, her weaknesses and strengths. This idle who I'm going to kill. Nausea rises in my throat and I barely manage to swallow it back.

Watching the text scroll across the screen, I'm reminded that I've done this before—too many times. The only thing that tells me I'm not reliving the past is that typical striker clients can't write up such a detailed, meticulously researched spec sheet. By the time clients contact strikers, they're well aware of time slipping away. Their spec sheets are punctuated by desperation.

I pick out the most relevant info and read it again:

Origin Point: 667 Hudson Street,
      Gaslight Ward
Time of expected contact: 20:00
Of special note: Alt has specifically requested this
      additional shift for extra payment.
      Calculated probability of a no-show: <2%

And then a picture of the idle.

I close the document, knowing the spec sheet will be automatically wiped away. The Board, covering its tracks. I tuck my cell into my jeans pocket and get to my feet. Go to pick up my bag where I left it by my door and carry it over to where I've laid out all the weapons on my desk.

The Roark gun with its vials of poison, my old gun, and the two switchblades.

I pick up the Roark and the vials and drop them into my open bag. My fingers gently skim over the old gun and blades. *Not for me to use this time.*

My hands are shaking as I tear a sheet from the tablet of watercolor paper on my desk and grab a pen from one of the buckets. What to say to Chord? I'm at a loss as usual when it comes to words. This time, it seems there's too much to say to even possibly know where to start.

So I do what I've always done. Let my actions and my weapons be enough to speak for me. I place my gun and the blades next to the piece of paper. With my pen, I scrawl this:

Chord, I'm okay, and I'm even leaving these behind to show you I'm perfectly safe. I'll be back in a few days and I'll explain everything then. Please don't try to find me. I'm asking you not to, all right? I love you.

—West

P.S. This has nothing to do with Baer or Dire, so there's no point in asking them about it.

And that's it. There's nothing else to be said.

I zip up my bag and sling the straps over my shoulders. They settle in easily, already familiar.

Downstairs, I force myself to eat something. Nothing that requires thought to put together—a granola bar, water, a leftover slice of the pizza from last night. When I'm done, I do what I do every night before going to bed. Twist the blinds shut, wipe off the counters in the kitchen, and sort trash from recyclables. I'm moving on autopilot again.

Three days. Less if I'm quick. Physically, I think I'm in good enough shape to do it—it's the mental part that I'm not sure about.

I turn off all the lights inside as I leave the house. It's starting to get dark out now, and the low gloom enfolds my home like a blanket, putting it to sleep.

I walk fast down my driveway. Hit the street at a near run as I make my way toward the outer ward train station, the one that will take me to Gaslight Ward. The faster I move, the less time I have for thoughts and worries . . . the less time I have to think of what I'm leaving behind and what's up ahead.

CHAPTER 8

I let the rain clean my skin as I stand on a street near the western shore of Gaslight, looking at the back lot of a strip of buildings. Not too far behind me the city barrier cuts across the sky. It's thin and almost spindly from far away, but I know up close its bars would be as thick as my leg, the iron black and solid.

Completes are on tour out there, monitoring their sectors of the barrier. Even just behind me, traipsing back and forth as they cover their appointed ground, looking for signs of intrusion, for signs of the Surround. I think of Kasey, who is out there right now, walking his sector somewhere in Jethro. They must feel the rain like I do, their uniforms turning dark with moisture, droplets glistening off their watch cuffs.

I can't see the ocean from here—it's much too dark out now—but I can smell it. The brine of an endless slate of bobbing gray, the end of land as I know it, no further place to go. Even if you find yourself beyond the barrier for some reason, the ocean only meets up with war on the other side . . . if you don't meet warships on the water first. The waves make a soft, hollow echo, and I imagine the distant slap of it against the aged signs nailed to posts shoved into the ground, right before the shoreline: THIS MARKS THE MARINAL AND MILITARY DIVISIONS BETWEEN KERSH AND THE SURROUND. DO NOT CROSS. THANK YOU THE BOARD.

There's a tinge of salt in the air, a stinging damp on my lips as I watch the front of the building across the street. I wonder with a kind of practiced, clinical distance what I could have missed. Something on the spec sheet that I must have misread. The mistake is on my end, absolutely, because there's no way any Level 1 Operator would have overlooked such a significant detail.

Because what I'm looking for isn't here.

A scooter. Which should be parked in the back lot of the beverage distillery where my target works part-time as a server, this idle who is supposed to be driving that same scooter home. This idle who is my strike, the Alt of a stranger I've decided to save. Guilt flashes again, and it's right to be there, but I push it away.

Think, West. You don't want to be chasing her all night, do you?

And I *am* thinking. So hard that I can feel the first twists of panic start gathering inside my gut. With no spec sheet left on my cell to fall back on, I'm stuck with my memory. Maybe it's not as ready as I thought it was—because she is not where I need her to be.

"Time," I say quietly on a low exhale. My breath is a puff of heat that splits the cool air.

My watch beeps back at me: *20:17.*

She should have been done with her shift seventeen minutes ago. I've been waiting and watching since a quarter to, but I don't think I could have missed her slipping out early. And

Sabian specifically noted her wanting this shift, so I have no reason to believe she just wouldn't show. So not only is she late to leave, but also her scooter's gone.

I swear under my breath. Resign myself to go inside. I can risk being seen by her because she is an unsuspecting idle, but I'd wanted to keep it cleaner than that.

Out of old habit—old but far from forgotten—I hitch my thumbs into the straps of my bag to tighten them. Run my hands over the pockets of my light rain jacket and those of my jeans to make sure my weapons are there. But they're not, of course—not the gun or the blades I know. The Roark gun, jostled with my searching hand, bounces against my waist, and the swing of its weight brings me back. To being an active . . . to being a striker.

Just three more. And what are three more when I've already killed so many? Especially three who are insignificant, unworthy, a threat to Kersh . . . though they hold my freedom in their hands.

Crossing the street, I carefully weave a path through the slow slink of traffic before heading down the side alley toward the front of the buildings, my feet are muffled echoes on the pavement. I turn the corner and walk along the storefronts.

As I enter the distillery, steam and heat form a warm wave. Too warm, and a coil of nausea starts to unfurl before I manage to snuff it out, leaving nothing but a bitterness in the back of my mouth.

Which quickly goes dry.

I see her.

She's near the back of the store, her face a match with the one on my cell: hair dyed a light violet and pulled back into a loose ponytail, eyes a coppery brown, skin flushed pink with the humidity that's like an invisible film in the air. She's vivid and alive against the hissing steel machinery of the distillers that line the wall, the long slabs of metal counters made dull by years of washing and wiping, heating and cooling. In the fall and winter, this place would be serving hot drinks to go; now that the weather's turned warm, she's serving cold drinks during her after-school shifts.

She's pulling a blue jacket over her uniform and talking to one of the workers. Fast and agitated, it's obvious something's wrong. She points toward the back exit, the one that would take her to her scooter. So she's realized it, too, then. Confirming that her scooter isn't where it's supposed to be.

I take a few steps farther into the shop, neither straying too far from the entrance nor getting deep enough inside to be mistaken for waiting in line. Looking at everything, yet nothing in particular, is the best way not to be noticed. It is the *between* where I don't exist.

It's impossible to hear what she's saying from where I am. The chatter of customers waiting to pick up their drinks is too loud to filter out. I move closer and against my will find myself holding my breath.

"I don't—" he says, frowning.

"—someone took off—" Her voice, angry and clipped.

"—should just call and report—"

"—not going to care, it's just a scoo—"

"—might turn it in."

A lull in the noise in the store and for a few seconds her voice is perfectly clear. "Whatever," she says, shaking her head. "It's gone. I'll report it in the morning. Inner ward train it is, then." A frustrated sigh and she's tying an airy yellow scarf around her neck.

Stylish utilitarian jacket for the rain and a summer scarf to soften the look. A heart or neck shot is still technically possible, but not being able to see exactly where I'm aiming is too risky. So I'm down to the temple now. I had wanted to shoot her from a distance there in the back lot, sight unseen. Catching her alone and distracted as she begins to climb on her scooter to drive home.

I went from having three options in which to make the perfect shot to just one.

She's waving good-bye to the guy and walking toward me. I can't help but watch her closely as she passes. Her eyes skim past me, no sense of doom or ill-fated connection—I'm just another customer in the store. Only when the muggy air stirs enough in her wake to lift strands of my hair am I somehow able to move. Propelled by guilt, need, and the knowledge that I'm doing what is best for Kersh.

I'm outside, moving steadily. The sight of her back thirty feet away on the crowded sidewalk is a beacon, and I follow it, keeping it in view despite the jumble of bodies flowing around us. Step for step . . . at first. Without even knowing I've made the decision, I'm slowly speeding up. Catching up.

Road traffic is a bit lighter, the cars moving so fast that no one dares to cut across. She's going to the corner to cross the street at the light. The train station is a block away, the inner ward one that's headed in the direction of her house. The memory of her address from her spec sheet burns with cruel finality, the fact that she is about to die, and for a second I wish more than anything that I can simply forget what I've learned about this idle. Because without a doubt she is the weaker Alt. The unworthy one. Against any normal Alt, she might stand a chance. Even at sixteen and with nothing more than the basic Alt Skills program to her name. But against an Alt who's not only from Leyton but also from the Board?

No chance at all.

I'm twenty feet behind her, and she's ten feet away from the corner.

Fifteen feet behind her, and I'm narrowing in at the perfect pace.

The light at the corner turns red, and the crowd gathers there, waits. It will be perfectly reasonable for a girl to suddenly stumble and fall with so many bodies moving all at once. Maybe she'll have dropped something and is groping around for it. There'll be no need for anyone to fight the crowd and go back and check if she's okay.

Slowly I lower my hand into my pocket. Fit the small gun into my palm, slip my finger around the trigger. It takes me more than one try to do it, my palm sweaty as hell, my nerves close to shattering.

Five feet behind her now, and she reaches the corner. Stops at the edge of the crowd and pulls out her cell as she waits. *I do that all the time,* I think, the realization vague and dim. I watch as she brings the cell to her ear, waiting for someone on the other end to answer. All the while, her yellow scarf continues to flutter in the wind, holding my gaze.

I'm at the corner, right behind her. We're both still, everything's still, as we wait. Only my breathing is erratic to my ears, jumpy and nervous. The gun in my pocket is heavy, pulling on my jacket, and I wonder how any of these people can miss what I'm carrying.

The light changes. Red to green.

Go.

All around us the crowd surges. She follows, and I'm swept up, too. The edge of her scarf—it's soft, flimsy—and tendrils of her hair flow out and brush my cheek.

We cross the street and are back on the sidewalk. I close the gap with her until we're shoulder to shoulder, at the back of the crowd. She's slowed, probably too distracted by her conversation to keep up. She's on my left, and I start to lift my elbow to knock her phone from her hand. I can see it already. How she'll stop dead, give me a dirty look, crouch down to find it at her feet. Her temple near my hand, the poison at the ready—

When her words make me hesitate.

"—coming home now, Mom." She pauses, listening. "Don't worry, I know which train to take."

Mom. Yes. Of course she's got a family. Why wouldn't she?

Someone nearly steps between us before falling back again, and I know my chance is slipping away.

Sweat is a thin dribble down my neck.

Someone in front of us laughs, someone beside me sneezes.

The breeze. It lifts her scarf again. Up close, I can see that it's actually a floral print, delicate and pretty against the blue of her jacket.

She taps her cell to sleep and is starting to tuck it into her pocket.

Now.

Do it.

I stick my left foot out and she stumbles over it. I lift my left knee and shove it into her hip. Off balance, she goes down fast.

"Hey—" she says. An abrupt protest.

I sense more than actually see some of the crowd turn around to see what's happening behind them.

I rush to bend over her. "I'm so sorry," I say to her through numb lips. "I tripped. I'm so sorry . . ." And I am. *I am.*

The crowd turns away, no longer interested.

Just me and her left on the sidewalk. For only a handful of seconds, though.

"You didn't trip, you pushed me," she says, scowling at me from where she's still lying on the ground. Her eyes, narrowed in anger. "I felt it, don't lie. It was your—"

The Roark gun is at her temple now. Steady as I've ever held any gun. Just the slightest taste of nerves in my mouth, the thin boom of my pulse in my ears. It tells me I'm still human, still West, still the girl Chord loves. I picture the clear poison contained within the tiny cylindrical dart, ready to be heated and given life even as it ends one.

Her eyes widen, the bright copper of them gleaming.

I'm so sorry. The words are on my lips, seemingly the only thing I can think to say to this idle I'm supposed to kill. *I'm so sorry.*

But what I say instead is this: "I'm supposed to kill you. But I don't want to do it. And you're in trouble. So if you want to figure a way out of this, then get up and follow me."

• • •

The alleys in this part of Gaslight are dirty and run-down, making me think of the Grid. Bricks and windows crusted with a thin layer of shimmery dust. They say if you swipe your finger along it and dare to take a taste, it's salty. I guess being this close to the ocean, sea spray is thick and seemingly on every single surface.

Another reason why this isn't the Grid. The alley is deserted. No one else here.

I still have the gun pointed at the idle, but I know now that I can't pull the trigger.

I've failed. Chord, Kersh, myself.

And this idle. Because even though I can't kill her, neither can I let her go. She's been marked for sure death by Sabian, whether it'll be by my hand or the next person he decides to hire.

"What did I do?" she asks, the question strung out on a long, shaky breath, as though speaking steadily would make me pull the trigger. "What do you want?"

"I've been hired to kill you." I'm repeating myself, no clue what else to say. Remotely aware that my own voice is just as low, just as uneven. Like I'm scared, too. "But I don't want to do it."

"You already said that, back on the street." She swallows. The pretty floral scarf wobbles, still knocked askew from her earlier fall. It's stained with dirt and the dark wet of her tears. "I still don't know what you want. Why am I in trouble?"

"Someone important wants you dead and your Alt alive."

"I don't . . . I don't understand what you're talking about." There's near hysteria in her voice now, which means soon she won't be capable of a rational response to any question or choice.

Choice.

And I think I already knew what I was going to do, deep down. But it's taken me this long to understand it, what it means for everyone.

"I'm going to give you a choice," I say to her. "Live the only way left for you now, or die."

The idle backs up until her back hits brick with a smack. Her face is sickly pale against the dull gray-red of it. "I don't know what you mean. What does that mean? 'Live the only way left'? I don't want to die!"

Dire's words in my head: *They became a non-Alt, a non-person. Incompletes might be dead, but at least they don't have to try carving out a life without an identity, sneaking resources they aren't qualified for.*

"Are you a striker?" The Alt's eyes are bright pools of panic. "Because I'm still an idle. You must have the wrong target. I'm not—"

"I'm not a striker." My gun wavers, making me doubt my aim, and it occurs to me that there won't be any choice left if she doesn't choose right now. My aim is going. I step forward and shove the muzzle hard into her temple. "Live or die? Choose! Now!" Each demand is a hoarse cry torn from my throat. "Don't make me choose for you!"

"L-live," she stammers. Her words are choppy, barely understandable. "Live, then, in whatever way you're talking about. I choose that—"

I swing the gun toward her face, steady my one arm with the other, no longer daring to breathe.

Don't let me miss. Please.

And I shoot her in the eye.

She shrieks just once, loud and sharp, and it shakes me back to breathing. I take a step back, the Roark gun now visibly trembling against my side, as she claps a hand to her eye, the other instinctively squeezing shut.

But she doesn't fall. She's still on her feet. She's not dead.

Relief is a gigantic swell that overtakes me, and I'm the one whose legs give out. I go down to one knee, breaths coming in thin gasps as I stare up at this girl who should be dead but isn't, and I don't know what this means anymore. It's starting to rain again, and it mixes with the heat of the tears on my cheeks, the salt in the air. My hair, dark, streaming rivulets that don't do enough to hide my face.

"My eye. It *hurts*. What did you do?" The idle takes her hand away, finally opening the other. And where once there was a pair of eyes the color of pretty old coins there is now a pair that has nearly no color at all. Just the slightest hint of their former copper, a reflection in the sun off a shiny surface.

No one in Kersh has eyes like this. No one. She's flesh and blood and talking to me, but what does any of that matter when in the system, she is officially an incomplete? She's alive without an Alt code, but instead of being a complete, she is a non-Alt—someone without worth, yet still alive enough to suffer the wanting of that, to know the wanting of that.

And Sabian's first Board Alt is now a complete. One strike down.

It has to count.

I slowly get to my feet, suddenly exhausted. "You are alive, but not," I say dully. "You are an incomplete in the system, but also a non-Alt, someone living without an Alt code. Your name is no longer yours. You have no identity anywhere in the city. *You are no longer an Alt in Kersh.* Do you understand me?"

A whole minute with the only sound the light patter of rain against the ground, on our heads. Finally she nods, but I know she doesn't. Not really. Her eyes are alien, hard to look at—my doing—but still human with confusion, shock.

Only time will lessen that. Nothing I say can comfort, can change what I've done.

"Get contacts to cover your eyes," I say to her. "You're going to need to get fake papers, a new life. Don't get caught—the Board *will* kill you."

I take a deep breath.

Because I can hear Chord explaining to me all over again. How an Alt needs the new disrupter alongside the remains of their spent Alt code in order to temporarily go neutral, momentarily become a non-Alt.

And Dire's words. How a loaded Roark gun obliterates each and every single trace of an Alt code, leaving someone permanently neutralized and no longer in danger of being burned by the barrier, disrupter no longer necessary.

Chord's newest key-code disrupter, put together on a whim, somehow capable of doing the unthinkable. A Board-supplied Roark gun, built with the sole purpose of ending someone's life, using vials of life-altering poison as its ammunition.

They should have very, very little in common.

But they do. One thing.

They each make it possible for someone to walk out of Kersh.

"The Surround," I say to the girl now. "If things get really bad, you can go there. From Jethro Ward, go to the barrier off Fireton Street. The electricity there is . . . off and on. You may be able touch it."

Now her eyes are truly huge, sharp with real, if fearful, understanding.

"Or dig your way out," I continue in a voice that sounds faint to my ears. I remember that news file, the one about the guy and his tunnel, and add, "Or climb, cut, whatever. You can do it, if you're smart about it. And fast." I taste the bile that's in my throat, blink away the rain that now feels cold. "You can't tell anyone about any of this. You'll just put them in danger, too."

"From the Board?"

I nod. And I have to be sure she understands. I'm the real threat right now, here with a gun still in my hand. The Board is a shadow—large, looming, but not as immediate. "And from me."

A heartbeat of silence.

"Where along the barrier?" she finally asks, blinking those horrible, non-Alt eyes at me.

I shiver. Suddenly recall her name from her spec sheet. I waited until she was a non-Alt to use it. It's too late, but I'm compelled to say it, anyway.

"Look for a huge tree, Gracen Beck. It's silver at night. I was told it's beautiful and that the way out is clearest from there."

CHAPTER 9

So very tired.

I stare up at the house with bleary eyes that miss sleep. Sleep doesn't come easily when all you do is dream about the dead.

I'm in front of *his* house. My next idle's. Strike two out of three.

When Sabian's text came earlier this evening, it was a muzzled bark along my leg, demanding my attention, making me finally look up and around.

I wasn't sure where I was. After my first target took off, chased away by my words, I climbed onto the first outer ward train that came my way. I rode it to the last stop and got off simply because I had to. It was all I could do just to walk. Put distance between myself and the idle I just made into a non-Alt. So I wandered. Reached a neighborhood I didn't recognize. I could have been in any ward; it could have been any time; I could have been anyone. Someone else.

But opening the text brought me back with a jolt. Holding my cell tight in my hand, I forgot about the ocean wind in my hair, the salt from Gaslight still on my lips.

Specs:

His name, Shaw Finley.

His face, thinnish but with well-shaped bones, hair dyed a white-yellow—a good-looking kid.

He's on the swim team, plays guitar for his school band, works part-time for the family farm.

I bet he's popular in school. I bet he's one of those rare kids who's cool and actually still nice.

All of this information, even the fact that he's left-handed, given to me so I know best how to strike him down, the parts to this person I'll either have to make an incomplete or non-Alt. I can't even give him the chance of fighting me.

And now I'm here in Calden—for him. The existence of this eighteen-year-old Alt of a Level 1 Board idle might be what finally pushed Sabian into action. With only two years left, assignment activation would happen any day. Better to head it off at the pass. What's the point of so much power if he can't use it to his child's advantage? Any parent in Kersh would do the same, if they could.

A single muttered request and my watch beeps out the time: *01:39.* Late enough that he's home.

Living in Calden means a life of seeding, growing, and harvesting. Or—in the case of this idle and his family—one of birthing, rearing, and butchering. The smell of manure drifts from the backyard to where I'm standing on the front curb, raw and pungent even in the cold air.

A small-scale farm. Chickens, most likely, given the size of the houses and the properties around here. Raise them, slaughter them, eat or sell them. It's a bloody business, but an honest one. I have blood on my hands, too. But how honest was my work for Dire back then, or for Sabian now?

I step off the curb and cross over the soggy grass of the front yard. I lean against the side of the house and slip off my bag. Unzip the side pocket and take out Chord's key-code disrupter, the one I've used time and time again.

I can never tell him how I'm using it now. And that other key-code disrupter he once put together, now safely destroyed . . . how would he feel about how I used what he told me about *that*?

I rub a fist over the ache in my chest and exhale. Breathe the thought of him away.

With the disrupter carefully positioned against the mark on my wrist, I press it onto the faceplate of the lock. The tumble and click of gears and I'm in.

I slide inside, shut the door quietly behind me. Against the wall, I wait for my eyes to adjust.

There's a staircase leading upstairs.

By the time I step onto the upper landing, I have the gun in my hand, drawn and ready.

Three bedrooms and a bathroom. One of the bedrooms is a master, and the door's open.

Silent feet carry me over. A careful peek and I know it's empty because his parents are on night shift this week.

A spare bedroom. Very neat and also very empty.

The last must be his. The door is left open just a crack. I move closer, nudge it open a bit more with my foot, step inside.

And freeze.

He's not alone.

Two sleeping forms in the bed. His and a girl's. They're

wrapped around each other, enclosed in the safety of idleness, the presence of each other. Here, where danger is not expected. I blink fast so it's not Chord and me I'm suddenly seeing instead. Not us about to be torn apart because his life will soon be altered forever, with whatever choice he makes.

Thoughts race through my mind, sprung from being caught utterly by surprise. *I can't do it,* I think frantically. *I'll come back in a few hours. Maybe she'll be gone and I'll be ready to force a choice from him with no witnesses.*

And maybe she won't be. Either way, he is the unworthy one. His training is nothing compared to his Alt's. Whether you let him choose now or later changes nothing, and whatever his choice, he will still be lost to her. And she'll keep quiet, if she doesn't want him gone before he has to go.

I press the gun against his temple.

Whatever training he already has can't be that poor because he wakes up instantly.

For a long moment, we simply stare at each other.

"I'm sorry," I finally say out loud. I need the girl to wake up now. She needs to understand, too.

She stirs at the sound of my voice, and the way her breath catches tells me she also sees the gun in my hand.

"What do you want?" he asks. His voice, halting and hoarse with both sleep and disbelief. The smell of fear in the air mixes with that of sleep.

I move the gun toward his eye. "Listen carefully."

I slide the gun back in my pocket and head down the stairs. The sound behind me is low, muffled, but unmistakable. Her crying, him consoling her.

Better than the sound of her crying alone.

Full-fledged rain has finally broken out. Heavy on the hood of my rain jacket and soaking into my sneakers as I walk down the street. Half of me is blind to everything but the need to keep going, seeking relief with distance. The other half is watchful of my surroundings, trying to decide which direction to go. Where to wait for Sabian's next text.

I should be able to find a room for the night, somewhere that isn't home. Much too close to Chord there. I hop on an inner ward train headed toward Calden's business core.

Just a few others on the train with me. I sit in the back so I can watch them. Though I know there's no way my marks can be seen from beneath my bandages and sleeves, they still feel obvious, dark cuffs proclaiming what I've done. My eyes touch on each passenger. How can they act so normal with me here?

The motel room I end up at is . . . fine. Neither run-down nor luxurious. In some ways, it feels like just another empty, one I might have stayed at when I was on the run from my Alt.

"Time," I whisper, my voice a rough croak as I slip off my bag and place it next to one of the pillows on the bed. Another habit that's come back to life. There is no reason to be worried about having to leave in a hurry, but here I am. Falling back on skills I thought were long behind me.

03:17.

I collapse on top of the bed, thoroughly exhausted.

Chord.

The thought of him is painful, but I don't push it away. I wonder if I should turn off my cell so he simply can't reach me. But Sabian will be sending me the last spec sheet any time now. It's nearly over.

Still, I owe Chord *some* kind of explanation. He won't accept a dead cell this time.

I fall asleep while still debating.

And am woken by the buzz of my cell in what feels like only seconds.

Morning light filters through the drapes into the room. I dig into my jeans pocket with groggy fingers and pull out my cell.

I'm already tapping the screen to answer when I realize it's not a text but a call.

Only one person would be calling me at this time of day, right before class starts, to see if I'd like a ride.

Cell to my ear, a hollowness in my gut. I'm wide awake now and at a total loss for what to say. Caught between the words to bring him here and the words to keep him away.

"West." Chord's voice, soft and wary. "Where are you?"

I take a deep breath. "Where are you?"

"Where do you *think* I am?" The image of him, sitting on my bed. My note at his side, my weapons in his lap.

It hits me. "The key I gave you . . ." My eyes blur. It took something like this for him to finally use it.

"When you didn't answer your door, I got worried."

"Did you find my note?"

"I did." That's all.

"Chord, I was really hoping you'd call before coming over."

"I'm sure as hell glad I didn't," he says flatly. "What lie would it have been? That you weren't feeling well and would skip school for the day?"

I say nothing. Confusion slices through me. That would

have been an easy way out, buying myself more time. Why can't I realize it's no longer simple to cut him out and still expect everything to be fine?

Chord's low sigh is full of worry and defeat, making my throat close up. "You left your gun here," he says. "Your knives, too. So if you're not working for Dire again, what are you doing?"

"I'm not working for Dire." A nonanswer, a West answer. But I already know it won't be enough anymore.

Silence. I can't stand it. "Chord, I'm sorry," I say in a rush. I've apologized more in the last two days than I have in my entire lifetime. My hand, a fist on the strange bedspread. "I don't know . . . I *want* to tell you—"

"Tell me."

"—except I'm scared."

"Of what? Are you in danger?" His voice goes hard, and in my head I can see his expression go dark, his eyes narrow. "West, *are* you in danger?" he asks again.

Yes. The reply is on my lips, wanting to be said. But if I say yes, then he'll be in danger, too.

"What are you scared of?" he asks.

You. Hating me. That my reasons for doing what I'm doing won't be enough for you to not walk away.

"Just . . . scared," I finally say. I flip onto my side, curl into a ball. The weave of the blanket is rough against my skin. I shut my eyes.

"Wherever you are, I can be there fast. You know that, don't you? Just say the word and I'm there, West."

No, I can't. Not now, when I'm not done yet—

"I don't want you to be scared, all right? Why can't you—"

"Chord." His name is a plea on my lips. "The Motel Ten on Moss Street. In Calden Ward. Room twenty-seven."

He barely even pauses. "Don't leave. I'm heading there now." And with that he hangs up, as though afraid I'll take it back if given the chance.

Outside the sun continues to lift. I lie on the bed and through closed eyelids watch the room lighten. The sun could blaze bright enough to blind me, but I'll still know the ghosts are there.

Seeing Chord again is what finally breaks me. I open the door at his knock and lunge at him. Feel tears rush to my eyes as he grabs me and holds me tight. My name in my hair as he presses his mouth there, full of relief, anger. Questions.

Without thinking about it, I'm already shaking my head. Keeping my arms locked around his waist, I shove my face against his chest. Let everything else fade away—the bland strangeness of the room, the weight of the gun not my own in my bag, the faces of the two idles I've essentially killed.

Chord kicks the door shut behind him. My arms go around his neck as he picks me up and walks us over to the bed. We drop down onto it, Chord sliding over until he's sitting up with his back against the headboard and I'm in his lap. I stare at his chin, steeling myself.

He tilts my face up and over so he can see me. Wipes off my tears with his fingers. Gives me one gentle kiss on my mouth. Sighs and says, "West. Talk."

"It's never as simple as I think it will be," I say to him, my voice hoarse from crying. Nowhere to hide as we look at each other. His eyes are very dark and very tired and lit with the unmistakable sheen of frustration.

"And sometimes not as complicated as you think it is," he says.

I lean against him, let out a breath. It does nothing for the storm of nerves in my stomach. "Sometimes."

"That was a pretty cryptic note you left for me, don't you think?" Chord's voice is almost casual enough to fool me.

I place my hand on his chest, feel his drumming pulse. "I know. I didn't . . . I just . . ." I take another breath, try to make some sense. "I'm sorry."

"I didn't come to hear you say you're sorry, West," Chord says. "I don't even know what you're apologizing for." His fingers in my hair to soften his words. "I *don't* think it's because of what you're doing. Only that I'm in your face about it now."

I shake my head. "I told you where I was, didn't I?"

"True."

"If I didn't want you here, I could have left. I didn't have to wait." Though I would have—I would have waited and waited and waited. To see him, to make time stop, to keep all of this from happening.

"Hmm." Chord brushes my hair from my face, lingers gently on my scar. "You're doing it again."

"Doing what?"

He sends me a pointed look. "Answering without answering."

How to say it? Like trying to disarm a bomb with a hundred different wires and no clue which one to cut. He's here now, though, and I need him, and I have to believe that his knowing won't be enough to make him stop loving me.

"Remember when I asked you about kids . . . about whether

you thought you'd be able to handle them becoming incompletes?" I ask him.

Confusion clouds Chord's face. My question comes from nowhere, and I have to back up.

"And you said if there was a way to protect them that was *right*, you'd do it?" I press.

"Actually, right now I'm remembering what you were asking me before *that*," he says.

I wait, already braced.

"You were talking about having to kill again." Too soft, his voice sounds dangerous. "When we're already complete." His arms are stiff around me, and his hands are unmoving on my skin. "What does that have to do with us and kids we don't have and what I can or cannot handle?"

"What I mean is . . . what I'm trying to say is . . ." I am stumbling in the face of Chord's suspicion.

"When I said I would do anything . . . West, you know you can't twist that."

No, that's not . . . you didn't— "You said if you knew it was meant to be, then you would do it." I'm talking too fast now. Wanting to backtrack and unable to. Speeding ahead to get it over with.

"Do what, West?" he says. Now his voice is pure ice. "Like kill?"

"It's not . . . you're coming at this the wrong way, Chord. Just let me—"

"Wait. Don't say it." Chord's words confirm my worst fears, my nightmare come to life. He's with me still, but it's not really him anymore. His face is . . . devastated. "Don't tell me you're striking again."

146

I'm about to say no, but I stop. What I've done, left loose ends in the forms of non-Alts—how is that any better? Who's to say what's worse? I still don't know, no matter how much I go back and forth. So I tell the truth. "Yes. I guess I am."

He says nothing, still in shock.

I move away to sit on the side of the bed, suddenly needing space from this Chord who is not Chord. This person who can't hide what he feels about how low I can go, who sees all too well the worst parts of me. "I'm sorry," I say again, knowing the apology is far from enough.

Chord slowly gets off the bed and stands up. Stares at me like he's never seen me before.

"Why?" His eyes drop to my wrists, my still-bandaged marks, and some misguided sense of defensiveness has me crossing my arms in front of me. "Dire could ask any of his other—"

"I'm not working for Dire, Chord."

"Not Dire," he repeats.

"It's . . . they came and asked me! I didn't—" *Shut up. You said yes. Who cares who asked who?*

"You can't even tell me who? For Christ's sake, West!"

I shut my eyes for one long second before looking at him again. "The Board."

"What are you talking about?"

I get to my feet, an attempt to close the gap between us, even just a little bit. "Two days ago, that night you came over in the rain . . . I had an order to go to headquarters in Leyton. And he made me an offer."

"*He.* Who's—"

"Sabian. A Level One Board Operator. He said if I work as

a striker for him, any kids I'd ever have"—and here my face gets hot, though it's the last thing I should be embarrassed about—"would be born complete. No Alternate, no assignment, just . . . life."

Chord shakes his head. His eyes are bleak, his mouth a line. "He lied, West. No way can he—"

"Who runs the Alt lab, Chord?" I say to him quietly. "Who runs the whole Board, the whole filtration system?"

Level 1. He knows the answer, but I can see him working it out now as though this is the first time he's heard it. Flipping it, twisting it, searching for a trap. "Who are the targets?" he asks. "How many?"

"Three. The Alts of the Board's kids. Level One Alts," I finish, my voice sounding weak even to my own ears.

Make sure you say Alts, not idles. You can't tell him that. Worse than a striker, you're a mur—

"So you're killing for a promise that won't be kept for years," Chord says. "For your kids to be completes from birth."

"Ours," I say quietly, suddenly needing to look at anything but him. The off-white walls, the thin drapes, the dirty tops of my shoes. I never took them off, not even to sleep, I think dully. "Maybe, one day."

Chord's hands touch the sides of my face, tangling in my hair. His mouth comes down hard on mine. Then he ends the kiss, puts his hands on my shoulders, and takes me in with an expression close to grief. "And you really believe a top-ranking Board Operator will keep a promise to a striker?" he asks gently.

"Yes." Tears singe my eyes, and I blink them away. "I have to believe that, Chord. That I'm not as selfish as I think I am, and that if I can give this to you, I would."

"You don't *have* to give me this, West." But I hear the longing in his voice. "And you're not selfish. Why would I think—"

"Because that's not the only reason why I'm doing this."

An almost imperceptible tightening of Chord's arms around me. Not stiff like before, but a defense. "Spit it out, West."

"Being a striker before, for Dire . . . I hurt Kersh, Chord. I killed without caring who was worthy. If I can do this job for the Board, by making sure those next in line survive, I'll make up for all that."

"Sabian told you this?"

I nod.

His hand along my cheek. "Is it that easy to make you believe you're so evil, when everything you did you did in order to survive?"

"Evil or not, does it change the fact that some of those Alts might be alive if it weren't for me?"

"Maybe, maybe not. It can't matter now. It's over."

"Not for me, it's not." My hands clench into fists at my side, and I force them open. Lift one up to look at my wrist and wonder if the marks have always been so stark, so encircling. "My marks. He said . . ." And here I falter, stumble over the ugly nakedness of the truth. That more than any children the future might hold for us, more than any guilt I need to appease, it's my simple wanting to start over. Pretend I'm someone I'm not.

Chord takes my hands and holds them in his. My marks against his skin, tainting the untainted. "What did he say, West?"

"He's going to have them erased."

Chord goes still for a second, and then he swears under his

breath, presses his lips to one of my marks. "They're nothing. They're just . . . ink and chips. I don't even see them anymore."

"Don't lie. You have to see them, because I can't *not* see them."

"I don't—"

"For a while, I could almost do it. Be able to look at them and not think 'striker' or 'assassin.' To just try to see them as parts of the past. But it never lasted for long. The shame always came back." I can't stop, as though I'm seeking salvation with a confession.

"So maybe you just need more time to—"

"And now it's too late for even that. Because it's not just 'striker' I think of when I look at them. It's 'killer of Alts, killer of idles—'"

Stop.

Stop.

Shut up, West—

Too late.

Chord's eyes, as dark and hollow as night. "You said idles. Not just Alts but *idles.*"

I hold my breath.

This is who you love, Chord.

"Idles. *West* . . ." The stunned look on his face makes my chest ache, and I'm desperate now. Mistake or no, I have to tell him.

"I didn't kill them, Chord," I blurt out. "They're not dead."

At his look, full of hope, I shake my head. Misery is bitter on my tongue. "Though they're not safe, either," I continue. "I wanted to kill them using this gun that meant they wouldn't feel anything. But I couldn't do it. So I . . . took out their Alt code instead. Their Alts became completes, just like Sabian wanted, but the idles I was supposed to kill . . . they're non-Alts now."

"What does that mean?" Chord asks, sounding numb, defeated.

"In the system, they're officially dead. Incompletes. But they're really still alive, which means whoever they were before . . . they can't go back to that now. They won't be recognized as anyone, now that they have no identity. And if the Board catches them . . . they'll be killed."

Chord shakes his head. "So you left them alive . . . to live that kind of life?"

"*Some* kind of life at least, Chord!"

"You didn't kill them, and that's . . . that's huge, West. But don't you see you might as well have?"

There's no denying it. I've fallen to new depths, where even he might not be able to save me. To strike down active Alts is to be a cheater; to strike down idles is to be a monster.

Chord drops my hands and runs his fingers through his hair, as though to wipe away my touch. It's agony to think that he doesn't want my hands touching him again.

"You weren't ever going to tell me, were you?" Chord says. Softly, like fresh skin over a wound. And I know then that it's not so much me doing what I did that's driving him away, but that I've betrayed him again. Doubting him. Us. "Were you?"

I'm simply unable to move. Not even to shake my head. Why make him hate me that much more? My heart—each beat is like another punch of pain.

"I can't figure out what else you need from me, West. To make you trust me the way I trust you. Isn't it enough that I love you?"

Chord's face blurs, and I'm suffocating beneath the weight of his hurt. The one person I hate hurting, who I hurt again and again.

"I don't care what you did, what you can do, what you're doing *now*, even," he says. "If that makes me as horrible a person as you think you are, then fine. We'll be horrible together."

"I don't want us to be horrible together, Chord. I just want . . ." And I stop. How can I tell him I want more? That I want everything when I'm the one who decided to lose it all?

Chord takes a step closer, his face a loved one's and a stranger's as he slides his hands around my neck and weaves them into my hair.

"Everyone *wants*. Don't you know that?" he says quietly against my mouth. "Except how many are willing to do what you've done for it? Or decide that being alive just isn't enough?" *Because you've decided, West. That you're not enough. I'm not enough.*

"Chord, I—"

He leans forward until our lips touch, as carefully as though it's the first time, and we are motionless for seconds that are too long, too short. Then he breaks free. He unwinds his fingers from my hair, lingers on my neck, before letting me go.

And he's gone, the door shutting behind him with a very final click.

And I'm alone.

My cell buzzes with an incoming text. It's an ominous sound in the heavy silence.

Sabian, with the spec sheet for my last Alt.

I stare at the door and am torn in half.

Though I know. There is no choice, not really. I've gone too far to go back now, and I'm so close to being done that the end is in sight. Just one more. Then Chord will understand. He'll *have* to. He wouldn't—

I pull my cell from my jeans pocket so I can stop thinking. Start moving so I can finally be free of the past.

I read the details, memorizing each one as though they are the difference between life and death. For this last contract, there is no room for mistakes. Even the tiniest statistical probability of something going wrong will have to be quashed. Because this is Sabian, this is Level 1, and this final Alt is the last thing standing in my way.

I tap the room checkout code into my cell and send it to the front desk before tucking it back into my jeans pocket. My bag is still lying near the headboard. I unzip it, take out the gun, and reload it with a fresh vial of poison. The final vial—I cannot miss, will not miss. Slipping my bag on and walking out of the motel, the gun a fresh weight in my jacket pocket, I can't help but notice just how calm my breathing is. How my hands are as steady as they've ever been, how my eyes are already looking for him.

The last Alt.

CHAPTER 10

Inside the reception area for a public training arena for Alts, I'm restless, wanting to finish things. That the training arena's located in Leyton Ward of all wards, and that I'm only blocks away from Board headquarters, sits easier with me than it might have if this was simply another striker contract issued by Dire. Seeing Sabian in person again would be far from fun, but it might be necessary if he needs to be reminded of his end of the deal.

Even as I'm thinking this, I'm scanning the room around me, taking everything in.

A handful of Alts, and I know without a doubt most of them will be idles and not actives. By the time an assignment is handed out, actives have to put any form of regular training behind them. Whatever they can do to keep their skills honed is squeezed between minutes of running and hiding, chasing and hunting. The Board-ordered eye scan at point of entry is another reason why actives stay away. These transactions are recorded and show up on the public Alt data log, which is made accessible to any active looking to locate their Alt during an assignment.

There's an attendant at the front desk, but he's busy scanning cells to reserve slots for the arena. I know the general layout of such places, even though I only ever used one a handful of times. There was never any point, when training with Aave and Luc taught me just as much. Maybe more, in fact—my brothers knew my weaknesses and called me out on them. I miss them, these brothers who weren't the worthy ones, after all. But if not for them, would I be alive today?

There's a laugh from somewhere, bringing me back here, reminding me to remain focused.

I recall the spec sheet. It doesn't take long, as it's much shorter than the previous two from Sabian. Missing addresses, gap-filled schedules. A photo that wouldn't open properly, leaving me with only a written description of what he looks like. The uneasy feeling that what's not on the spec sheet might be just as important as what is.

I should feel more cautious. But it's the very opposite of caution that electrifies my nerves now, making it nearly impossible to keep still. It's reckless and foolish, but there it is.

The front desk is free and I walk over and hold out my cell to the attendant. "How long until the next available slot?" I ask him.

"Uh, after this group goes in"—he gestures to the Alts still hanging around with a quick point of his chin—"a couple of minutes, probably. Another group is heading out now, so . . ." He waves the scanner over my cell, and there's a sudden spark of panic; surely a complete would draw attention for being here? But when the scan goes through without the attendant giving me another look, it's relief that I feel instead. Sabian knew I would have to come here—he must have preapproved my entry somehow. Along with participant registration and automatic withdrawal of payment from my bank account, an entry scan also means I understand, agree, and accept the risks of being in a place like this. That accidents can still happen, no matter how unlikely.

In many ways, it can be safer in here than it is out on the streets. In the arena, no tired and half-starved actives let loose with wild, desperate shots. Here, idles are actually *more* careful with their aim, trying to improve.

But a good striker moves fast and smart. Slip in and out without a trace. A good, fast striker will take advantage of a sectioned-off training arena, full of little pockets where prey can be quickly cornered and finished off.

I tell myself this is why I've chosen a training arena for this last Alt. That it's not because I have no other choice, given the spec sheet and its strange lack of info. At seventeen, he clearly understands that time is running out, and using an open study period after lunch for additional off-campus training can only help. As it is, I have little on him. His schedule reads:

12:45 Alt public training arena, Leyton Ward, arrival.
14:00 unable to verify
14:30 unable to verify
16:00 unable to verify
17:00 Alt endurance training facility,
    Leyton Ward, arrival.

His arrival here is my first opportunity, one I didn't want to pass up. I'm ready for this to be done already.

The attendant hands me a flimsy black paper vest and a white label, the kind with a peel-off back. It has a large 27 on it in thick strokes of black ink; in smaller print on the bottom is a line with the time and date. And across the top in bright red text is the word *STOP*—a warning to others that I'm not a target.

"This is your registrant tag—it has to be worn on your vest and be visible at all times. When your time is up, just deposit both in the recycling bin on the way out." He holds out a pair of safety glasses. "These will go in the disinfection unit."

For a second, my mind is blank as I take in the safety glasses dangling from his fingers. Because I didn't think of that . . . why didn't I think of that?

He must be aware of my surprise, because he shrugs. "You don't have to wear them, but we're required to ask, anyhow. Most Alts don't want them because—well, let's face it. Out there, who's going to be walking around with safety glasses on? Not to mention restricted visibility as a shooter."

"Right," I mutter to him. "No, thanks, then." This Alt is a Leyton Alt. He would skip the glasses, too—I hope.

With that, the attendant drops the glasses in a bin behind him and is already looking past me, already focused on the next idle in line.

I move away from the counter, vest and tag in hand, and glance up at the numbers scrolling by on the clock on the wall. Minutes until I'm cleared to go in, and minutes until he arrives—*12:45.*

I decide to stand by the hall that leads down to the arena— it's not so far that I can't see who's coming in or so close that I'm crowding the people signing up at the front desk. Leaning against the wall, I do a quick rundown of what he's supposed to look like, replaying that portion of his spec sheet in my head.

Dark brown hair with a reddish tinge, medium-length on the top, shorter in the back and along the sides. Dark brown eyes. Skin, noted to have olive undertones. Height is five feet eleven inches. Weight is one hundred and seventy-eight pounds. His name is Auden Parrish.

At the sound of the front door opening, I look over, eyes narrowed, wondering if it's finally him. But I can't tell because the group of Alts still waiting has sidled over to fill my sightline. Talking, laughing. I walk up and stay on the fringes of the group, finding the *between* that makes me here but not here, just like in the distillery in Gaslight. I listen to the attendant and the person he's now talking to.

"—it going today?" Definitely not the attendant's voice. It's faint, fading in and out because of the noise in the room. But younger, smoother . . . and also somehow familiar, like having something on the tip of your tongue.

"—surprisingly busy, though—"

Another burst of laughter from the group of friends waiting their turn, and I inch closer to the attendant and whoever he's talking to.

"—you doing here, anyway?" the attendant asks. "You're registered to use this place? It's not nearly as good—"

A short laugh, and there's that same twinge of familiarity. It lurks on the fringes of my mind, pulling at threads of memory—

The attendant, talking again. "—your number is thirty-four, so make sure it's visible—"

A sudden drop in noise level as the Alts move from laughter to low chatter, so I can't miss what's said next.

"—lots of newbies today, Auden, so watch your—"

It's him. Auden—the same name as on the spec sheet.

He'll be wearing the number 34 on his back, in an arena filled with shooters—though I'm the only one shooting at a live target.

The cells of the laughing group all beep simultaneously to indicate their start time. They begin to move, heading toward the inner entrance to the arena, and with my face averted, I shuffle along behind them, leaving Auden and the attendant to finish their conversation at the desk.

My own cell beeps just seconds later.

It's my turn, too.

I enter the arena, hoping it will be the place where things will end so I can make my way home. The training arena is similar to the ones I've seen in the Grid—and at the same time, nothing like. I'm in Leyton, after all. And even its most practical corners have to meet aesthetic approval.

The space is huge, a rectangle that must measure at least a couple of hundred feet long by a hundred feet wide. Instead of bare plywood flooring, it has solid concrete, and its walls are covered with yellow sound-absorbent panels. Thick wood beams are set in neat parallel lines overhead instead of exposed ducts. Brightly painted lines instead of layers of cheap chalk mark out lanes and direct foot traffic. And dotted throughout, just like in the Grid arenas, just like in Baer's classroom, are the familiar individual stations, each designated for a different weapon or skill set.

Every other one is walled off for safety. I'll need to find my target in one of those.

As I walk onto the floor, I purposely fall back to let the group of Alts pull ahead. Reluctantly, I follow what they do, setting down my bag along the wall off to one side of the room.

It feels strange to leave it behind. But I have no choice. I need to blend in with the others, and wearing the vest over a bag just won't work. My jacket is pushing the limit, even, but how else to hide the Roark gun in my pocket until I need it?

I let Auden pass me, too, instinctively tilting my head so that my hair shields my face.

That faint unease stirs in my gut again as I watch him walk away. The width of his shoulders, the gait of his stride . . . *something* . . . like trying to remember a dream upon waking.

I keep moving until I reach the middle of the arena, standing with the others and waiting to see how everyone disperses. I'm careful to keep my back to him. Slapping my 27 tag onto the back of the vest, I slip the whole thing over my head.

Idles crowd around me, still sorting themselves into position and deciding which station they want. Voices and laughter echo off the main walls and there's the sound of clothes being adjusted as tags are smoothed and vests donned. Personal guns are loaded with clicks and snaps.

Auden breaks free of the crowd and heads off toward the stations. As a Leyton Alt, he's quick to load his weapons; I shouldn't be surprised by that.

I follow him, keeping just enough of a gap between us that I don't lose sight of him and, at the same time, don't give him reason to suspect I'm tracking him. I'm just another idle in a busy practice arena.

His thick hair is dark brown with a red tinge. He wears it smooth on the top and hanging slightly over his forehead. His skin is olive beneath the beginnings of a summer tan. The number 34 on his back has *STOP* written on it in huge letters. The warning means nothing to me.

He stops in front of two adjacent stations, deciding. Both of them are still available; the movement detectors on the floor in front of their entrances are still green.

One is fully walled, the other only partially so, its cement partitions only reaching shoulder height at the most.

Choose the correct one, I will him silently. *Let this be over.*

Seconds later, he turns into the fully walled station and I can no longer see him. The station's movement scanner switches to yellow. It's a station meant for two Alts at a time, then.

Relief is a heady drug. Everything is close now, just a little bit farther to go. I take the same steps he did until I, too, am within the station's walls. I don't see it behind me, but I know the detector marking the entrance now burns a bright red, a clear warning. No one else will enter until it's either yellow or green again.

It's a shooting station. The two walls flanking the entrance have painted wooden spheres hanging in front of them, made of pine because it's soft enough to give way to bullets, rather than dangerously deflecting them. Suspended by thick twists of rope from the overhead beams in random intervals, the spheres are challenging targets, given how they would sway and bobble with the passing or impact of bullets. Hitting the bull's-eye proper cracks open the sphere and drops it to the ground.

Auden is standing at the broad painted shooting lines in the center of the station. They run parallel to the targets, the numbers painted next to them signifying the distance between shooter and target. He's chosen to face the wall a dozen feet away, his stance perfect for the handgun he's holding as he prepares to shoot at the row of targets lazily spinning in front of him.

He fires: one, two, three, four, five. There's the sound of falling targets hitting the ground: one, two three, four, five. Reloading, he moves back to stand behind the next shooting distance.

I head straight toward the center of the station, where the lines for my targets are . . . where he is. My hand reaches into my pocket for the Roark gun. As I draw it out, the fit of it against my palm has never felt more seamless. For one second I can almost mistake it for one of my paintbrushes, how the feel is just as natural in my fingers. Is it my imagination that it actually feels hot to the touch? Will this final shot of poison destroy the gun from the inside out and me in the process?

I'm five feet away, carefully angled away from his line of sight so that he won't know my intentions until I round upon him from his side.

This close, I'm finally able to see his profile clearly.

A chill ripples down the length of my spine.

That nose, that jaw . . . hold on . . .

He moves again to a new shooting distance from behind a different line and finally notices me—and the gun in my hand that's pointed right at him. He goes absolutely still for a handful of seconds—one, two, three—before turning toward me.

I can see his face fully for the very first time.

And the world stops. Time stops. *I* stop.

Because it's not Auden I'm seeing but his Alt.

My dead brother, Luc.

Shock like a live current blasts right through me. The gun tumbles from my fingers onto the ground. I stagger back a step, then two.

No. *No.*

How can I hurt this Alternate who is also partially my brother? To wipe away the last parts of Luc left on this earth?

Everything else in the station fades, like static from a dead broadcast. His eyes are wide and stunned and far too familiar.

"Who are you?" he blurts out. Luc's voice, but not. His gun is no longer aimed at the wooden targets but at me.

I'm unable to move, even as his gaze falls to the gun on the ground. I can't miss his surprise as he stares at the weapon on the ground between us, the dawning realization that it's not a regular gun. When he looks up at me, confusion comes off him in waves.

"Who are you?" he asks again, demand clear in his voice despite the question. "Why were you pointing *that* gun at me?"

Still frozen.

He reaches for the Roark with his free hand.

I lunge for it, my fingers scratching at the concrete as they grab hold of the gun. My lungs are on fire from not daring to breathe, and now my breath escapes from me in a rush as I point the gun at him again, aiming for his eye. No denying that the gun's barrel is wavering now.

Luc's eyes.

The barrel shakes hard. The gun feels hot against my skin, fighting me.

Too late.

I back away. One step. Two. From outside the station's walls are the sounds of chatter, muffled thumps and booms as training goes on as usual. It's only in here where things aren't going according to plan.

"Hey! Stop!" Luc—*Auden*—moves closer, and anger's

replaced his confusion. His gun is still absolutely steady in his grip, and the dark, deadly tunnel of its barrel does not move from my head. *"Who are you, and what do you want?"*

I run.

Out past the entrance and back onto the main floor, toward the side of the arena where I left my bag. Never fully stopping, I dig it out from the pile with my free hand and stuff the gun into my jacket pocket with the other. Curious voices chase me out of the arena and into the waiting area. Judging me, deciding someone who obviously can't handle training will stand no chance against a real Alt.

The front attendant watches me rush past him, his expression so surprised it's no wonder he can't think of anything to say. Am I really the only person to ever leave this place running?

I shove the door open, my heart pounding, my blood a furious roar. I don't know where I'm going, who to be—

And I come to a full dead stop at the chaos in front of me. A completion taking place right around the corner from the training arena, and I've run into it blindly. Not even time to do an FDFO.

Two Alts, girls no older than me. One's on the ground in front of me, just a few feet away, downed and gasping. Blood drips from an exit wound in the back of her thigh. As ugly as the wound is, it's nothing compared to the one right below her left shoulder blade. Still gushing with each pump of her heart, a coursing river of blood. Lying on her side, she lifts her gun by shaky degrees. It's much too little, much too late. In this war of Alternates, she is not the one. She is not worthy.

A thin crack in the air as her Alt shoots from down the street. The first shot misses and I swear I can hear the whistle of the bullet as it flies past me. The second makes its mark, and the Alt in front of me collapses fully.

A hand on my arm drags me back into the mouth of an alley just off to the side. Two thoughts rocket into my brain, one barreling over the other within a fraction of a second.

One: That at any other time, I would have seen this alley on my own. That I wouldn't have been so slow to get out of the way and let myself be so vulnerable.

Two: *Sabian.* He knows I've failed, has found me already, a warden sniffing out an escaped prisoner, fast even for a Level 1.

But it's Auden, half out of breath from chasing me down the street and just as angry as I left him back in the arena. His face is livid, barely tempered by the confusion that's starting to creep back, the questions that must be running wild in his head. His bag is in one hand and his gun is still in the other. No longer pointed at me, but out nonetheless, and for a second my own confusion has me unsure of what to do next. Go for the gun in my pocket or tell him how much I've missed him. But I sense no real threat from him, so I do nothing, just stare at him and feel completely at a loss.

At my silence and the obvious fact that I'm not going for my weapon, Auden slowly drops his gun, his arm lowering to his side.

"Where did you get your gun?" he asks. Auden's voice is smoother than Luc's, more refined, though his mouth has a harder set to it, his eyes sharper. Even at his angriest with me, it was impossible for Luc to be truly cold. I cling to this difference between them.

"Why were you trying to shoot me?" This time his voice is edged with agitation, unable to stay so perfectly level.

Much more like Luc's.

Without letting myself think too much about it, I take an aggressive step toward him, a move I used to pull on Luc to get him to back off. It works. Auden steps back with a scowl. That scowl is the exact replica of how Luc would look at me when I got in his face about something, and instead of feeling the rage that I want to feel at my brother not being the one alive, I'm crushed. None of this seems possible. None of this is bearable.

"It's my gun—most Alts have one." I don't yet know how to answer his second question. And it's hard enough to say even that—how to talk to a stranger who isn't exactly a stranger?

He shakes his head, watching me very closely. "I've never seen an Alt use that kind of gun before."

"It's just a normal gun," I lie. If I don't show it again, he'll have to believe me. What he saw of it in the arena was so fleeting, he might not be sure of what he saw, or thought he saw.

His eyes narrow, full of blatant mistrust. "You and I both know it's not. It shoots poison, not bullets."

How did—

"Only the Board has access to them, and only for testing," Auden continues. "They're not ready to be used for completing."

He is no ordinary Alt.

"Who are you?" I blurt out. Nothing makes sense. Why would Sabian want me to kill a complete?

A short and harsh laugh, completely devoid of humor. "Who are *you*?" Auden says. "And you still haven't answered my question: Why were you trying to shoot me?"

Think, fast. "I was just getting my gun into position for the targets. My mistake for drawing too early."

"I know how to use a gun, and it's obvious you do, too. You were aiming at *me*. Why?"

I have as many questions as he does, and we're not going to get anywhere unless we quit dancing around the truth. It should be more difficult to trust Luc's Alt, who I'd hate under any other circumstance. But it's not, and I don't know what that says about me.

"You're Auden Parrish." I recite the words tonelessly. "A seventeen-year-old idle from Leyton Ward whose Alternate has been declared the one—worthy. My name is West Grayer and I've been hired to make you an incomplete."

He goes absolutely still, and to his credit, does not turn and run. "That's my name, but I'm already a complete." His eyes automatically drop to my wrists, though my marks are hidden beneath my bandages and the sleeves of my rain jacket. Standing on a street in the middle of Leyton, it's best they stay that way, too. "I thought strikers never made mistakes."

"We don't. Not like this. And I doubt Sabian makes—" I stop. I've said too much.

"Sabian?" Auden looks at me, renewed confusion on his face. "You mean Sabian from the Board?"

"How do you know him?" I ask. Only those within headquarters would know Level 1 Operators by sight, and even fewer by name.

"My father's a Level Two Operator. He and Sabian work together."

Thoughts shift and slide in my head, trying to find some kind of explanation for why Sabian would want to assassinate the child of another high-ranking Operator. And without my ever finding out.

And another realization, this one thick and painful. Luc never had much of a chance after all. Not compared to a Board-trained Alt. It's a devastating blow, and I hurt for him, this brother who was never meant to live for long.

"Why were you even at that public training center?" I ask Auden. "You're a Board Alt. You've got all the facilities you need at headquarters. I know because I've seen them."

"Level Two trainees were told the training facilities were being cleaned for a few days. Sabian assigned each of us to different ones here in downtown Leyton."

I nod. Of course. Auden wasn't training for an assignment to beat his Alt, but to become a full-fledged Board member. "Not only did Sabian need to find a believable excuse for you to leave headquarters so I could get close enough to you, but he also needed to keep you apart from the others. Less chance of someone noticing anything."

"So why didn't you do it?" Auden asks. He pulls a jacket from his bag and puts it on, stuffing his gun into one of the side pockets. The fact that someone other than his Alt would ever want him dead has made his face pale. "Why didn't you kill me back there, when you had the chance?"

I decide to tell the truth. "Because your Alt was my brother. And killing you would be too much like killing him again. And I can't do that, striker or not."

A clearing truck turns on its siren as it heads in our direction. Which means Operators of the Board won't be far behind. Level 3 or not, I don't want to be seen. The warning sound jars me back into the moment.

To have killed idles who had no warning is bad enough; the same—and, admittedly, maybe even worse—goes for making them into non-Alts, destined for a life hiding from the Board. But at least I can tell myself they were doomed to be incompletes. But to have come so close to killing a complete, someone who's survived the Alt system and properly declared himself worthy, is another thing altogether.

I need to get as far away from Leyton and Board headquarters as possible. And take Auden with me, too. It's too dangerous to let him walk back into headquarters and act as if things are normal while waiting for me to come up with a plan to save him. We'd risk having Sabian finding out before the deadline that I have no intention of completing the assignment, and then he might send someone else to finish the job. Not just to kill Auden but to kill me, too. I'm a loose end. I've seen and heard and done too much to go back and beg for mercy. The Board doesn't know the word.

I rip off my paper vest and ball it up in my hands. "Follow me," I say.

He stays behind me as I walk out onto the sidewalk and toss the vest into a green can sitting on the edge of the curb. I slip my bag on and tighten the straps, then look over at him.

His face is still dazed, perplexed, and my irrational anger disappears. It's not right that he has to go through this when he's already a complete. The look on his face . . . is this how Luc would have looked at getting his notice of assignment?

I have to stop thinking this way. Luc's gone, and this is all that's left of him. I can't kill him or make him a non-Alt. I can't go through that again. It's a terrible, awkward thing— knowing that to kill him would give me everything, and in letting him live, I'm letting it all go.

"We need to get out of here," I say to Auden, looking

around for signs of Operators, signs of Sabian. Here on the sidewalk, we're just two people among many. But I feel uneasy and on edge, something I haven't felt about Leyton since I started my internship at the art gallery, with my weekly trips slowly buffering smooth the raw memory of killing my Alt's boyfriend here.

"And go where?" Auden asks harshly. "These are Level One guys you're talking about. We can't run forever—they *made* this freaking city."

I know where. Though it's known to the Board, it's the best place I can think of. At least until Sabian figures out what's going on. But time is time and we need to take what we can.

"Underground" is all I say to Auden.

"Underground." He says the word as though he's never heard it before.

I eye his vest. "You might want to get rid of that first, though. The number on the back isn't exactly subtle."

I need to see you.

My words float on my cell screen, waiting patiently for a reply. Though I'm not patient inside. I'm wired and jumpy and desperate to see him again, and if will alone could make the train move faster, we'd be there by now.

That is, *if* he'll see me.

Seconds pass, driving me crazy. I'm about to text him again when Chord's reply comes through with a buzz.

Where are you?

Three simple words and something aches inside my chest, squeezes hard. I've messed up, and badly, and I don't know if I can fix it.

The sudden surge of my own selfishness is bitter in my mouth. How I push him, then pull him without ever letting go of him. Through their coverings, my marks simmer like the flush of a mild fever, a persistent rash. I couldn't even get rid of these, I think dully. Or give him that future I was so close to making possible. Because I couldn't kill the Alt of his dead best friend.

Can you meet me at Dire's? In an hour? I press SEND.

Nearly a minute later. Not the *Why?* I was dreading but a simple *If you're sure* and I breathe out a sigh of relief at his understanding. Because I know he's never been there, the place where I first became a striker. Like asking a person in pain if it's okay to keep ripping off the fresh scab. *Yes, I'll explain everything later,* I tap in.

I'll wait outside for you.

I won't be long.

I'll be there.

His text forgives too much, and now self-disgust joins self-ishness. That infinite patience he has for me will be his undoing one day if I'm not careful. I tuck my cell back into my pocket, wishing even harder for the miles to pass quickly.

"He never said why I'm supposed to die?" Auden's question is blunt and matter-of-fact beneath the harsh interior lights of the outer ward train.

I decided to take Auden home to the Grid. Completely unable to guess how Chord's going to react. I came close to telling him earlier in my text but I made myself shut up.

There is nothing I can say or do that will make things easier, to keep Chord from instantly thinking of Luc's incompletion when he first sees Auden.

Easier said than done. I should know. To look over, see my brother, and tell myself I don't know this person.

"Sabian," Auden says stiffly. "When he hired you. He never said why?"

"Only that you were an Alt to one of the Level One kids and needed to be assassinated for the sake of Kersh as a whole."

He shakes his head. His smooth cap of hair that is so different than how Luc wore his, though the color is identical. "I don't get it," he mutters.

I don't tell him that I think we'll find out soon enough. Too soon, probably, when it comes down to it, our lives being on the line. So I tell him what I *have* figured out.

"You already being a complete actually explains a lot," I begin. Carefully, the way I would with anyone I've just met, who I know nothing about. "Now I understand why Sabian had to get a total outsider to do it. The other Board members know you, and they know you're a complete."

"So Sabian told you I was still an idle. *Would* you have accepted the contract if you knew I was a complete?" His eyes are suddenly wary again. Just because I've made it obvious I'm not going to kill him doesn't mean I'm not a danger to the system, to the barrier.

"No, I . . ." I trail off, suddenly no longer sure how deep I would have fallen. If Sabian promised me the same thing, and somehow convinced me that killing Auden would be for the good of the city, would I have made the same decision? Would I have let myself be convinced? "I didn't know," I add lamely. This much is true at least.

"What was he like, your brother?" Auden asks.

"His name was Luc," I say, my voice flat. I turn away, look

straight ahead. There's an elderly couple at the front of the train watching us, and I wonder what they're seeing. Two people who resemble each other enough to be siblings. I bet anything they haven't come close to guessing the truth: a fifteen-year-old striker with her target, who also happens to be the Alt of her dead brother.

"You're not betraying him by talking to me, you know," Auden says when it's clear I'm not going to continue.

His logic makes me feel foolish, immature. It must be a big brother thing because Luc managed to do that a lot, too. I exhale. "Luc was a good guy. He had a really great sense of humor—way better than mine, though I'm sure you would never have guessed."

Auden laughs, but it's abrupt and over quickly, as though he feels bad for forgetting even for a second that we're in deep trouble.

"I miss that a lot, just having him around to make me laugh," I add. "He and Chord were best friends, and they used to get mixed up in all kinds of—"

"Who's Chord?"

"My boyfriend."

"Is that who you were texting earlier?"

"Yes."

"So does he know who I am? About Sabian or any of this?"

"Some. Just . . . some." I think back to Chord in that hotel room and watching him learn to not trust me. "But we're meeting up with him now, and I'm going to have to tell him everything."

"It's going to be weird for him. Don't you think?"

"I don't have a choice," I say. Suddenly I feel defensive and mean. "And if Luc had been given the choice to become an active, he might be the complete and not you." Before I'm done saying it, I already know how unfair I'm being. I rub my eyes. "Sorry, I didn't mean . . . that came out wrong."

"I didn't kill him," Auden says.

"And you want to hear that you could have?" I ask, very serious.

"It doesn't matter now."

It doesn't.

"When the notice came in that I was a complete," Auden says, "I was shocked."

"And relieved," I murmur.

"Well, wouldn't you be?" Silence, and then he says carefully, "It said he was a PK." So curious about this person who could have meant his own death.

"Yes, he was, all right? I was there. I saw the whole thing."

He has no response to that, and I'm glad for it. What can he say? That he's sorry? That he's not? My hands tighten on my bag, and I don't want to think about Luc anymore. It feels wrong to talk about him with this stranger.

Auden sits up straighter in his seat. "Wait. Did you ever ask Sabian why he wanted *you* for this?" he asks. A thoughtful expression on his face. Something's crossed his mind.

I glare at him, wanting to know what he's thinking, hating to ask. "Because I'm good, that's why."

He coughs into his hand, doesn't bother to cover up the slight roll of his eyes. "That's nice, but anything more specific?"

"He said because I don't have any family left, it makes things easier," I mutter. "No ties to worry about."

"Level One didn't know about your brother being my Alt

because he was a PK," Auden says slowly. "All Sabian cared about was that I was already a complete. When Alts become incompletes through anything other than a natural completion, their assignment numbers don't get fed into the normal Alt data log, the one that Level One monitors. They go through legal first, who checks things out before passing them on. By the time Sabian and the others would have gotten to Luc's number, he would already have been filed as a PK."

I remember Sabian's watchful eyes as he told me the same thing, back in that café in the Grid. "I guess so. But what difference does it—" Now I sit up in my seat, too. Outside the train windows the streets fly by as we leave Leyton behind and enter Jethro.

I look at Auden. "When Luc died, your half of the shared assignment number automatically deactivated." Things become clearer as I speak. "So even if I did kill you, your number wouldn't show up on the Alt log for Level One to see. Since it's already gone from the system."

"And if you *didn't* kill me, they wouldn't know that, either."

"But it also means I have no way of convincing them that I did it," I say to him. "Only my word."

"So if I stay hidden, he'll never know I'm still alive."

We only have a few hours left until Sabian expects to hear from me, one way or the other, and making him believe Auden's dead would be easier if I knew why he wanted him that way.

"You'll have to figure out pretty quickly why Sabian wants you dead," I say to Auden. "Because if he finds out I didn't kill you, I might as well be dead, too. We'll both be on the run." I wonder if I should tell him about the other two Alts. But I decide against it—what's the point when we might end up living that kind of life, too? And what's the point of reminding him that Sabian really *did* intend to save Board Alts . . . just not him?

Auden nods curtly, and his face shuts down, goes bleak with frustration.

The train enters the Grid.

This is where I'll find Chord.

And where Chord will find a ghost from the past.

Chapter 11

I see Chord as soon as I turn the corner. True to his word, he's standing against the chipped brick wall between Dire's place and the store next door, his hands shoved deep into his pockets. Against the late-afternoon sunlight his familiar profile makes my heart hurt with wanting.

"Stay back for now, okay?" I hiss over my shoulder at Auden.

He stops, sighs. Makes a face and looks so much like Luc that for a second I feel my hand curl into a fist so I can punch him in the arm. "Where do you want me to go? Just . . . hang out on the sidewalk?" he asks, so out of his element here.

"Yes. Whatever. Five minutes, that's all I need." I'm distracted, staring ahead at Chord, willing him not to turn this way and see Auden. Not yet. Not until I know what to tell him.

"Fine. I'm waiting." Auden stands right where he is, looking ridiculous and uncomfortable and somehow still refined as the crowd swirls around him, some people giving him dirty looks as they're forced to adjust their course.

"No, not there." I look around. We don't exactly stick out, but Board Operators move like smoke. I grab Auden by the arm and steer him toward a café that's so full the front window is steamed over, making it hard to see inside. Perfect. "Just get in line or something, all right? I'll be back as soon as I tell Chord—"

"West, it'll be fine," he says quietly, suddenly very serious. It's the first time he's said my name, and it's like Luc's voice is yanking me back in time. "I know they were best friends. You told me that on the train ride here, but I didn't kill Luc, remember? Do you really think Chord's going to have a problem meeting me?"

"I don't know. I really don't." I don't want to tell him it was Chord's Alt who killed Luc and that the sight of Auden is going to bring back those terrible moments in one massive rush. Chord would have died for Luc; for him to see Luc's Alt alive and well . . . I just don't know.

Auden pulls open the café door, muttering to me under his breath as he leaves, "He's coming over."

He disappears inside, and I turn to face Chord.

I meet his eyes, and they aren't filled with hate. They take me in, waiting, and I move closer. My heart in my mouth, I wrap my arms around his waist and simply hold on.

"You're late," Chord says quietly.

"I'm sorry."

A low, rough curse. "Me too."

"I feel like I keep saying that, but it's true."

"I know."

Our mouths meet in the middle and the heat chases away whatever lingering fears I might have had.

"West," he says against my skin. "Are you okay? How many left? Are you done?"

I feel my face start to give with the impact of his questions, the weight of his wishes, what I can't give him yet. "I never finished, Chord."

"So you still have to—"

"No, I don't." I squeeze Chord as hard as I can, to make up for the words that never come easily for me. "I don't have to hurt anyone else, all right?"

He nods slowly. "I'm glad," he says.

That's all, and it's enough.

But now I have to tell him. Auden, Sabian, both of them in my head now, demanding my attention. "Chord, there's something else."

A flicker of exhaustion crosses his features. "How is that even possible?"

"About why I didn't finish."

His hands go still. Drop to my shoulders. "That's something *you* decided, West."

I take a deep breath. "The last contract, the Alt I couldn't kill—or couldn't make into a non-Alt—it's . . . it's . . ."

"I don't want to know about who you kept yourself from killing, or who you didn't kill but still ended up destroying, anyway." Chord's face goes tight, reminding me again that though he accepts my being a striker because it's who I am, it still doesn't change what a striker is. "You don't need to tell me that."

"I *do* have to tell you this, Chord." Rushing now, before it's too late. "It's—"

"No, you don't. I . . ." And he goes absolutely still. Chord is looking over my shoulder as though he's been pulled into the past and is no longer here with me.

"—Luc's Alt," I finish weakly, the words still foreign on my tongue. I turn around slowly, careful to keep myself between the two.

Auden is just leaving the café, a coffee in one hand, a tray with two others in the other.

"Wait," I say to him as he nears. Behind me, Chord's stunned silence is loud, a living, breathing thing. People are moving all around us, only inches away, but they suddenly seem very far away, nothing more than a faded backdrop.

"I *did* wait," Auden says, one eyebrow lifted. "Here." He holds out the tray.

I yank it from him, the coffees wobbling. Holding it awkwardly, I watch Auden glance over at Chord standing behind me. The look on Auden's face switches from confusion to curiosity to defensiveness in reaction to Chord's silence. I'm guessing he's wondering if he should say something to Chord first, regardless of my asking him to wait. He has no way of knowing why Chord's shock is as great as it is.

And Chord . . . there is no mistaking he's reeling. As always, it's when he gets very quiet or goes very still that I know he's losing it inside, and right now he's both. He's absolutely frozen, just staring at Auden like he's watching a ghost come to life. Which isn't that far from the truth.

I take a step back until I'm right beside Chord, grabbing one of his hands with my free one. "Chord, this is Auden. He's Luc's Alt. Obviously, I mean." I look from one to the other and the moment is surreal, off-kilter.

"Yeah, I figured out that much," Chord says stiffly, still holding Auden's eyes with his own. His expression is wrenching, speaking of emotions I know all too well. Guilt, love, hate. "I'm . . . Chord."

"Hey, I'm Auden." He sounds casual enough, but no way can Auden miss the tension in the air, connecting the three of us. "West tell you everything? It's a lot to take in, all at once . . ." I can tell he's more nervous than he shows, the way he's rubbing his upper arm with his free hand. Luc used to have that same habit.

Chord nods, a flicker of pain rippling across his face at the sound of Luc's voice. His hand around mine is very warm, and holding on tightly enough that I know his nerves are stretched thin, ready to snap. Strange to be his anchor for once, when he's always been mine. "You should be dead," he says bluntly to Auden.

I wince. Whether he means by my hand or Luc's, I don't know.

Auden studies the cup in his hands. His face is full of unease again. "You might be right about that," he says to Chord as he reaches over and tosses his still steaming drink into a nearby garbage can. "We'll find out soon enough, I guess."

I take Chord with me as I move over to the same garbage can. But instead of throwing away the tray of untouched drinks, I balance the whole thing on top—it's hot, and free, and it won't be long before an active comes by and finds it.

The sun is lowering bit by bit. Close to late afternoon now. Close to when Sabian has to hear that I've killed Auden.

"We've got to go," I say to them, walking fast toward Dire's place. I don't stop to check if Auden's keeping up or slow down so I'm not dragging Chord. Auden's sharp command for the time is the only way I know he's still behind us, and the heat of Chord's hand in mine tells me that he's still with me. We weave around knots of people.

"How did you find out it was him?" Chord asks me in a voice low enough so Auden can't hear. "When?"

"Right before I was about to shoot him."

His hand squeezes mine. "That's . . . pretty timely."

When we reach Dire's place, I'm the first inside. Chord follows, his features hard and full of resentment as he looks around the store, taking in the plug-in and download stations, the mostly-shorted-out holograms lining the walls. Despite how normal everything seems, this whole floor is nothing but a front for Dire's base of operations downstairs—recruiting and tracking strikers, tattooing marks, and—even though Dire did this unknowingly—the source of my learning how to kill without killing.

"So what's this place and why are we here?" Auden asks me, looking around like Chord. Except while Chord's eyes can't hide his suspicion, Auden's eyes are filled with questions—and troubled confusion. How can this dingy place play a part in saving him? If Auden was out of place before on the street, his being an outsider to the Grid is even more obvious in here. "This is what you meant when you said underground? Because I'm not so sure this is—"

"For someone who hates this job, you sure can't stay away for long."

I turn around at the familiar sound of Dire's voice. Both relieved and wary to see him—but mostly relieved. No better person to help me counter the Board than someone who makes a living doing it.

"I need your help." It's all I dare to say to him up here, with customers throughout the store. Too many ears and eyes. And in the far corner of the store, Hestor.

Dire lifts one eyebrow. "Again?" He glances over at Auden. "Who are you?" he barks. Squints as he does a once-over of Auden's face. "You her brother or something? You look alike."

I shake my head, trying to answer but unable to, my breath stuck in my throat.

"He's not her brother," Chord snaps as he moves to stand behind me.

Dire sends me a look. "Another guest, Grayer? It's practically a party in here."

"I know, it's kind of"—the front door opens, and the gust of incoming wind plays with my hair, puts chills down my spine, reminds me what needs to be done—"hard to explain. But we need to get out of sight for a bit."

Dire scratches the side of his beard. He knows what I'm asking, and I admit it's a lot. I had Baer to vouch for me when I first showed up here, and I've slowly earned Dire's trust, but Chord and Auden mean nothing to him. And Auden has Board ties, a potential threat. The enemy is at the door, and I'm the one who showed him the way.

"You have to give me more than that, Grayer," Dire finally says. He scans the room, turns his back to it so he can't be heard by anyone other than us. "Does this have anything to do with what you were here for last time?"

My questions about the Roark gun. I nod. "Everything to do with it."

"Who's after you?"

Against my will I glance over at Auden before facing Dire again. "The Board."

"The Board?" Dire's eyes go flat, like liquid blue ice. "Don't tell me your last visit had anything to do with them, Grayer. That I helped them by helping *you*." Quiet disappointment in his voice, and it's worse than any kind of anger.

I nod, then shake my head. Words failing me, *again*. Whatever skills I have with weapons, I fall far short with those meant for communicating.

"Who on the Board?" he asks.

"Level One. An Operator named Sabian."

The name has Dire swearing under his breath. "Not smart, Grayer. Not smart."

"You know him, don't you?"

Instead of answering, he looks at Chord and Auden again. "You two. What's the story?"

Chord glares at Dire, says nothing. Not a good decision, and I can tell Dire's about to lose it.

I grab Chord's hand, know that Dire can't miss me doing it. "This is—"

"If you know Sabian, then you probably know my father."

Auden's rash words have the effect of grease on a fire. The air turns thick and dangerous, though Auden is oblivious.

"And who is your father?" Dire asks.

Auden looks from me to Dire. Whatever is on my face has him going very still, bracing for Dire's inevitable bite. "Meyer Parrish. He's a Level Two Operator."

Dire blinks and says calmly, "Just a Level Two?"

Auden shrugs. Still guarded.

"Well, your dad was never overly ambitious. If he weren't already a member of the Board because of his folks, Meyer might have been just as satisfied slumming it out here in Jethro, doing something else."

"How do you—" I ask Dire, too stunned to stop myself from interrupting. Dire's about as far removed from the inner workings of the Board as I can imagine.

Dire ignores me. "Your old man aside, how are *you* involved with all this?" he asks Auden. "With Sabian? And Grayer?"

"He, uh, hired her as a striker to kill me."

This time when Dire swears, he doesn't bother trying to be quiet. When he's done, he pulls out his cell and taps out a text.

"Who is he texting?" Chord whispers in my ear.

I shake my head, frowning. Who else could Dire want involved with this? "I don't—"

"Baer," Dire says. The name from him is nearly a curse, his voice resigned.

"Who?" Auden asks, looking from Dire to Chord to me and back to Dire again.

"Baer," Dire says again, still tapping away. "He used to work for the Board with your old man. If we're trying to figure out what Sabian's up to, having Baer here will help."

The bizarreness of what's happening is a storm in my head, and it's Chord who manages to ask, "How do you know all this? About the Board?"

"Because I used to work there, too." With that, Dire shoves his cell back into his pocket and motions for us to follow him as he moves past the front counter and disappears down the stairs.

Her back is to us, but I know who she is. The only other person I've seen in here, other than Dire.

Innes. Even her posture is elegant as she works at one of Dire's computer stations, and I still remember the catlike green of her eyes, the way her lips curled as she tattooed the marks on my wrists. She couldn't quite hide her disapproval over Dire's choice to accept me as a striker.

Innes turns around at the sound of Dire's approach, standing up as we enter the room. Her expression cools as she looks from Dire to us. Lingers on me for seconds longer, and I can't miss the surprise in the lift of her brows, the slight widening of her eyes. Maybe she's simply surprised to see me back here. Or that I've lasted so much longer than she expected.

"Dire," Innes says to him, a warning tone behind the smooth tones of her voice, "what are you doing?"

He shakes his head. "It's fine. They're fine. Having a meeting down here is all."

"I have work to do."

"We'll stay out of your way."

"Hmm." She's annoyed, but also curious. "See that you do, then." Innes sits back down, spins around in her chair, and continues doing whatever she was doing. Matching up clients with strikers, extracting finder fees, tracking those who might not be so eager to transfer said fees. Her fingers tap out a light staccato on the screens. It's soothing, like birds chirping.

I watch as Chord and Auden take in the room and see what they see.

A small basement with dingy gray walls. There are no windows, the only light coming from the three cheap bulbs hanging from the ceiling over the beaten metal table in the center of the room. Mismatched chairs are scattered loosely across the concrete floor. A cool, earthy dampness in the air that I can feel against my skin.

It's jarring to see anyone other than Dire and Innes in here. If I let my eyes blur just a bit, it's Chord and Luc, scoping out the potential of new tech pieces to bring home and refurbish, reconfigure. A scene from life Before—as in, Before Chord got his assignment, Before Luc died, Before I ever killed my first strike.

I blink and it's Chord and Auden again. Chord, much as he was upstairs: wishing he didn't have to be here. And Auden, seeing for himself the rival of the very system that feeds him, makes him who he is, who he will be. As a future Operator of the Board, this will be a threat, but right now, as an Alt running from that same Board, it might give him a chance at safety.

"My father," Auden says. He looks at Dire. "Do you think he's in danger?"

"I don't know. Depends on why Sabian wants you dead."

Auden feels for his cell in his jeans pocket. "I should warn—"

"If Meyer is the same Meyer I remember, you don't want to call him. He'll never be able to keep himself from confronting Sabian. Your old man wasn't one to climb rank and had the most laid-back attitude of anyone I ever knew at the Board, but he was also a hothead when he had to be. Right?"

Auden exhales. "Yeah, he is." Reluctantly he lets his hand fall from his pocket. I know how he feels. There's nothing harder than watching from a distance as a predator approaches someone you love. That the smart thing to do is to let it happen.

And I'm startled to realize that Meyer is also Luc's father, as much a part of him as the father he and I shared. So that's where Luc got it from, then—that easy way he had of always sensing what were the little things that could slide and what was worth sweating over.

Dire mutters a command for the time: *14:48.* "How much time does that give you?" he asks me.

"Seventeen hundred is the next given time on Auden's spec sheet. An endurance training facility in Leyton. After that, the only other possibility is tomorrow morning, when he's signed up to leave headquarters for drill training."

"So that's when Sabian's going to expect you to complete the strike, seventeen hundred."

"Right. Sabian would never expect Auden to be on guard enough to kill *me*—as a complete, Auden wouldn't suspect an attack. So since I haven't reported Auden's death from my first opportunity, when he was arriving at the training arena, Sabian's probably thinking I either passed up the chance or just missed it. He's going to assume I'm simply waiting now and that Auden's about to head out to endurance training from"—I look at Auden, double-checking—"headquarters, right?"

"School, yeah," Auden adds. "Normally I would just take off right from the class wing. We never see any of the ranking Operators during regular school hours."

"Which is why Sabian won't expect to see you until after you get back from this next session," Dire says. "From endurance training."

Auden nods. "But I'm not supposed to get there, am I?"

"No, you're not," I say. "He didn't want me trying to track you on your way *back* to headquarters, because then I would find out you weren't just any Alt. So it's either this chance tonight or the last entry on the spec sheet—early tomorrow morning, when you're supposed to arrive somewhere else. Which means you'd have to go home and hope you can fool Sabian."

"Not going to happen," Dire grunts. "Like tossing sheep right to the wolf."

Footsteps come down the stairs and Baer enters the room.

He's grim and weary-looking. Beneath the bare lightbulbs strung from the ceiling, his skin is a landscape of scars, all bleached crescents and pale red moons. His clothes are wrinkled from the drive over, and I wonder how fast he must have driven to get here so quickly.

It hits me that this is the first time I've seen both Baer and Dire together in the same room. Both of them play such significant parts in my life—it seems wrong that it took this long to happen.

"Dire," Baer says with a curt nod and a slight narrowing of his eyes. "It's been a while since we last saw each other."

Dire scowls. "Not long enough, I'm thinking."

"Fourteen years, if I'm counting correctly."

"That's all?"

Baer nearly grins at that. Nearly. Smiles don't come easily to someone like Baer, who is surrounded by classrooms half full of the future dead, day after day. "I've missed you as well."

"Of course you miss me. When you gotta settle for being around your sunny self all the time?"

Laughter wants to bubble up my throat. Sadness, too. What had happened to end what must have been a close friendship?

"I was surprised to hear from you," Baer says. "To say the least."

Dire shrugs. "Grayer's involved. I knew you'd want to help."

I hate knowing that my decisions have affected my friends.

"You were with the Board longer," Dire continues. "Might know something about Sabian I don't."

"Just by months."

"Might be enough."

"Hello, Baer."

Baer looks over at Innes. She's turned around in her chair again, and as his face warms, I begin to wonder more about this woman who's shown nothing but disdain toward me. "Innes, how are you?"

She gives him a smile that actually reaches her eyes. For one second. Then her face turns serious again. "I'm sorry it's been so long. And now this."

He turns, sees Auden, and the sight of Luc's Alt leaves him visibly shocked. Luc was once a student in his weaponry class, and an exceptional one. How strange for Baer to meet the very person he once hoped Luc would beat.

And now the one he has to help.

"So Dire says you're Meyer's son," Baer says quietly. "Auden, correct?"

"Yeah." Auden looks puzzled and a bit annoyed. Too many people, too many questions, not enough answers. "Who are you?"

"My name's Baer. I used to work with your father, a long time ago. How is he?"

A cautious shrug. "Fine."

"You were three years old when I left the Board, and the loudest kid in the whole damn building."

Dire barks out a laugh at Auden's expression.

"Once you learned how to talk," Baer says to a dumbfounded

Auden, "believe me—you were not above tattling. It seems you've learned to rein in the talking a bit."

I feel a pang of jealousy. My history with Baer and Dire is far from these happy childhood memories.

At the sight of Chord, Baer nods in greeting. Not happy to see him here, but not unhappy, either. For me.

He turns to me next.

Baer walks over. I don't let myself back down from his glare, though I think I can hear every single thought going through his head. Each one is well deserved. For all their animosity, in this Baer and Dire can agree on their disappointment, anger, and worry. I escaped a beast only to willingly stroll right back into its den.

"As a complete, you were done with the Board," Baer says to me, his voice flat. "You should have been satisfied with that."

Echoes of what Chord's already said to me, and I can only nod.

Dire pulls out one of the chairs from the table in the center of the room and sits down heavily. "Okay, Grayer, let's hear it. Tell us what the hell you've gotten yourself into."

I shake my head, make no move to sit down. My thumbs are hooked tight into the straps of my bag, the canvas digging into my skin—proof that this is all real. "Why didn't you ever say anything about working for the Board? That you and Baer *both*—"

"Not so fast. That news is old enough to sit a bit longer. You came to me asking for help. *Twice.* Your turn."

So I start talking, right from when I saw that Operator standing outside of Julis's office. I hide nothing. Auden grabs a chair and sits at the opposite end of the table, away from everyone else. Chord is too wound up to keep still; his pacing follows the flow of my words. Only when Dire throws him a pointed look does he force himself to lean against a wall.

It's when I get to the part about not killing the idles that someone else finally speaks.

"So *that's* what you got out of my telling you about that gun?" Dire's disbelief has me hunching my shoulders.

Everyone in the room is still. Innes, even, has given up all pretense of work to turn around from her computer to listen quietly as we discuss what she herself created.

"First of all," Dire says, "me telling you that the gun created non-Alts was supposed to scare the crap out of you, Grayer, not show you how to do it."

"I did mean to kill them," I say. "Right up until the second I was about to pull the trigger. When I couldn't, I had to think of a way out for them."

"For you, too, as it turns out," Dire says. "Don't forget that part of it."

I know he's thinking about what he said to me about a striker not leaving loose ends. I've failed him, too.

"Grayer, you told them to go to the Surround?" Baer now. He sounds more uneasy than angry, which shakes me up even more.

"West, you didn't," Chord says. He takes a step closer to the table and then stops, falls back to lean against the wall again. His face is very pale. "Please tell me you didn't tell them about the disrupter."

"I didn't because they don't need it to get through," I say weakly. "The poison permanently neutralized *everything* about the Alt code, even its shell. *We're* the ones who'd still need the disrupter to neutralize what's left of our Alt codes if we wanted to get past the barrier. And the effect would only last as long as we were holding it."

"What's a disrupter?" Auden asks, sounding absolutely confused.

"A mistake," Chord says.

"That was very poor advice, West," Baer says. "Sending them over there."

"I said *if* they had to escape—"

"The Surround is *no* escape." Baer's tone is cutting. "If these kids are discovered over there, you can be sure that our enemies will try to re-create that breach in the barrier. Somehow."

"You better hope those targets of yours decide to stay right here in the city," Dire says. "Not that we'll ever be able to ask them nicely. Roark guns wipe out any way of tracking them."

"So now you're on the run, with Sabian on your heels and short on time." Baer exhales heavily and says nothing else, as if there's no point. Because it's not long until Auden's expected to show up, either dead or alive. And figuring out Sabian before he figures me out means doing something that still comes hard for me—staying still and not running, asking for help instead of thinking I can do it all myself.

"Getting involved with the Board was your first mistake, Grayer," Dire says. His voice has an unmistakable edge to it. "Thinking you could win was your second."

I swallow thickly. "I know that. *Now.*"

"You don't know the Board like I know it," Dire says. "So if you want a chance to get out of this alive, then listen. Because I have a story to tell you."

CHAPTER 12

"I was twenty-one years old and still a Level Three Operator alongside Baer and Meyer," says Dire. "Meyer was five years older than us, but like I said, content enough just to float along with wherever the Board wanted to place him. Sabian was the same age as Meyer and already a Level Two.

"I was in no hurry to advance, even though the Board already told me I showed enough tactical skill that they intended to push me through to Level Two soon. Thought I had all the time in the world, you know? I was complete, a Board member living in Leyton—and I had Freya."

I pull out a chair to sit, letting my bag drop into my lap and positioning myself directly across from Dire so I can see him and make sure this is real. Dire as a recruiter of killers makes sense; Dire as a young man in love does not.

"She was eighteen, the daughter of a respected Level Two Operator. If things went the way they were supposed to— meaning she'd complete when she finally got her assignment— Freya would have been a Level Two tactical Operator within a few years. As it was, she still had lots of training to finish and qualifying exams to pass. She was doing some research in the data logs, studying techniques and strategies, when she came across a bunch of old miscoded files that had gotten dropped into the wrong data log. Turns out one of them was about a side project conducted by Kersh's bio lab fifty-five years ago."

Dire breaks off abruptly and glances over at Innes, who's listening as intently as the rest of us, her work at the computer forgotten. Then Dire continues as if he never stopped, as if we couldn't have noticed.

"Finding cross-filed data itself wasn't that big of a deal. There were lots of different data logs, and sometimes mistakes happened. But Freya had never heard of this side project before, so she kept the file to analyze later. It was just a partial one, just bits and pieces of jumbled, miscoded information that didn't mean anything in and of itself. It was innocent curiosity, that was all."

From the corner of my eye, I see Baer start moving across the room, pacing. Now he's the one too restless to stand still. "Start from the beginning, Dire," he mutters.

"As a Level Two Op in training, one of Freya's Board duties was to check on the training facilities throughout the ward. Make sure the equipment was still working fine and all that. There were usually enough trainees at any point that a schedule was kept to track who was going where and when. So it wouldn't have been hard to figure out where Freya's next check was going to be. Where *she* was going to be."

I rub at the sudden chill on my arms. Dire's words tell me he's haunted. And beneath the room's cheap lighting, he looks old, worn down. Not strong.

"It was a brand-new building, not yet open to the public," he continues. "The skill stations were still being set up. Freya was there looking over the latest shipment of bullets that had come in when the whole place just blew."

There's a noticeable break in Baer's step before he continues pacing. I look over at Chord to see him watching me, eyes very dark. Auden is pale. Innes doesn't react at all.

"Gas leak," Dire says, his voice harsh. "They eventually said it was because of a glitch in the computer program that regulated the gas flow. But, you know, nothing like that's ever happened since. Not in Leyton, or any other ward in the city.

"I had my own facility to be checking at that time, at the other end of the ward. But I wanted to be with Freya and decided to go with her instead. It was five weeks before I woke up in the hospital. Nothing but minor burns that were already healed. And Freya—" Dire's voice breaks off.

"Was she okay?" Chord asks.

"Freya was . . . fine." Dire frowns, and he rubs the side of his face, as though to wake himself. His blue eyes are very bright as he looks over at Innes. Her expression is impossible to read. "She was more than fine actually," Dire says slowly. "She told me that while I was recovering, she got notice that her Alt had been killed in a train accident. So she was finally a complete, just as I'd been for nearly four years.

"For weeks nothing was clear, like I was looking through fog, and my head felt like crap. But Freya helped me get through it; pain aside, things were good. We had both made it through a freak accident, both of us were completes, and our future positions in the Board were secured. Eventually I felt right again. Except the more right I felt, the more wrong Freya started to seem."

My throat, dry as dust. "'Wrong'?"

"Off," Dire says, correcting himself, the word curt. "Different. At first I thought it was just me still recovering. Then I thought it was just her worrying too much. But, yeah, different. Small things, like forgetting the name of someone she'd known for years but hadn't seen in a while. Tilting her head to the wrong side when she laughed. Not eating her favorite foods."

I guessed the truth then. "It wasn't Freya, was it?"

"No, it was her Alt."

"Her Alt." Chord repeats the two words, as though doing so would make it less crazy.

"Something about that side project from the bio lab that she found," I say to Dire. "Was that it?"

He nods. "Someone was threatened by what she found, or *would* find if given more time. When I was okay again, her notes and the file were gone. And her Alt had, of course, lost interest in it."

"You're saying the *lab* was behind the explosion?" Chord asks. "Because we all know the Board runs the lab."

"That makes no sense!"

Heads swivel toward Auden. His face is still pale, but set. This is his world we're dissecting and deciding it's rotten inside.

"Level Operators are valuable assets," he says. "Years of training, inherited in-house knowledge, access to elite facilities—all to form the best soldiers. The best citizens. It makes no sense why they would just kill Freya and then go to such lengths to save Dire. Not only save, but also trick into thinking nothing had changed."

Dire lifts an eyebrow. "You're sharp, kid," he says. "It took me a bit longer to reason that out, and then to discover the answer."

"So? What did you come up with?"

"It wasn't the Board," Baer says quietly, finally stopping his pacing. "It was only a single Operator, acting on his own."

"Sabian," I mutter.

"Sabian," Baer says with a nod.

Dire says nothing, and as though sensing Dire's weariness, Baer continues.

"After Dire got Freya's Alt to confess—that it was Sabian who bribed her with life as a complete, as a Board member, and a guarantee that her family would never run out of resources, all to impersonate someone else for the rest of her life—he confronted Sabian at headquarters with everything he'd learned.

"Freya's lab project actually uncovered data about Kersh's true beginnings. It had been accidentally miscoded to look like a lab project, don't forget."

"'True beginnings,'" Auden repeats. He sounds about as cold as when he was demanding answers from me, out there on that street in front of the training arena. "You have *got* to be kidding me."

"Kersh provides safety for its people from the Surround," Dire says, still sounding tired. "But it's also a prison. Now listen, this city really started out as an off-limits zone, a place for prisoners of war, criminals, the diseased. You have to remember the Surround was chaos, anyway—it made things easier just to lock up those they didn't want around. The Board could control the amount of resources going in. And what did the Surround care about the prisoners eventually dying out?

"But things were going from bad to worse out in the

Surround, and three members of the Board began to be particularly vocal about trying to change things."

"The Founders," Chord says.

"You bet. Cris, Jackson, and Tamryn. They decided they had to start small if they were going to make much of a difference in the long run. What better place than a prison, already barricaded and self-contained? Over time, they convinced the prisoners to fight back against the Surround. The Founders left the Surround for the last time, crossed the barrier, and Kersh was born. And so here we are—and the Surround continues to want the land back under its control."

"The part about us being prisoners now, though," I say, shaking my head. I glance over at Chord, and then Auden. They look about as lost as I feel. "How?"

"We're still prisoners because the Board keeps us here in order to make sure they stay safe from the Surround."

"But if it weren't for the Board, we wouldn't even be here," Auden says. "We'd have died out ages ago."

"We also wouldn't have any Alts to kill."

Auden says nothing.

"So Sabian was acting on his own when he killed Freya?" Chord finally asks. "Why? And how did he know this about Kersh, when you and Baer didn't?"

"Only a few of the most senior Level One Operators are ever supposed to know the truth about Kersh once being a prison," Dire says. "At the time, one of them . . . well, she had a major weakness for smooth-talking younger guys and eventually got sloppy about keeping Sabian away from her records. And once he knew the secret, he went from not even qualifying for Level Three to becoming Level One within just a couple of years. I'd already left the Board by the time he got there. And the Board wasn't aware that Freya had found anything—only Sabian knew after he overheard Freya telling me about that damn file she was so curious about. When his plan went to hell because I got hurt, the Board was furious that he took matters into his own hands and not only lost one asset but also perhaps two. And that's why they decided to bring in Freya's Alt. Damage control. I would never have to know."

"What did you do when you found out about her Alt?" I ask him. Suddenly this, of all the things I just learned, seems most important of all.

He sighs, rubs the back of his head. "The mind's a messed-up thing, Grayer. I believed what I wanted to believe. And by the time I realized I was wrong, it was too late. Freya or not, I did love her, even as I was devastated to lose the person I'd thought she was."

Chord shakes his head, his eyes black fire, lit with indignation. "You're saying one Alt is interchangeable with another. That one isn't different enough from the other to matter." I can guess what he's thinking. Chord wants nothing to do with his own Alt, the person who killed his best friend.

"I'm saying I was too sick to notice," Dire nearly snarls at him.

"In the beginning, maybe," Chord says. "Not later."

"Listen, kid—"

"Just looking like someone and sounding like them and behaving like them—it shouldn't be enough to *be* them," Chord says. "Loving that Alt as though she were Freya, you're saying everything that happens after birth means nothing."

"Loving her Alt didn't mean I felt less for Freya, you got that?"

"You really loved both, then?" I ask Dire. "Her Alt lied to you. How could you . . . how could she—"

"I did lie, but only at first." Innes's sharp voice cuts through the room.

Shock strangles us into momentary silence.

Innes is Freya's Alt.

It's Auden who breaks the silence first. "But now you're both here, recruiting strikers to work against the Board." He glances between Dire and Innes. "Why did the Board let you leave, if they wanted so badly to keep you both as Operators?"

"I knew the truth. About Kersh—about Freya and Innes. Sabian confessed to the prison, to the explosion, and to switching Alts. My knowledge was enough to make them let me walk." Dire glances up at Baer. "And I told them that I left all that info with a friend. So if anything happened to us, every bit of dirt would come out."

Baer. He's still standing there, listening, and it's hard to imagine him as a twenty-one-year-old. I try to picture him and Dire both at that age, and Baer keeping such a secret for so many years to secure safety for his friend.

"Did you blackmail the Board so you could leave, too?" I ask Baer now.

He nods. "Not long after, a few months. And then I found out Dire was a recruiter of strikers. I understood his grievances against the Board—what I couldn't understand was his chosen method of fighting back. He called me a weakling."

Dire snickers. "Actually, the word I used was—"

"Hush, you two," Innes says. She turns her head to look at

Auden. Her green eyes make me wonder about her Alt, how different or similar Freya would have been. How I'd feel living in the shadow of another, forever trying to be both. "So now the question is," she says, "why does Sabian want *you* dead?"

For a second, Auden says nothing. Then he pulls out his cell from his jeans pocket. He taps it awake, opens it to a file, and hands it over to Innes.

She takes it from him, and whatever she reads there has her green eyes widening in shock. "These are Freya's notes on that old file." Her finger slides across the screen, moving across the page. "And the miscoded file itself."

"What?" Dire's voice is uneven. He steps over and looks at the screen with Innes. "That's Freya's handwriting . . . and a copy of that file she found. . . ." He shakes his head and stares at Auden. "Where did you get these? The file went missing after she was killed."

"I found them in a folder in the old research section of the lab," Auden says. "They were old enough that . . . well . . . I read some of it, and I got curious, so I scanned it all with my cell before putting everything back. It's all gone now, anyway. They've just cleared out that whole paper section to make room for digital storage."

"Why were you in the lab in the first place?" Innes asks, surprised. "Most Level Alts choose active training to fulfill their qualifying hours."

"I think the technical side of things—like our gene maps and why we're still sterile—is pretty interesting, too."

"I agree." And now Innes is looking at Auden more curiously. The more she talks, the more I can see past her cat-like beauty so she's less intimidating, more human. "It's just another way to approach a fight, isn't it? With a different kind of weapon—knowledge."

I think of Innes and her tracking chips in striker marks, her binding agent to speed healing, her poison in the Roark guns. I never thought of knowledge that way before—how it's not whether things hurt or help that's important, but the knowledge that led them to exist in the first place.

"How would Sabian know you saw those old notes, though?" Baer asks Auden. "Sabian must know you have this knowledge and want you stopped, just like he stopped Freya."

Dire still seems unable to speak. Caught in the past. I watch as Innes reaches over and touches his arm.

Auden shakes his head. "I don't know. It just doesn't seem possible. I think it must be something else."

"He did say the Board wanted to make sure these Level One trainees completed," I add, picturing Sabian telling me this, back in the meeting room in headquarters. "The ones I was contracted for. Because the Level Two Alts weren't good enough to take over if something happened."

"So he wants me killed just in case?" Auden asks. "I couldn't care less about rank."

"It's possible Sabian sees that," Baer says. He looks thoughtful but touched with doubt. "He always did find fault in Meyer for not caring more. He said it was an unworthy trait for a Board Alt, let alone a Level Alt."

"Well, whatever Sabian's reasoning, it's not going to give us any more time," Innes says. "For now, I can study those notes with Auden. Perhaps there's something more to them than Sabian told me about, that first time he came to me. Something he's scared about someone finding out."

"Maybe Sabian had been lying about Kersh's origins as a prison," Chord says. "It's all miscoded, right? So the notes could mean almost anything."

"No, that was no lie." Innes's eyes are very green, suddenly catlike again, and I'm reminded of her own skills in a lab. "I was there. The top Level One Operators at the time confirmed it."

Baer utters a single command into his watch: "Time."

13:18

"Cutting it way too close, Grayer," Dire mutters. "Barely enough time to get back to Leyton and be where you're supposed to be to kill Auden. Take the outer ward train, walk the same route you would have to get there, wait the same way. Sabian will be expecting that, and we can't risk raising his suspicions as you go to him to get your marks removed." His words are eerie echoes of many past instructions for strikes, of preparing to go under. "Time to learn how to lie—and lie *well*. Well enough to fool even yourself."

I stand up straight. Heartbeat amped, pulse skipping. My hand reaches for Chord to settle me. "What about Auden? Where will he go?"

"Pull this off first. He can stay here for now."

"The Board knows about this place, though. I just didn't know where else to go."

"Sabian has no reason to believe you won't kill Auden, Grayer," Baer says to me. "He doesn't know you suspect anything. We'll deal with that after you get back from headquarters."

Headquarters. The idea of going back there sends new chills through me. But Sabian agreed to erase my marks; changing my mind all of a sudden, for something that I pushed so hard for, would be a huge red flag.

I have to go. No simple text to confirm completion this time. The first time I'm to break striker protocol and meet a client in person after I've killed for them. The first time I'll walk in and be more afraid of them than they are of me.

"Remember," Dire says. "Get in, finish the job, get out. It's as simple as that."

I take a deep breath. *Slip in and out. Leave no memory. Leave no footprint.* The last strike I'll ever do and the one that carries the most significance. No target, no gun, no blade, just my weak words and transparent face.

At least I won't need the Roark anymore.

"Dire, wait." I pick up my bag from the ground and unzip it. Pull out the gun and hold it out. "I don't want to take this," I say to him. Auden's off to my side, and I feel the weight of his emotions as he watches what would have been his instant death be passed from his striker to her recruiter—disbelief, embarrassment at having to be saved, gratitude.

Dire only shakes his head at the gun. Pushes it back at me. "It'll set off alarm bells if you don't have it on you when Sabian asks for it back. And also . . . well, just keep it on you for as long as you can."

"Just in case, you mean." I still have one vial. Am I to finally use it on Sabian the way it's meant to be used? Does Dire *want* me to make it meant for Sabian?

His eyes are hard but worried, and I know I'm wrong. "Just in case." *To take care of you, not to take care of Sabian.*

So I slip the gun back inside my bag, slide the straps over

my shoulders. Horrible to admit that the renewed weight is a relief. Completely empty of weapons, my bag had felt too light.

Dire and Innes head upstairs, and I'm left looking after them. Wishing they would stay, if only so time could stop.

Auden gets to his feet. "West, I . . ." His gaze moves from me to Chord and then back to me. "I don't really know what to say. Except thank you for not killing me, back in the training arena. I know you could have, easily, from what I saw."

"I wasn't going to kill you," I say to him. "Not exactly."

"Thanks for that, too, then." He nods, exhales. "Don't get killed." And then he follows Dire and Innes up the stairs.

Baer walks over to me and I'm careful to not look too closely at him. I don't want to see traces of that earlier doubt because if I do, I know it can only be doubt for my survival.

"Not all weapons are made of metal," he says. "It's not just a gun or blade that makes you capable, Grayer. You're a complete, and you have earned it."

I have earned it, haven't I? All of it, all of this. The possibility of everything going wrong.

"Chord," Baer says, "I know you want to go with her."

Chord's shoulders stiffen. "And?"

"That's all I'm going to say. You both know what to do. We'll be waiting upstairs. Make it fast."

Chord and I, alone. I turn to face him.

"You think that's Baer's way of telling me I should go with you?" Chord asks. His smile doesn't reach his eyes. They're carefully shuttered, all emotion banked down so the fire of what he's feeling won't escape, burning both of us.

Because I have to go, and he has to stay, and that is not something that can be argued.

Still I nod and smile, wanting to pretend for just a bit longer. "Yes." Our shared lie on my lips.

He sighs. "Yes." Comes closer, puts his hands on the sides of my face. "I know you'll be okay, West," he says, his voice rough yet soft enough to make my chest ache. "You will be okay." His desperation won't let me believe otherwise.

"I know," I say.

"Lie like you've never lied before." A hint of a smile on his lips. "Better than you ever did with me, okay?"

"I will." I force a small laugh. "And who says I've ever lied to you?"

Too many memories of too many close calls flicker across his face, and I know he's haunted by her, my Alt who won't stay dead. She's only ever one blink away, that one degree separating who she was from who I am. How to tell him she can't go quiet yet? That it's she who makes that part of me work, kill, lie?

"I can go out there with you," he says suddenly, fiercely. "He won't even see me. I'll be—"

I shake my head. "You can't do that, Chord. You can't do any of this. Only I can. If Sabian even—"

"He won't. I *swear* he—"

I kiss his words away. Absorb his fear with my hands in his hair, draw it from his skin with mine. Like a sickness threatening to cloud his judgment, a thorn pricked with good intention . . . a drug to make him vulnerable.

Not this time.

"West," he says against my temple, my ear, my neck. "Please." And I know it's not a plea to change my mind, but for me to come back.

I wrap my arms around him, make a new memory of how

he feels against me, a different kind of mark than those on my wrists.

A soft trill of my watch—felt against my arm more than heard—and my pulse, already racing, speeds up even more.

"I have to go, Chord." The words are wrenched from me. The last thing I want to say—the only thing I can say.

One final hard embrace and he's the one who lets go first. It's right and what has to be done, but it hurts just the same.

Chord's lips on mine. The last parts of us left touching now because it's good-bye and it's so very hard, so excruciatingly painful. "The faster you go, the faster you get back," he whispers against my skin. "Just remember that I love you."

CHAPTER 13

I'm rushing out the front entrance—*cutting it way too close, Grayer*—so I run right past him at first. Only the sound of my name has me coming to a stop.

I recognize that voice.

I turn around and see Dess sitting on the curb, waiting. His face shows the impatience of an eleven-year-old who's found himself waiting much longer than expected.

I walk over to him, force my face to look normal, however normal it can get right now. "Dess? What are you doing here?"

He gets up, swipes at the street grime on his clothes from sitting on the ground.

"You weren't answering your cell." The sharp edge of accusation in his words, and something that runs much deeper than plain annoyance at having to wait for me. I stare at his face. See what I missed earlier, maybe even made myself miss on purpose so I could keep moving and not feel guilty. His eyes are rimmed with red, his mouth small and set with anger.

A queasy feeling in my gut.

"Where were you, West?"

"I told you." The cell's easy enough to explain—I ignored

all incoming calls apart from Sabian's spec sheets. The one from Chord that slipped through caught me off guard. But I'm scrabbling for the other details, barely able to remember what lie I told him. Lie on top of lie and I can't find the one I want when I need it. "I was . . . busy."

A stream of bodies cuts between us, giving me a few seconds to try to remember. Was it only two days ago that I talked to Dess? A lifetime between then and now.

I narrow my eyes at him. "How did you know where to find me?"

"I followed that teacher from your school here. I know you work for him."

"Baer?"

"Whatever. I don't care what his name is." A huge scowl on Dess's face, a thousand times worse than what I'd ever seen on Ehm's face when she'd gotten angry with me, and it's like being sideswiped from two directions. Old memories, new anger. "But I followed him inside that music store," Dess says.

Queasiness turns to full-blown nausea. "You went inside?"

"Yeah."

"That's fine, Dess," I say quickly. "It's just a store, anyway. Did you find something to buy—"

"That worker Hestor told me you were downstairs. He said I could wait for you."

Stunned, then the bitter film of rage on my tongue. Tinged, of course, with fear. Of all the Alts I've killed . . . I could gather them together now, each and every one of them, and the emotion I would feel still wouldn't come close to touching the depths of what's in my heart for Hestor. Sheer hate that it's Dess he's toyed with now.

"Where did you wait for me, Dess?" I ask him. *What did you hear?*

Fresh tears trickle down his cheeks. "You're striking again, West."

I cringe at the hurt. It's all over him, like a giant bruise. "Dess, I—"

"You said you wouldn't anymore."

"I know, I—"

"And you saved *him*."

"Who?"

"That guy. Your brother's Alt. Who you were supposed to kill."

Auden. How to explain that I was supposed to assassinate a complete, the one, the worthy? "Hold on a second, let—"

"West." Dess swipes at his nose with an arm. "You could still do it, you know."

I shake my head. Denial turns my voice hollow, the passing of crucial minutes relentless and unforgiving and somehow muffled now. "What are you talking about?"

He glares at me. "Finish the job. You're too close to getting what you wanted. Then you'll be done, and things will be normal again."

More people cut across, and I can't see him anymore, and I don't want to believe this is the Dess I know. But when the path clears again, nothing's changed.

"Dess, I can't. I can't do that."

"Why? He's not your brother! He's just his Alt. He would have done it, if he had the chance and your brother wasn't already dead."

"But he didn't, Dess," I whisper harshly to him.

"So if you aren't going to do it, why is he still here?" Dess's eyes are dry now, bright and hot.

"Dess, Auden's not—he's just another complete, all right?" The words are awkward. It's still not easy for me to talk out loud about things that matter. Auden is more than another complete; he has pieces of my brother that are still here, alive.

"Are you and Chord going to start hanging out with him?"

"I don't— No, he's not family." Lie, not a lie, I don't even know anymore.

And it's time to move.

"The Board's not going to stop looking for you if you don't do it," Dess says. "You have to or they'll come after you. And what they said about your kids not having Alts? Why *wouldn't* you do that if you have the chance?" Dess blinks, caught in the past. "I'll never forget what it was like. Having to kill him. I would *never* want my own kids to go through that, if I could do anything to stop it."

"I'm sorry, I can't do it," I say. Just those simple words and they resonate inside my head like clarity, like waking, the breathing in of new air, and I know I'm done. No more. "I just can't—"

"You said that before, and you lied. So what's one more?"

"It's not just one more, Dess. It's—when does it stop?"

"Then you're already dead, West. Just like my Alt, like your Alt, like your brother!"

Before I can say another word, he's running down the sidewalk, along the street. Getting lost in the crowds, trying to hide from me.

I swear under my breath and chase after him. The wind is

surprisingly cold and whips my hair against my face. I know time is ticking away, and I have to catch the train *right now* if I'm to even have a chance of making it out to Leyton to kill a phantom Auden. But I'm going in the wrong direction for that and my mind's eye can't see past Dess's face.

The cell in my pocket goes off, and I swear even louder as Dess disappears between the lines of cars.

I yank my cell free and without glancing at who it could be, speak into it. Only half paying attention as I try to catch sight of him again. "Hello?"

The voice on the other end hits me like a slap.

"Grayer," Sabian says flatly. "What is the status of the last assignment?"

I'm standing on the sidewalk, watching life in the Grid happen—cars, bodies, thin hisses of black factory exhaust billowing into the darkening sky—and seeing none of it.

He's early. And catching me off guard.

"Why are you calling me?" I ask through numb lips.

"After this you will be done. Are you where you need to be." Steel in that last sentence. Not a question.

The stink of soot in the air, the chaos of movement all around, broken brick and cracked pavement. I take in the Grid and answer, "I'm in Leyton, yes."

"Be ready," Sabian says. And the blunt command in his voice, the satisfaction at being so close to getting all that he wants—idles of the Level 1 Operators made complete and Auden dead, all by my hand—takes me by the throat. It leaves me both cold and hot with fury. Fair or not, whether I came to be here willingly or not, I see all too clearly the gun that's still in my bag. Feel all too easily that small yet heavy weight in my hand. If I were to waver even once from the absoluteness of knowing I never want to strike again it would be now.

The stark need to be finished with Sabian engulfs, overwhelms. It drives away all else.

Including reason.

"It's already done," I say into my cell. My lie, out before I can spin it perfectly. "He's dead."

A pause. "It's not quite time. He's not supposed to be there yet."

"Good thing I got here early and waited, then." Auden said he would be leaving from school at this time, usually with no contact with any of the Operators on the way out. Please let him not be wrong, or exaggerating. It should work. It should make perfect sense.

More silence coming through my cell, each second stretched out.

"I believe there was a . . . glitch while sending out this particular spec sheet to your cell, West," Sabian says, sounding friendly now. "Please confirm the Alt's physical appearance so we can be sure there's no mistake."

Of course. He needs to confirm Auden's death since he doesn't have the benefit of an active assignment number to pop up on their Alt log. My answer, and how I answer, is the very last thing to stand between my escape or running forever.

No point in trying to pull up a spec sheet that was automatically erased after my first download. I shut my eyes, picture Luc in my head as I remember him. My description is of both him and Auden.

"He was tall, nearly six feet," I say evenly. "On the thin side with broad shoulders, probably from training or playing sports in school. Between a hundred and seventy to a hundred and eighty pounds. Dark brown eyes, and dark brown hair that was nearly black."

"Anything else?"

I open my eyes. See Auden now. "He wore his hair smooth on the top so it hung a bit over his forehead. Shorter in the back and along the sides."

A briefer pause this time.

"Completion confirmed, Grayer," Sabian says.

Relief is a visceral thing. It makes my eyes sting, my guts unclench, my marks burn. They are the last link in what chains me to the Board; the faster they are gone, the faster I will be home.

I wonder if he's forgotten our deal, even as I wish *I* could forget. But forgetting would be suspicious, and giving Sabian even the smallest reason to be suspicious is too much.

"My marks," I say to him. "When can I come in and get them erased? And I want a written guarantee about my children with the signatures of each of the Level One Operators and a stamp bearing the official symbol of the Board." I'm pushing it with these demands. But it's what I need to do to make him believe—that I'm a striker done with her contracts who is now collecting payment. Normal.

"Yes, there is the matter of payment, isn't there," Sabian says. I imagine him sitting at that table, drumming his fingers in thought, working out how best to fit me in, exact my silence, and then get me out. "How soon can you come back to headquarters?"

Never is too soon. "Give me an hour to clean up." It'll take almost as long to get to Leyton from here, but any longer would be strange. Better to just arrive late if I have to. "It got messy."

"Fine. I'll be in touch." He disconnects and I'm left with dead air pressed to my ear.

Tucking my cell back into my pocket, I step off the sidewalk and cross the street to the outer ward train station. I hope hard that the next one is going to be here soon, to take me from wild safety and back into the cage.

Standing in the middle of the waiting crowd, my cell buzzes again. A low, almost soothing purr passing through my jeans so I can feel the rumble of it against my leg.

It's a sound that can only mean one thing. Not a normal text or call. But the Board, sending out a Kersh-wide news file.

My mind whirls. I'm back standing in my kitchen, watching the television with Chord and listening to the Board talk about the Alt who got caught.

A black contract for someone who has overstepped.

Rebels.

Strikers.

Like me.

A splinter of ice threads itself through my veins, leaving me frozen to the spot.

My hand clumsily pulls out my cell, taps the screen awake, and opens the file. I read it, and I almost don't believe it. Except that I can feel dozens of eyes—watching me, boring into me, matching my face to the one that's on the screens of their cells.

The picture is clear; there is no mistake. It's me. The camera in that meeting room at Board headquarters was a good one.

Who: West Grayer
Why: Confirmed Assassinations of
    (1) Level 2 Board Operator, Meyer Parrish and
    (2) Level 2 Board Operator, Trainee, Auden
    Parrish

Meyer, dead? I don't—

Can barely grasp that, what it means, when I realize there's more at the bottom of the news file. This is wrong. Every black contract I've ever heard about, it was already over. Level 2 Operators already took care of it, and whatever we learn of the results is up to the Board.

But not for me. For me the black contract continues.

Offering: One (1) Unlimited Pass to all offered
Alternate Training Sessions, Elite Level, held at
select facilities throughout Leyton Ward. Valid until
Assignment of Pass-holder is rendered Complete (or
Incomplete).
In Exchange For: Confirmed Death of West Grayer

It's all I can do to simply start walking. I'm careful to look at nothing, face no one, knowing only that I have to escape.

I turn the corner and run.

I'm an active again, my Alt every single idle in Kersh who could ever want for extra training.

It's fully dark out now and what was once bone-deep fear has morphed back to anger.

Sabian.

I scowl deeply at the thought of him, this person who has already taken so much at the expense of those I know. And now the successful killings of those Alts, the purity of the Board nicely secured for the future, and me—scrubbed away like an ugly, telling stain.

The rolling blare from a clearing truck a few streets down startles me, and I pull my hood down even farther over my head. Keeping my eyes on the ground, I walk down the street. I'm neither in the Grid proper nor in the actual suburbs of Jethro now, but somewhere in between, straddling a blurred middle ground. It's still crowded here, but the stream of people makes it easier to disappear.

Why kill Meyer? *Who* killed him? The questions fill my head.

That Meyer was assassinated makes me believe Sabian is in this alone. No way would the Board turn against one of its own so blatantly. But I can't be sure.

What I *do* know is that I was never meant to get out of this alive. My fault for not listening to the warnings until it was too late.

There's a shout from someone on the sidewalk behind me and I jump. I'm strung too tight. The Roark is still in my bag. But I have nothing else on me, not even a blade.

It takes me a handful of seconds to come back down and realize the shout has nothing to do with me. That not everyone out here is an Alt looking for what most will consider a sure path to completion.

But some are. And I have to get off the street, if only so I can decide where to go from here. Part of me thinks I should head to Leyton Ward; its Alts are already much better off and maybe less tempted by the reward. But Leyton is also where headquarters is.

I find myself veering deeper into the Grid, leaving behind Jethro's suburbs. These parts of the ward are mine—I can move through here in the dark and never get lost, even if it no longer feels quite so safe.

I'm careful to stay clear of my place, Chord's place, and Dire's place, making a point to head in the opposite direction. Chord's likely to still be there. Probably being held back from looking for me. Probably wondering why I haven't answered any of his many, many texts and calls. The ones I'm no longer receiving now that I've turned off my cell.

Not yet ready to talk to someone who can break me in so many ways. Who can make me believe there might be another way out, when there is no such thing—only a way *through*. Chord, who would come with me at one single knowing look, no words needed.

My eyes scan basement suites and low-level condos as I move past. Looking for a flash of that telltale white hanging from a front doorknob or shoved into a door frame. Empties in the Grid aren't common, but my chances are still better here than they are in the rest of Jethro. Lots of shift jobs and cheap work means plenty of piecemeal housing—one-bedroom apartments crammed in here, a makeshift studio sectioned off there. I have to believe I'll come across something soon.

Ten minutes later and there's a peek of white shoved into the worn door frame of a first-floor apartment. I reach the front door and yank the tag free. If clearing hasn't come to sign off on the place by this time of the day, odds are they won't be back until the morning. Which means I should be fine here for the night. For a few hours of sleep, maybe, even if the idea of sleep seems far off now, a mythical thing, a reprieve I don't deserve. But I learned to get over that as an active once before, and as a striker, I can do it again.

My fingers are clumsy with the need to hurry as they unzip my bag and find Chord's key-code disrupter. I press my wrist against it and the lock plate. Listen for the tumbling of gears and then I'm inside.

Strange smells, unfamiliar shapes and shadows in the dark. A bleak hopelessness crawls up my throat. It feels too familiar, walking into an empty again.

I lock the door from inside by flicking the latch over and hang the tag on the back of the doorknob so I don't forget to replace it later when I leave. The action is done before I even know I've decided to do it. Like blinking.

I'm careful to put the key-code disrupter safely back in my bag, knowing I'll have to use it again before long. Just like I know I'll have to get more weapons somehow, and soon.

My hand touches on a light panel near the door, but I don't press it, not even to check for electricity. Better for nothing to be seen from outside, and it won't take long for my eyes to adjust so I can see more clearly. Though I don't really want to. Places left behind by incompletes all have the same sense of grim, flat emptiness. I'm the dazed soldier wandering onto a field to look for survivors, knowing there won't be any.

It's a single room that can't be more than four hundred square feet in size, a studio apartment built for one person. Along the left wall is a narrow glass patio door, its drapes lit just enough from the streetlamps outside that I can see a bit into the room. Directly across from me is the kitchen and eating area, marked by a strip of tiled flooring, a mounted cupboard, and a square table with two chairs. Appliances and dishes and a tablet are positioned neatly on top of a rectangular counter. There's a closet door and a carefully made bed with dark sheets on the right side of the room, and the lump on the floor next to the bed is a pair of guys' work shoes. They're big—he must have been tall, the guy who used to live here.

I move into the kitchen.

The fridge is still running, and inside there's yellow cheese and apples. I slice off some of the cheese and eat it; the soft, salty texture reminds me of childhood. Rinse an apple beneath the tap—the water is ice cold—and eat *that*. Wash it down with a glass of water because who knows when they'll shut off the supply.

In the cupboard I scavenge an unopened sleeve of energy bars and place it inside my bag. But that's about it. Everything else is either too heavy or too messy to eat while on the run. Not that there's much to pick from. The size of the cupboard is in line with the dimensions of the rest of this place.

I walk toward the bed and sling my bag down onto the bed-spread. Let myself collapse next to it. The mattress is firm and the sheets smell clean and I curl up into a ball on top of them, holding my bag against my chest. Wrapped inside its worn cotton canvas is death, a wad of fresh clothing, my wallet—full of useless cards now that the Board will be tracking them—and little else. But it's all I have that's mine, so it has to be enough.

Shutting my eyes, I wish for the sleep I know won't come. The faint sounds of the Grid outside come through the walls, too constant to ever be completely shut out. Signs that life continues to move onward, no matter how much I've messed things up. Is it already over and I just don't know it yet? Against the Board, I'm little more than a brief, ugly disturbance, no matter how much I might have to hold over them. Sabian is no typical Alt to beat, and I'm no longer a striker at her peak. My odds suck.

A soft rasp at the front door and my eyes fly open. Heart in mouth, panic is a huge wave that smothers all thoughts except for one: I've slipped somewhere, somehow.

I was right to think I had no chance.

At the sound of the flimsy secondary lock starting to come undone, I throw myself off the bed. I hit the ground in a roll and the place is so small that I'm already at the wall behind the front door.

Which swings open before I can even get to my feet.

CHAPTER 14

So slow.

Why am I so slow? When it's my life to save now and not some other Alt's that I'm ending—

Someone steps into the room. A guy, with wide shoulders. And he's tall. I picture the large shoes from beside the bed and for a long, crazy second I'm sure it's him. That this was all a trap laid by Sabian, a trick to make me think this was an empty.

"West?"

Chord's voice coming through a dark that's suddenly lifted by moonlight and my mind is absolutely blank.

He walks into the apartment, shutting the door behind him. The room goes dark again but not before I get a glimpse of his face. The hard set of his mouth, his eyes frantic with worry as he looks around. His hair a wavy mess from the wind and the rush to get to me.

I manage to sit up. "Chord." His name is a rough whisper, low and desperate. "Down here."

He's next to me in a second, on his knees. *"West."* His hands run all over me, too much and not enough, checking for whatever damage he thinks he must have done to bring me to the ground.

"I'm okay, I'm fine," I tell him. "You just sur—"

"I'm so sorry." Chord's voice is too quiet, the surest sign of his anger. Slowly his hands on me go still, as if afraid to believe I'm really not hurt. But he keeps them on my arms, holding them tightly, and I know his fear was—and is—as great as mine. "I couldn't warn—" He breaks off, swearing under his breath, then says furiously, "You've got to stop turning off your damn cell, all right?"

I check the sleeping weight of it, still in my jeans pocket, and press my thumbprint against the home switch until it vibrates. "I meant to turn it back on earlier," I tell him.

"Don't lie." His tone scalds me even as his hands are gentle on my arms. "You don't need to lie. I know why you did it. No one in Kersh missed that news file."

A shudder runs through me at the memory of that moment. All those eyes on me, seeing me as a cheater, a murderer. And they would be right. "You're still mad, though."

"You just took off," Chord snaps. "You expect me to be okay with that?"

"I had to. This is—"

"No. Quit it with the excuses. I think I've heard them all by now."

"This is different."

"It's not. It's still about your survival, isn't it?"

I shake my head. "It's not my Alt this time, or Sabian, or even just the Board anymore, Chord. It's *everyone*."

"If it only takes one person to kill you, what does it matter?" The words are torn from him, raw and hollow. His hands tighten on my arms again, just for a second, before they let me go.

"What about Baer and Dire?" I ask him. The room is colder now without his touch, and I shudder again. Pull my knees to my chest, wrap my arms around myself.

"What about them? Do you really think they're afraid of Sabian?"

It's so easy for Chord to dismiss Sabian, having never met him. He's never heard that false, friendly voice, seen the void in those hazel eyes.

"West," Chord says, and I can hear the frown in his voice, even if I can't see it on his face, "however much you fear the guy, Baer and Dire can handle—"

"I think they have good reason to be afraid," I blurt out. "They've been watched this whole time, all these years. Who do you think Sabian's going to talk to first, if I stay under long enough that he'll stop waiting for an idle to come along and fix his mess? What Baer and Dire don't know might be enough to keep them safe."

"You know they wouldn't care about that, if they could help you."

"I care, though! Just like I care about the same thing happening to you, all right?"

Even in the half dark I can't miss how his eyes go narrow, hot with a fire of his own. "Then you care too much, West, if it means putting yourself in more danger."

"I'm scared, Chord," I whisper hoarsely.

His fingers against my face, over the raised streak of my scar. "I know," he says simply. And that's all. Not *Don't be* or *Why,* just his acceptance of how and what I am, how I think and feel. It's this that cuts me apart and gives me away to him, pieces of me he'll take better care of than I ever could.

"Then stay," I say against Chord's mouth. "Please." It can't be wrong to want *this*. If it's a weakness to want Chord with me now, to ask him to stay instead of making him leave or having me leave him, then I'll be weak.

He pulls away just enough so he can meet my eyes. Are mine as naked as his, stripped by the darkness of the room even as it conceals? "I didn't find you only to leave, West," he says.

It hits me then. What I missed in the rush of seeing him.

"Chord, how did you find me?" I think of my cell, wonder if he tracked me that way, the way he once did. Though shouldn't the fact that it's sleeping make a difference? If not, then what's stopping anyone from—

He takes my hands, traces the marks around my wrists. "Tracking chips, remember?" he says. "I was at Dire's."

I nod, my relief immense. "For a second I was worried that I missed something, or left something behind."

Chord pulls me to my feet. "No, just me."

I squeeze his hands and then wrap my arms around him. "What about the others? What happened after you guys got the news file?"

"Auden lost it, of course, when he heard about Meyer. The official statement from Sabian is that the Board believes it to be a political thing and that you were hired as an assassin. That ultimately they are dedicated to tracking down who hired you, but in the meantime, their best lead is finding *you*. Baer and Dire had to physically hold Auden back from rushing out to find Sabian. Guess he really does take after his dad with the hotheadedness."

"Luc was a bit like that, too," I say. Maybe not to the same extent as Auden, but still . . .

Chord nodded. "He was."

"What then?"

"Auden wanted to go and let everyone know he was still alive, that you didn't kill him, but Baer and Dire stopped him." His words have an edge, telling me he had no say in this decision.

"Chord, they had to. Auden proving that he's still alive doesn't mean Sabian's not going to try some other way to get to me. And it won't bring back those two Alts I've already hurt. Sabian would still want me dead because I know too much."

"I know that. It doesn't make it any easier."

"Not for Auden, either," I point out. "He also can't prove Sabian killed his dad."

"Or had him killed," Chord says. "Maybe tactical—"

"If Sabian didn't do it himself, he'd get someone from way outside the Board. Not a Level Two Operator. Too dangerous."

"And we still don't know why he did it, when it was Auden we thought he was after."

"Maybe he was really after both the whole time." My hand curls into a loose fist in his hair, holding on. "I think Sabian's planned all of this, and not the Board. He was never going to let me go, whether I killed all of them or not."

Chord sighs. "Maybe. Probably."

"And Dess?" An image of his face as he ran off, wanting nothing more to do with me because of what I was doing, what I wouldn't do. "Did he come back?"

"Dess?" Chord pulls back, surprised. "I didn't even know he was out there. Was he with you when you got the news file?" I wonder if he's thinking about Taje, his little brother who was made an incomplete over a year ago now. And if he pops into his head at times like these, just as Ehm still does for me.

"No, he . . . left right before that," I tell him. "But, Chord, he found out about everything. He heard us talking while we were at Dire's."

"How were you planning to explain your missing marks to him, West? I think lying hurts you just as much as it hurts the person you're lying to." His hand brushes my hair off my face to take the sting from his words, make them not an accusation. "Especially when you're trying to keep them safe."

"I don't know, I wasn't thinking about what to tell him. Only that I would." And that I could only hope he'd be okay with it—because it was never about Dess, or even Chord, really, but me, my own selfishness. "Dess wanted me to finish the job. To kill Auden."

Chord swears under his breath. "He said that?"

"Yes, but only because he was worried about the Board coming after me if I didn't. Also . . ." I'm on the verge of telling him the rest. About Dess's jealousy of Auden—something I don't think even Dess knows exists—and his insecurity over being displaced by someone who's actually related to me by blood, Alt of an incomplete brother or not.

But I don't. It seems like a betrayal of sorts to reveal these parts of Dess to another, though I know he's comfortable with Chord, too. But Chord is not the person Dess met while on the run; he isn't the person who could have walked away without a word of encouragement and didn't; he isn't the person who gave him blades out of nothing more than free will.

So I stay quiet, and I know if Chord knew, he'd more than understand.

"Also?" Chord prods, waiting for me to continue.

"Nothing. It's just . . . I want him to be okay."

"If Dess is smart enough to have figured that out about the Board, then he'll be okay."

"Yes." My one hand is still caught in Chord's hair, and I force myself to let go. I rest my hand against the back of his neck, my marks against the vulnerability of his bare skin there, and tell myself I can't damage him.

"Time," he asks softly.

20:57

"It feels later than that," I say, just as quietly. For whatever reason, it seems right for us to grow hushed now. As though any kind of safety to be found here is the borrowed kind, tenuous and finicky. The sleep that eluded me before is creeping in. I yawn hugely behind one hand.

"Hey, don't fall asleep on me yet," Chord murmurs into my ear. "The bed's right over there."

My pulse kicks up a notch, cutting through the blur of fatigue. "The bed's . . . small."

"I know. Good thing I'm not a bed hog." He brings me over to the bed and sits down on the edge and pulls me down next to him. There's a thump of something falling to the ground.

Chord picks up my bag from it where landed at his feet. He passes it to me. "Did you have to use it on the way here?"

It. The Roark, of course.

I shake my head as I move the bag onto the foot of the bed—on the other side of me, away from Chord. The weight of the gun no longer seems so noticeable now, as though its time had come and passed, no longer of use. But I still don't want it anywhere near him. "No, but I might have, if I had no other choice. I didn't have anything else."

His hand rests on my face, on my scar. "I'm not judging you, West. Even if you did use it. How can I judge you, when you've managed to keep yourself alive for this long? Doing whatever you need to do, or felt you had to do?"

I lean against him. He's solid, and unbearably close, and more than anything I wish we weren't here. I should have known the past isn't changeable, or fixable, especially for a future built on even more death. Like building something on an already cracked and toppling foundation. Fighting fate.

Even though I don't see him doing it, I can feel Chord reaching into his jacket pocket. "I had to go out to your place first," he says. "Otherwise I would have been here sooner." He finds my hand, places something in my palm. "For this."

My gun. The feel of it is instantly familiar, like a piece of jewelry that's been worn close to the skin for so long that it's no longer felt. Simply there—silver bone, steel tissue.

"And these." My blades. Chord gently folds my fingers over everything. "To do what you need to do. I don't care who you have to kill. As long as you're the one left standing."

A fistful of weapons on my lap, what I'll need again to help save myself. Chord can only be my shield in so many ways.

I put the gun in my jacket pocket. One blade goes in the other pocket, the other in that of my jeans. "Thank you," I say to Chord.

He kisses me slowly. "You're welcome." Then he takes off his jacket and tosses it on the floor next to the bed. Reaches over, unzips the front of my jacket, and works it off my shoulders.

"What are you doing?" I ask him, doing my best to keep my voice level.

Knowing what my jacket holds, he's more careful with it than he was with his own, and drops it down slowly onto the floor next to his. "You're tired, aren't you? I thought you wanted to sleep."

Sleep. Squished next to him on a bed that feels smaller than ever, so not touching is impossible. Not wanting him impossible.

A curl of heat in my stomach even as cold logic has me shaking my head, trying to clear it. "I can't sleep. I have to decide what to—"

"You're dead on your feet, West." Chord shifts me over so we're both lying down on the bed. "A few hours, that's all."

I turn onto my side, fit my body against his. He pulls at the covers and flips them over so they lie over me. And he's right. I can't deny that my eyes are heavy, my words slower in coming. Even my thoughts seem less than clear, too raw. Being so close to him leaves me vulnerable, but also safe. "I need my gun," I say against his neck. "I've never slept in an empty without it close by."

"It's okay. I'm not going anywhere. And I'm not tired." His mouth on my temple. "So good night."

"Hmm." I move my hand up to touch his hair, then down along the back of his neck, before I wrap my arm around his chest. Like marking what's mine. "I'm glad you're here, Chord."

"Me too."

Sleep. There is no worry about the nightmare coming back tonight, of seeing my Alt—my mind is too full of other unpleasant things. The sound of distant sirens, tripped alarms, and the occasional gunshot. At some point, I must say something in my sleep, because through the haze of dreams Chord's telling me not to worry, it's not for us, they're not coming for us.

They are, even if we're completes. It doesn't matter—

Skin against skin, soothing me. *I love you, and we are fine.*

When I wake up, it's still dark in the room, and I can tell I'm alone in the bed.

I sit up and the covers and Chord's jacket slide off me. It'd been spread out on top of me as another blanket.

Chord.

Where is he? My eyes are still fuzzy and it's hard to see and his name is on my lips—

His hand clamps over my mouth. I can just make out his face. He's crouched over the side of the bed closest to me and he's holding a finger to his lips. *Don't make a sound.*

Someone's outside. At the patio door. There's a slight shifting of moonlight from behind a shadow.

Fear works its way up my throat and shakes me fully awake. Chord's low, soft whisper in my ear as he leans closer to me. "Take this and get out of sight. Wait for me."

He presses my gun into my hand, the grip warm enough to tell me that he's been holding it for a while now, letting me sleep under his guard. He gets up and slips out the front door, around the corner from the patio. A flash of something in his hand as he leaves, and both relief and dread fill me.

Chord's good with a knife. But he's never used them for me, or over me. What if his emotions get in the way?

I scramble off the bed and stay low to the ground as I shuffle over the few feet to the wall along the patio door. Flatten myself against it as much as possible as I straighten up again. I clench the grip of my gun.

Now that I'm closer to the patio door, I hear it: from behind the cheap drape pulled across the door there's the thin, high-pitched buzz of a glass cutter at work. Then the nearly silent snick of the small panel of scored glass being lifted away.

I watch—admiration and frozen panic fighting a battle of their own in my head—as a hand reaches in through the new hole in the glass, pushes aside thin cloth drape, and feels for the locking mechanism.

Flips it open and begins to slide the door over.

I lift my gun, and it trembles in the dark. It wavers, unsure.

Shoulder or knee? Shin or elbow? What's the best way to slow down without killing?

I don't know. *I don't know.*

My lungs are straining from not daring to breathe and my mind is frantic with thoughts of Chord and where he could be and what he could possibly be doing. The barrel of my gun is still undecided when the Alt steps in, perfectly silent, perfectly smooth—exactly as I would have done it.

Without warning, he's flying into the room with a broken shout and landing on the floor in a clumsy heap. Caught off guard and pushed from behind.

Something I would *not* have done.

Chord steps into the room from the patio. His knife is still in his hand, ready to be put to work, as he readies himself for the Alt who's already on his feet, gun beginning to aim. Not at Chord but at me.

Fast recovery at least. In that, I can still be an equal.

My flying leap takes him down at the knees, his gun flying across the room, and only for the most fleeting of seconds does it cross my mind how slight he feels, how his weight can't be much more than mine—

And then I'm pointing my gun at his face. His face, twisted and harsh.

And see that he's a *her*.

A girl not much older than I am, with vivid copper eyes and long brown hair in a sleek ponytail. But in my mind I'm back in that alley in Gaslight and the eyes I see are bleached of their copper color, the ponytail messy and dyed violet and tangled up with a yellow scarf that has a floral pattern.

This Alt. This is the Alt of that idle I hurt. This is the Alt who I saved . . . who now wants to kill me.

Confusion turns to cold fury and that dark part of me hisses sharply in my head. *Just finish it.*

I push the voice away and ever so slowly lower my arm, let my hand go slack. My gun drops to the ground next to me, next to her. This Alt who owes me her life.

"Why are you here?" I ask her. I hate the sound of my voice, full of doubt and hurt, sounding younger than I am—and much too innocent to last much longer in this match. "How did you find me?"

A long beat of silence. "The Roark," she finally says. "Prototypes are built with a shadow system so they can be recalled for testing. You forced my father to withdraw one for you to use. But it's not hard for a Level One Operator trainee to access tracking and restart a shadow if they know there's a missing one to look for."

My father.

This is Sabian's daughter.

"I don't understand." I'm confused, reeling, thinking about that black contract and Sabian knowing exactly where I was this whole time. "Why did Sabian send you here to kill me if he could just track me down himself? And you're a complete. You don't need any more training. You don't need the reward."

"This isn't about that stupid reward." Her words don't hide her anger, or disgust, and beneath it all I hear her Alt, speaking on her cell to her mom, that she was going to be home soon. "This is about what my father hired you to do."

"He hired me to save you."

"You had no right to save me."

"West, who is she?" Chord asks as he helps me up, his other hand grabbing my gun. Even in the flickering, uneven light, the confusion on his face is obvious.

I hold on to his arm and pretend to be steady. "A complete. Sabian's daughter."

A single indrawn breath. "You mean one of the ones Sabian hired you for?"

"Yes."

"But you got rid of her Alt for her. Why would she want—"

The girl gets to her feet, careful to move slowly. Two against one, and neither Chord nor I are easy targets to overcome. "A complete at the hands of a striker means nothing," she says fiercely. Fire in her voice, laced with hate. If words could kill, I would already be dead. "You took away our only real chance to prove ourselves worthy! Everything we've trained for and worked for since birth! *You had no right.*"

Only Chord's hand on the small of my back keeps me from physically backing away from her rage. I'm struck dumb at her venom, and it's he who speaks next.

"Watch it," Chord says to her. His voice is deceptively quiet, pushed nearly too far. *"She saved your life."*

She ignores him, glaring at me. "You and our father took away what should have been ours."

"You say 'ours.' You and your brother's?" I need to be careful. I can't mention Auden yet, not until I know why he's been set up to be killed. Not until I know he's not going to be in danger by her finding out, this daughter of Sabian's.

"Mine and my brother's," she confirms. "The two contracts."

So she doesn't know how far Sabian's plans really go. But what *does* she know, then? What to say without saying too much? Because there's more than guns and blades involved in this game.

"You don't have an answer, do you?" she goes on. "What made you think it was okay to decide who was worthy and who wasn't?"

"What difference does it make?" I say. "You're a complete, what every Alt fights for. And not only a Leyton one, but also a Board one. Exactly what Kersh needs to stay strong."

"I still need to prove that! I don't know how strong I really am or that I'm what Kersh needs. All you've done is put everything in doubt."

I wrap my arms around myself, wholly chilled, not only from the cool night wind blowing in through the open door, but also from the depth of what she believes. *I* don't even know what to believe anymore. Didn't I make everything stronger? How could I prove it? What could make this girl believe it?

I look at her. Feel the wind find its way into my guts and deep into my bones. "Why are you here?" An echo of the very first question I asked her. I'm not going to let it go unanswered again.

"You killed our Alts." The glint of faint moonlight off her

eyes, which are all too sane and full of determination. The same kind that I've tasted myself, lived off of, made me keep going. "So *you're* going to be those Alts now."

"What are you talking about?" I ask her.

"There's only room for the best. If we can beat you—the striker who killed our Alts—then we'll know we'll have killed them for sure, if we had the chance. And I need to know we would have won, if not for you." Full-blown pain reaches her eyes, obliterating the logic and the will that was there. "Besides, if not for you, *Auden would still be alive.*"

Beside me, I can feel Chord's entire body go tense.

"Who was Auden to you?" I ask her.

"I loved him, *and you killed him.*"

She sounds broken, hollow, and for a second I think of my Alt. She must have felt like this, holding Glade's necklace in her hand and knowing it meant I'd killed him, the boy she loved.

"Auden is—" Chord begins.

I squeeze his arm, hard, to make him stop talking. As much as I want to tell her Auden's still alive, I can't. She's Sabian's daughter—no way I can trust her to keep such a secret. It's still possible to save Auden. His being alive is the one card I have left to play in making sure he stays that way.

But now I can also add revenge for Auden's death to her list of reasons of why she needs to fight me.

"Why would I ever agree to your challenge?" I ask her.

"Because we're not giving you any other choice. With this black contract out on you, you're dead either way, whether it's going to be some idle or our father."

"Unskilled idles don't scare me, and neither does Sabian." A lie, if only so I can make myself believe it.

"What about *him*?" she asks, her voice rough and savaged as she looks at Chord pointedly. I know she's thinking about Auden, wondering why he's gone and Chord's not. "He might be an accidental PK. It could be tomorrow, or years from now."

My hands are fists at my side. The only thing keeping me from attacking is knowing that I would do the same if I were her; I would say the same, think the same, if not worse. The idea of Sabian going after Chord makes me raw, furious. "If you win?" I ask her.

"You can die knowing that Kersh is in good hands after all," she finishes. Not even a trace of arrogance there, just the simple fact of truth. She's an idle of the Board, born and raised to be the best. You'd expect being complete to be enough for any Alt; that it's not for her, this future Board member and Level 1 Operator, speaks well of her eventual intentions for Kersh. I also acted for the city's sake, but it'd be wrong to say my reasons were entirely selfless.

"And if West wins?" Chord asks.

"My father lifts the contract. No more being hunted."

"You can't force Sabian to do it afterward. You'd be dead, remember?"

She turns to him. Her look is withering. "It's not hard to set up a news file. And tapping into our broadcast system as future Level One Operators isn't that hard, either. A news file about our father hiring her in the first place is already triggered to go public if he doesn't call the contract off. And if she dies, I'll delete the news file myself. I'd have no reason to shame the dead."

Such a threat can only mean one thing.

"Sabian doesn't know you're doing this, does he?" I say to her, another piece slowly falling into place.

"Even if he did find out, he couldn't stop us. Not with what we know now."

"West." My name on Chord's lips, full of warning. "Don't listen. You don't need to do this."

I shake my head. "Chord—"

"She does need to," the girl says to him. "She owes us."

Chord swears at her. "What if she told you your Alts are still—"

"They're dead, Chord," I blurt out, cutting him off. I know he wants to save me, but not by setting the Board after the non-Alts instead. I've already taken away too much from them. "They're gone."

The girl shakes her head. "Nothing you say will—"

"What if she wasn't the one who killed Auden? Or Meyer?" Chord snaps at her. "What reasons would she have to want them dead?"

She looks over at me. Her eyes are very hard. "So then who hired you?"

I can't tell her, as much as I'm tempted to scream her father's name in her face. I remember Sabian's warning about what would happen if details of the contracts ever leaked—how he would hurt those important to me.

I look down and say nothing.

"And if I killed you first?" Chord says to her. The coldest and calmest I've ever heard him—he's furious at my silence. He's pointing my gun toward the girl. "West doesn't have to do it. No one would know the difference, if you're going to die anyway. No one could stop me."

"*She* would stop you," the girl says, her gaze moving from Chord back to me, as though already sure he's no real danger. "A part of her knows she shouldn't have done it. That it's absolutely gutless to kill an idle without any warning. She's already wondering how she's going to live with it."

Chord's shaking his head. The flickering of filtered light is to his back, leaving his face in the dark, but I don't need to see it to know his look of defeat. In this, he can't help me. "West, just say the word, and I'll do it," he says.

But of course I can't, because she's right.

Chord stares at me, my silence my answer. "*West—*"

"No, Chord. I have to do it." My words are impossible to take back. Not that I would, because Chord's safety is not something I'm willing to play around with. Revealing Auden wouldn't save him for long, and claiming innocence over Meyer's assassination means nothing without proof.

"I win, you get rid of Sabian's contract on me and no one touches Chord," I tell her. "You win . . . well, I guess it means I'll finally have paid for what I've taken."

She nods, cool in her success, more Level 1 Board Operator than sixteen-year-old complete now, and the movement is almost regal, reminding me of Auden. Both of them born and bred to be the best, and what she says next, succinctly and matter-of-factly, puts ice in my gut: "But you won't win."

I probably won't. No spec sheets to work from means going in cold. No memory of fighting their Alts to draw from, and all I can remember of what Sabian told me back in that diner, lifetimes ago, is the fact that they are the ones; they are worthy.

"What are the rest of the terms?" I ask her, sounding much calmer than I feel.

"We have a twenty-four-hour window when we're expected to be away from headquarters for off-site training." She says nothing else, and I don't miss what it means.

Twice as many Alts, in half the time.

Two chances of dying, with twice the danger.

"I choose Point of Origin," I say quietly. "If you're looking to get as close to a natural completion as possible, then you know odds need to be more level than what you're giving me."

She takes a minute to consider, then gives another elegant nod.

"Keep your cell turned on. It won't be long before we contact you," she says, and it's Sabian I hear again. She bends down, looking for her gun on the floor, but Chord steps in her way.

"Go," he says to her, his voice low and hot and about to break from wanting to tear something apart and not being able to. "Tactical will have replacement guns for you."

Without another word, she walks away, steps through the open patio door, and is gone.

Chord drops my gun and the blade he was holding onto the bed and takes the single step that separates us. He stops just short of touching me. Like he's almost afraid to—as though I'm going to fight him, hate him, leave . . . or worst of all, stay and love him and still go through with it.

"I love you, West," he says, each word hollow, raw with feeling. "But right now I almost hate you, too."

"I'm sorry." Again and again. It might never be enough.

"You don't have to do this." His dark hair is tumbled and chaotic, his eyes bright with insistence.

"I do. Too many people involved—"

"The only one—"

"—you, Baer, Dire, Auden—"

"—who matters to me—" Here he comes even closer.

"—even Dess, who I know might hate me now, but he can't hate me forever."

"—is you, West Grayer." And now Chord does touch me. Slowly he wraps his arms around me so I don't break apart. He takes my mouth with his and doesn't let go. He makes us fit together and breathe together until it seems even our heart-beats run together.

"We could," he says against my lips. "We *should,* damn it."

The traitorous salt of my tears tinges my tongue. "We should what?"

"Run together." Chord brushes my face with his fingers. "We could just take off and not come back."

I lean back and look at his face. *The Surround.* "No, that's not—"

"West, I can put that key-code disrupter back together. And then once we get through, we'll destroy it so no one over there would ever know about it. And everyone here would still be perfectly safe."

"Don't do this, Chord."

"It'd be a way out."

"Chord . . ." The hope in his voice is hard to listen to. It tells me of his desperation, that he's willing to give up safety for me. "You heard Dire and Baer. It'd be like being active again, except it wouldn't stop."

"But we have a better chance if we just wait them out, don't you think? If we stay here . . . walking into a cage match against two Board Alts . . ." One more kiss. "West, you might be a striker, but you're also human."

I press my face into his neck. The scent of him makes me hurt. "I know, but that doesn't change anything. I have to fix this."

He tilts my chin up so I can't refuse to listen to the brutal truth that will not be left unheard. "*You* of all people know what it's like to be driven by the need to survive. How it takes over, makes you think of nothing else. These guys, they'll have revenge on their minds, too—not only for killing Auden and Meyer, but also for what they think you took away from them. Now they think this is their right—that they deserve this fight. People can be made to do almost anything if they tell themselves they're doing it for all the right reasons."

His words, intentional or not, are sharp as barbs. "But that's what I did, Chord. That's what I was thinking when I changed those idles. I thought making their Alts completes would be enough. How is that any better than what those Alts want to do to me now?"

The buzz of my cell in my pocket and both of us freeze.

Chord pulls back so he can see me. Shakes his head, silent and already looking haunted. *No. It's too soon.*

I lift my cell to my mouth and speak, trying not to think too much.

When I hear Sabian's voice and not his daughter's, shock is like a single, well-aimed jab.

"Grayer." Suppressed rage makes my name sound like a curse. "Did you really think you could get away with it?"

My hand goes to my throat; it's so hard to breathe all of a sudden. "What are you talking about?" The most distant sensation of Chord leaning close, knowing something's deeply wrong.

"You lied about your last contract. That last idle is still out there, weak and unworthy and of no help to this city. You will finish that completion, Grayer." Not a request. Just fact.

"I don't want any of it anymore," I say to him. "None of it." For a brief second I clench my eyes tight, making a child's foolish wish, willing it to work, for him to say I've done enough, that I'm free to go.

"What you want and what you agreed to are very different things."

"Tell me why you wanted me to believe Auden was an idle and not a complete. Then maybe we'll talk. Because right now I've got just as much on you as you have on me."

"Ask yourself this," he says. "How did I find out Auden is still alive?"

"I don't know. Someone saw him and told you." A wild guess, but other than Auden giving himself up in some way, intentional or not, what else can it be?

"And if that person happens to be someone you know very well?"

Someone I— And when I know the answer, I must make some kind of sound because Chord's arm is around me, keeping me from falling.

Dess.

"I don't believe you," I say to Sabian. "He wouldn't do that."

"He would, and did. Though to be truthful, Dess did not come simply to tell us where Auden was. He came to offer to finish the job of killing him. Without further consequence to you."

No, Dess. You are no striker. You are no killer. And in my mind, I see two of him. The boy with hurt shock in his eyes at finding out what I once was and then started to be again and the boy who could barely control his fury at what I could no longer do, for his sake as well as mine.

"But even though he's a complete, he's no match for Auden," Sabian says. "He might . . . get hurt."

"Don't let him do it, Sabian." I'm begging and hating myself for it—my doing. My fault that Dess would even think about killing any Alt other than his own. "Because if you do, you're not safe. For that, I'd easily kill again." And I would, no matter what that meant for me.

"I'm assuming that I have an answer, then."

"The whole city is going to be looking for me!" Desperation— I'm scrambling. "I don't know if I can get to Auden."

"Already admitting defeat? What a shame—especially when Dess seems like a very nice boy. Very loyal."

"You were the first to lie! And then you set me up for Auden and Meyer."

"I admit to being deceptive, but I had no real choice. Would an insincere apology make it better?"

I feel sick.

"I'm still waiting for your answer, Grayer."

The one you knew I'd give you. "I'll complete the last contract and then you'll let him go."

"Three dead Alts and then I will let him go."

Three dead Alts.

The phrase echoes in my head, each word vivid and sharp, and suddenly I know what I have to do. The only thing that can be done.

I need to move. Fast.

"As with any striker contract, you have twenty-four hours."
With that Sabian disconnects, leaving me listening to nothing
but the details of a plan being laid out in my head.

I shove my cell into my pocket. Grab my gun and blade and
bag from the bed, my jacket from the ground. I toss Chord his
from where I dropped it after getting up. The urge to hurry
leaves me winded, as though I'm already trying to catch up.

"Tell me what's going on," he says as he pulls his jacket on.

"We've got to go, Chord. Can you text Dire, tell him we're
on the way?" I zip up my jacket, make sure my gun and blade
are still in their pockets. Where I need them to be again. And
without a doubt they will be shields this time, and not weapons. Can I walk that fine line between killing and saving, know
which way to lean when the time comes?

I'll have to. Standing on the edge of that precipice again, I
can't fall. Not if Dess is to be saved.

"West, you've got to talk to me."

I touch the side of Chord's face, an apology for moving too
fast again. My marks against his skin are simply there. Bearable. "Sabian's got Dess."

Chord's expression, full of shock. "What? How did he— Is
he okay?"

"He is, for now." I grab his hand and pull him toward the
open patio door. The thin drapes catch on us as we wind our
way through them and out of the apartment.

Chord holds me back as we come to a stop right before we
step onto the open sidewalk. People are walking by even this
late, and I'm reminded that I'll be an open target again out
there as we make our way through the Grid and out to Leyton
and headquarters.

It's hard to keep myself from simply racing out there and do what needs to be done. But I have to talk to Auden first. It's too risky having him leave Dire's. Dess's life is at stake just as much as Auden's is, and asking Auden for tips on how to take down the best should be done in person.

"Sabian wants Auden for Dess, doesn't he?" Chord asks. The cool evening wind tosses my hair. He traps it down into the neck of my jacket, pulls the hood over my head. So he's remembered I'm still a target, too.

I nod. "And not alive, either."

"So what are we going to do?" His hair is wild in the wind, matching the rising panic I can see on his face. *Who are we giving up? Because you're not in this alone, West. We'll be horrible together.*

I didn't miss his use of that word: *we.* But nor can I use it, no matter how much I want to. The issue of whether I do this alone might not be up to either of us anymore.

"Sabian's not getting either one," I say. "And I still need to find out why he wants Auden dead."

"Will fighting Sabian's kids give us an answer?"

"I don't know—I hope so. By the end of it, I'll have to make Sabian think he has no choice but to tell me."

Chord's eyes narrow just the slightest. "Tell me how and we'll make it happen."

"I'm going to give him something more important than three dead Alts or Auden dead. More important than the integrity of the Board." I press a kiss on his lips, fast and light. "I'm going to give him back his kids—alive."

CHAPTER 15

Dire locks the front door behind us as we walk in.

Strange to see the place actually empty. Like a lot of the businesses in the Grid, Dire Nation keeps long hours. It can't afford to rest in a place where sleep doesn't come easy or stay for long. That the store is closed means we're right in the middle of the short lull that separates one day from the next.

With a bleary glare he motions us downstairs. "Figures Sabian would make this as difficult as he can. Auden's downstairs, sleeping."

I think of Dire's basement. The concrete floor, metal table, hard chairs. "I know a motel wasn't a good idea, but I hope you gave him a pillow or something, at least."

Dire slides behind the front counter. Pulls out a tablet and yawns. "Hey, I've been sitting here all night, waiting for news. Can't even go home without worrying about him busting out to get to headquarters."

"How's Innes doing with Freya's notes?"

"Made her shut down her workstations and leave to get some sleep. You don't want to see her when she's running on nothing but fumes, trust me."

Downstairs, Auden's not sleeping. He's at one of Dire's computers, staring at the screen.

Sitting there like that, with the shimmery light of the screen turning him ghostly, he looks so very much like Luc that beside me, I feel Chord tense up. Between the two of us it's hard to keep Luc at rest—so many years and memories.

Auden turns around as we come in. His eyes are red beneath the flimsy bulbs strung across the ceiling. Not only from fatigue but because Meyer was killed just hours ago. I recognize all too well the signs of guilt over a death you couldn't prevent but still feel responsible for. It lingers, bites, haunts. Sympathy gnaws at me, but I set it aside. No time for that.

"You guys here to break me out of this place?" he asks, his voice a croak from lack of sleep, and from crying, most likely. "Between Baer and Dire, I'm wondering if I'm ever going to see daylight again."

Chord pulls out a chair, but I stay standing. Too wired. "Tell me about Sabian's two kids," I say to Auden.

He blinks at me. "Bryn and Hollis? What about them?"

Bryn and Hollis. I roll their names through my mind, the names of those I already saved once and am forced to save again. For a second I think of Bryn's reaction to Auden's death, and wonder if he's even aware of how she feels. "If you were their Alts, how would you kill them?"

His exhausted glance turns into a glare of suspicion. "What kind of question is that?"

"The only one that matters, if you want to get out of this alive."

"You fighting Sabian's kids is going to save me?"

"Yes." My impatience is a living thing, steamrolling his

confusion, but I can't help it. "So tell me. I don't have their spec—"

"How does that even make sense?"

"It just does!"

"No, it—"

"Hey," Chord says mildly. His voice cuts right through Auden's and mine, and my chest goes all hot inside. Because for a second I *believed*. I believed wholly and thoroughly that Luc was here again, and we were arguing like we always used to, and Chord was having to break us up like he always used to as well.

Auden looks stunned as he takes in my face. I blink fast and look away. Not so much wishing he was Luc, but that he was some other Alt altogether, so none of this was happening.

"Auden, listen." Chord saying what I can't say, again. "You don't know him, but there's a kid out there named Dess. He's kind of like family for us now, especially to West. He was here yesterday and he overheard us talking about what was going on. He caught up with West when she went to meet Sabian and didn't understand why she wouldn't finish the job."

"You mean kill me."

"Dess doesn't know you. You're just the Alt of West's brother who he never even met. He also knew it meant she'd be giving up whatever Sabian was offering her."

Auden gives me a look, knowing if he were anyone but Luc's Alt, he wouldn't be here right now, but he says nothing.

Chord goes on. "And he knew the Board wasn't going to let her go, you know? He just . . . lost it. So he went to headquarters to talk to Sabian."

"To give me up."

"No—to offer to kill you himself."

"A lot of people wouldn't mind seeing me dead, it seems," Auden says quietly.

Chord shakes his head. "Do you honestly think Sabian would trust an eleven-year-old to assassinate a Board-level Alt? Think, man. If he can't use Dess—this kid who Sabian knows means something to West—as a striker, how else would he be useful?"

Auden swears under his breath, his face going grim. "So Sabian's got him and won't let him go until West kills me."

"Exactly," Chord says, and the harsh edge to his voice gives away just how much this is tearing him up.

"I guess the fact that you haven't done it yet means you're not going to," Auden says to me, his words careful and measured, as though one slip could set me off. He looks vaguely sick, and for one shameful moment, I'm glad to see it. Why does he have to be who he is? Why should I even care about him living?

"I'm not going to kill you, all right?" I mutter. "But I do need your help." Where Auden's words were careful, mine are stilted and awkward. Still hard to admit out loud that I can't do it alone. I doubt I've ever said those particular words before: *I do need your help.*

Auden nods. "Go."

"Your friends Bryn and Hollis are pissed off at me for completing their assignments for them," I begin. No point in stringing things out. "So in exchange for getting Sabian to lift the contract he has out on me, and to avoid having Chord somehow end up a PK, I have to fight them. So they can prove their worthiness. Just like a real assignment."

"You can't, West," Auden says, pale and stricken beneath his tan. "You can't just kill them. Bryn . . ." Her name on his lips and I wonder again whether he feels the same for her as she does for him; it's clear he feels *something*. "She and Hollis wouldn't—"

"I'm not going to kill them, Auden—though they can't know that until it's over. I just have to hurt them enough—"

"Hurt them?"

"—to make them shut up and listen to me. Because they're going to be my way out. The way to get you out. And the way to get Dess back."

"You're going to use Sabian's own kids against him?" His eyes go wide with astonishment, then flat with defeat. "It's not going to work."

I glare at him despite the twinges of doubt that are starting to flex in my gut. "Unless you can tell us why he wants you dead in the first place, then there is no other way. If I die and he gets away with all of this, you know he's not going to stop. He'll find someone else to come after you. So tell me what I need to know to do everything *but* kill Bryn and Hollis."

He looks at me, his expression hard. "Is that a guarantee?"

"There are no guarantees," I tell him, "but I'm still going to say yes. Because it can't end any other way."

Auden exhales. Looks drained but starts anyway. "They're both trained to the hilt since they're Alts of the Board. *Level* Alts. But they're still human. Bryn's weakest at one-on-one combat and close-range blade handling." Talking about Bryn has Auden's voice going rough, as though the words themselves are betrayals of what they might mean to each other. "She's got an adequate eye with her gun, but it's her throwing arm that's the strongest."

"And her brother?" Chord asks.

"Hollis." The change in Auden's tone has the hair rising on the back of my neck. "He's Sabian's son through and through. There's never really been any doubt, even from the beginning, that he's the stronger half, the worthier Alt. His skills always measure high, clear across the board."

"What's his best technical skill?" Chord asks. "If you had to pick one."

"He's very strong with a gun. Better than a lot of the Level Two tactical Operators already."

"If he's so strong, why didn't Sabian just let him complete on his own? Chances are he would have won."

"Because it's Sabian. He doesn't take chances. Not when he's thinking about the Board and Kersh's future at large."

"And he's not just coming at this as a Level One Operator but as a dad," I say. "Wouldn't any parent with his kind of power do the same?"

Chord's eyes meet mine, and I know he wants to deny it but can't. Because haven't I done the same thing?

I turn to Auden. "Being outnumbered, I get to pick the Point of Origin. You know them—you all went through the same training. Tell me what they're expecting me to pick."

"I think you already know," Auden says slowly. "You're not that different from us, West, Board training or not. You don't know how to try to *not* win."

"I'm nothing like any of you." Yet another lie. I wanted more, just like Bryn and Hollis. It wasn't enough to be complete. And if winning means killing, then he's right about that, too. It's what I know, and who I am.

Because I *do* know what they would pick.

"They expect me to pick a place I'm familiar with, that I think will give me the best chance," I say.

Where else but the one place I still hold a gun or swing a blade on a daily basis? Where I know what's around each corner, what's held within its spaces and walls?

"The school," I say to Auden and Chord. "Torth. Where I teach weaponry."

"Makes sense," Auden says. "Though I also know it's where you *won't* be going."

I look at him. Nod. "If I move fast enough, I can get to the last place they'll be expecting me."

Chord stands up. "Board headquarters?" His face, stricken with denial. "West, you can't. Somewhere in the middle, at least."

"That won't be enough, Chord. You know that." I already have the worst of odds. Not one Alt but two, in half the time, no spec sheets to work from.

"I know there's three of us and two of them," Chord says. "Why does it matter who takes them down, as long as we get them to Sabian for Dess?"

"Chord, didn't you see how she looked at me? *I'm* the one who cheated them. It's not just them beating anyone—it's me they need to fight to prove they're worthy."

"You made them completes. It should be enough!"

"But it's not!"

"Chord, she's right," Auden says. "Bryn, Hollis, me—*how* we become completes is just as important as being one."

"So Sabian is the one who should be dealing with this," Chord says. He gives me a look that leaves me hollow inside. "Not us."

Auden nods. "If this works, he'll have the Board to deal with."

And that's it.

I place my bag on the table. I'm done with it; this will end quickly enough. I take out my key-code disrupter and slip it into the back pocket of my jeans. Then I pull out the Roark gun and pass it to Auden. "Bryn's been tracking this, ever since she found out what Sabian planned. It doesn't matter anymore—she might as well think I'm stuck here for the next little while. But I need you to give this back to Dire after I leave. I think if I tried to do it, he'd make me take it. I can't use it now."

He takes it. "Not even for Sabian?" He's not joking. Despite the person Auden knows Sabian to be—a long-serving Level 1 Operator, the father of Bryn—he can't forget he's also the killer of his father.

To use the gun on Sabian . . . I have to believe I can't be pushed that far. Only failing to get Dess would do that. And failure can't be an option.

"Not today," I say to Auden, putting my bag back on. Tell myself the odd lightness of it is not why I feel defenseless.

Auden starts to head for the stairs but stops after a step. Turns back. "West, you're sure you'll know when to pull back?" Fresh desperation in his voice, on top of what sounds nearly like anger.

"Yes. I'll have to, won't I?" His anger has me curious, and I look at him carefully so he can't miss my wondering.

"I saw my Alt once, years ago," he says to me. "Your brother."

Luc.

My insides go cold.

"You didn't kill him," I say slowly. Early Kills, the rarest of all unnatural completions. Gated city or not, Kersh is large enough that the chance of running into your Alt before your assignment goes active is slim to none. But a chance is still a chance. Luc had been close to death, and none of us had even known it.

Auden shakes his head. "I was here in Jethro, checking on a training facility for my dad because the regular tactical Operator was . . . I don't know, gone that day. And I was just . . . I looked across the street and there he was. With his friends, walking into a café." His eyes are distant, remembering what it was like to see himself so close, the person he'd either have to kill or be killed by. "I guess I could have tried to complete. I mean, the Board wouldn't have excused me just because of who I was, but maybe a part of me wondered about that. It wouldn't have been too hard to convince myself it was possible."

"So why didn't you?" I ask him. Seeing Auden in a new light now. That he let Luc live.

"Because I didn't want my life to be over, that's why. I know how EKs are punished." Auden's anger flares up again. "And because he wasn't ready, and taking him down then and there wouldn't have been any kind of challenge at all. It would have proved nothing—not to myself, to the Board, or to Kersh."

"Prepared or not," Chord says, "Luc wouldn't have been an easy completion. Far from it."

"The point is, I didn't try to kill him," Auden says. He looks at me, his face drawn with both fear and helplessness for his friends. "I let your brother live when I didn't have to. Keep that in mind when you're looking at Bryn and Hollis through the sight of your gun and instinct is telling you not to hold back."

I look at the reason why Luc lived as long as he did and I can only nod. I would have done my best not to kill Bryn and Hollis anyway. Now there's debt on top of that, and it's harder to breathe through its weight.

Auden nods back at me, shoulders slumped. "Thank you."

"Auden?"

"Yeah?"

"I'm sorry about your dad."

His shoulders slump even more, and he nods again. He turns and disappears up the stairs.

Chord doesn't say anything right away, and I'm not sure what to say, either. Finally I manage, "You know it has to be me in the end, don't you?"

Chord's eyes are darker than normal, braced for what he knows must come next, what can't be changed. "Yeah, I got that."

"You know I can do it." This is what he needs to hear.

"I have no doubt you can do it, West," he says. "But you're asking me to do something I don't know I can do. To sit and wait and *do absolutely nothing.*"

"You just said I'll be okay."

"And if you're not, then I might not be."

I grab his hand. " 'How can I have so much faith in you, when you have so little?' Do you remember saying those exact words to me once?" The night before I killed my Alt. When Chord and I hung in the balance, too.

Chord leans his forehead down on mine. "That's not something I could ever forget."

"Then don't." I kiss him, and it's supposed to be good-bye.

Because it's here and now when I would do what I normally do. Break off and run. Not just for his sake, the way I would tell myself, but also for mine.

I need your help. Saying those words to Auden earlier, the shape and feel of them seemed foreign to me, another language altogether. And it's true that I can't remember the last time I said them out loud, if I ever did. But now I realize I have said them before—to Chord, in other ways, not lesser, just different.

I pull back just enough so he can see my face. And the words definitely come easier this time. "Please don't go yet. Not when I need your help. Not when I need you."

Chord's hands in my hair, pulling me even closer. He kisses me, so slowly and thoroughly that it makes me cry, and I know he understands. And when he finally releases me, it doesn't hurt quite so much because I know it's not for good. "Yeah?" he asks.

"Yes."

"Then we better hurry. We don't want to keep them waiting."

Chapter 16

By the time we climbed out of Dire's car in Leyton, a light rain had started.

And it's still raining now, minutes later, with no sign of Baer. He's supposed to meet us here, and he's barely even late, but my nerves are shot.

I shiver inside my damp jacket, and beside me I can feel Chord doing the same. Here in the alley between two clean, sheer walls of two nameless, glossy office buildings deep in Leyton Ward, there is no overhang or awning to hide under. Just the dark of night as it slowly draws closer toward dawn.

Across the street is Board headquarters, and while the city sleeps, there's only the regular grind of wheels against the track as trains move in and out, the smooth whir of cars driving down roads, the occasional siren of a clearing truck.

"Time," Chord mutters into the night air, his eyes busy watching both the main entrance and the street for Baer.

04:13

He shakes his head. "Baer should be— Wait, here he comes."

The sound of footsteps on pavement and Baer ducks into the alleyway next to us. He slicks rain off his near-shaven head and gives us a baleful look in greeting. He is not amused at the time. "Auden's back at the Grid, I hope."

"Still at Dire's," Chord says.

"Good. He's probably going insane having to share close quarters with Dire for so long, but we're almost done here." Baer turns to me. "You ready, Grayer?" he asks, gruff as always, though I don't miss the underlying tension in his words.

"Yes." Too hard to say any more when terror is brimming in my blood, a stampede of nerves and dread.

"Remember this: they might be Alts of the Board, but you're a weaponry instructor, and a striker." Now Baer's voice softens a bit, a rarity in itself and yet another reminder of just how bleak the situation is. "Go in there knowing you're their equal."

"But I won't be their equal," I say to him. "I *can't* be. You know killing them means losing Dess, too. And backing off when they're going to be doing the oppo—"

"All these months of being a complete and working for me and you still question?" He frowns, and the hint of disappointment there is worse than any frustration. "That part of you— whether it's technical skill or instinct—that lets you kill is the same that knows when to show mercy. How you decide to use it is up to you."

All of this a feverish drone in my head, so I can only nod. *Yes.*

"Auden gave you the key code for the back entrance?" Baer asks Chord.

"It's on my cell. We have his number, too, in case something goes wrong. You sure you remember the layout of the place?"

Baer peers over, takes in the sight of headquarters. I know he spent years of his life there, would be there still if he hadn't felt his passion for the Board slip away. "It's been a long time since I wanted to think of that building, let alone retrace the paths inside. But unless they tore the interior walls down and rebuilt them again, it won't take that long for the place to come back to me. Everything's centered around that damned elevator."

"Okay. Remember we have to find Sabian in there and make sure he stays put. We can't have him suspect something's going on." Chord's jaw goes tight. "It has to play out, all the way. Or it's not going to end for West."

Baer pulls out a gun from his jacket pocket. I recognize it from weaponry class, and I wonder if that's what took Baer the few extra minutes to get here. He hands it to Chord. "While we're making our way through."

As Chord pockets it, Baer turns to me again, and when he speaks, that softness is gone from his voice. As though he knows it's not what I need to hear from him right now. "You're a complete, Grayer—don't waste that. And those Alts in there are only completes by your hand. That stands for something."

"Their Alts were nothing like them. It doesn't even compare."

"Don't be so quick to decide that. How do you think it feels to be them? Knowing they have to defeat someone who's already defeated parts of themselves? This isn't just a battle of muscles and reflexes, but a game of the minds as well. Can you remember that?"

His words hit close to home. "Yes."

"I'll be waiting over there for Chord. Don't take too long, Grayer—either out here or in there." With that he crosses the street and veers off toward the back of the main building where he and Chord are going to get inside and find their way to Sabian. Where Sabian is, Dess will be, too.

The rain's getting harder, and it sprinkles my lashes as I look up at Chord, doubling him. I blink the image away. Already enough memories of Alts to deal with. And if this is the last time I see Chord, he's the only one I want to see.

"So this is it," he says softly. "Are you ready?"

Instinct kicks in and I start to shake my head, but I make myself stop. "I have to be."

"That's not exactly the right answer."

I push my hood off so I can see him better. I don't even care if I'm spotted now; an idle out here is less danger than the Alts in there. For this good-bye, we're as alone as we're ever going to be. "I will be ready, then."

"Not just for Dess or me. But for *you*, right?"

Rain running through my hair now, streaming down my face and trickling into my mouth. Only the fact that it's salty tells me I'm crying.

"I'm so scared of screwing up, Chord." And of dying. Or not dying and coming back more striker than anything else.

"I think it's better than not being scared at all. Because it means you know the stakes and it'll just make you think twice before doing something stupid." He takes my hands, touches my marks with his fingers. "These are you, but it's not all you are. You know that. It's that simple."

I lean into him, and we're touching, and the sudden want and need for things to be right again is overwhelming and ferocious. Like a cleansing fire, or a giant breath being released, it calms and steadies me.

"You and Baer keep Dess safe, all right?" I say to Chord against his neck. "Just keep him away until I'm done."

"Dess will be fine." His words are rough. Too full, about to break.

"And you, too. Don't . . . save me."

A ragged sigh before he nods. Understanding does not make it any easier. "West, be careful. Please."

My hand on the back of his neck brings his mouth to mine, and our kiss is both too much and not enough. How else to describe something that hurts even as it loves?

I make myself let go. I push his hair, soaked from the rain, off his face and do my best to not see the grief there. "You go first. Baer's waiting at the back entrance for the key code."

One final heated glance and he turns away. I watch him slowly disappear into a dark that's close to lifting. And though I can't see him anymore, I know he won't be far. Chord, Baer, and Dire back at the Grid are like a safety net laid all around me, and I'm still learning that it's okay to fall.

I run across the street and head off in the direction of the northeast wing—the training wing. If it's logic that tells me Bryn and Hollis won't be sleeping while getting ready for a completion, then it's gut instinct leading me to where they *would* go. They have the advantage of numbers and space, while I only have surprise. It can't be wasted.

I have to enter through the end of the wing, as far away as possible from the main structure and the residences, for two reasons. First, Sabian's too smart to break routine, and if he's even remotely human, he'll be asleep at this time of night. Except he'll only be pretending to sleep, being forced to keep an eye on Dess, and at the same time making sure the rest of the Board stays unaware. While this is good because it means

Chord and Baer won't have to deal with other Operators, it's bad because if Sabian is outnumbered, he might feel cornered. And cornered animals never back down.

Second, if *I'm* cornered, I have no choice *but* to back down. Going from lobby to wing leaves me wide open to be tracked from the rest of the building; coming in from the opposite direction means only having to worry about each room as I cross.

If my gut instinct is right about them being in this training wing at all. Otherwise they could be anywhere and I will truly be in enemy territory. Just as much chance of them stumbling upon me as I would them. Advantage lost.

I reach the door at the end of the wing. From memory, I tap the key code Auden gave me into the lock plate above the doorknob. The lock clicks free.

Inside. The filtered air is cool and scentless in my nose. The hallway is empty.

But not fully dark. Light is hard to contain. It's like air, or dust, and right now there's a sliver of light along the bottom of one of the steel panel doors down the hall. Bryn, Hollis, or both must be here.

When I get to the light, I immediately know what room is behind the door. It hasn't been that long since I was last in there, after all. The only place where my Alt could ever come back to life.

All those mirrors inside.

I put my hand on the door. The cool steel against the heat of my marks anchors me to this place, this moment. In my other hand is my gun. I have to remember to aim low and wide—the opposite of everything I've learned. To avoid head and torso and aim for a limb.

The door is open a tiny crack, just a skinny slant of light. As I step in front of it, it cuts across my face, blurring my vision as it splits me in two.

Quickly, I lean against the door, listening. No sound except my own pulse beating in my ears, reverberating against the steel my skull is pressed against.

I do what no complete ever wants to do, should ever have to do: I slide the door open and walk knowingly into danger. My gun held low, cowed and restrained.

But the room is empty.

Except for the maze, of course. The replication system still has to be triggered, but from here the effect of so many mirrors so close together produces a dizzying effect on its own. Ceiling and floor and everything in between doubling, folding in on itself.

Footsteps behind me.

I hit the maze at a run. My breath is tight and hot in my lungs as I yank out my key-code disrupter from my pocket, press it against my striker marks on my wrist, and slam both against the control panel at the maze's entrance.

There's an audible click from the panel, then a series of beeps, and that's all I have time for. I drop my hand, shove the disrupter back into my pocket, and dive between the mirrored panels just inside the entrance. And hide.

My reflections are all around, and already there's too many others of me, Alt upon Alt. I sink into a crouch and wait. Let my breath out in a soundless stream of air that fogs the mirror in front of me. The soft smear of condensation is the only thing that separates my reflection from the others, and I shiver.

Because I also did not miss the soft whir in my ears as I dove past the entrance, or the bright flash of light across my eyes. And behind the now fading spot of moisture on the mirror, I can see her—my newly replicated Alt.

I turn around. Her coiled eyes are nothing like mine, but the rest of the face is an exact match, and it makes my skin ripple with goose bumps. She's crouched over as well, waiting for me to act so she can start the chase.

If I'd managed to reset the program.

The soft footsteps I heard in the hall now stop in the doorway to the room, and I know it's Bryn. When she speaks, her voice is more controlled than it was back in the empty. More like her father's. "I know you're here. There are wet footprints on the ground."

I swear silently to myself and at Bryn for pointing out how I've already made a mistake. My eyes half on my still-dormant Alt, I slip off my shoes and socks and kick them to the side. Bare feet have more traction than slippery cotton. The ground is cool, but not cold. My Alt stands up in reaction to my movements, and her reflections ripple in the mirrors surrounding her. It's almost difficult to see where mine end and hers begin and I suppose that is meant to be a good thing, considering the purpose of this place.

Even as I hear Bryn move closer toward the maze's entrance, I'm already turning and beginning to run toward the far end.

Nearly two thousand square feet in size, Sabian had said when he first showed me this place. It's all the space I have in which to show my Alt what to do, what needs to be done.

The more engaged you are in the training session, the faster she learns. And so I let my fear break loose, no use hiding it—my heartbeat is a drum, my pulse wild in my veins, each step of mine spurring on one of hers.

I need my Alt to learn how to chase.

The maze's paths aren't the least bit straight—mirrored panels turn and twist, making me think of how a snake moves along the ground. I weave among my reflections, our long dark hair streaming everywhere, our faces winking in and out of sight . . . and the whole while, my Alt keeps pace behind me. Not quite fast enough, though . . . still learning.

"Grayer?" I hear Bryn yell from the mouth of the maze that falls farther and farther away as I keep running. She is indignant, angry. "I'm not stupid—I'm not going to be distracted by a program!"

I stop to test my Alt and when she slows to a near stop and gives no sign of trying to make contact with me to put an end to the chase, I know she's not ready yet. From somewhere behind me there's the sound of Bryn's footsteps. She's moving through the maze now, given away by the light brush of leather soles against concrete, matching the ins and outs of my own uneven breathing.

With panic wanting to dig its way through me, I yank my cell from my pocket with a hand that's surprisingly steady. I tap the cell awake and hurriedly type in three short words. But I don't hit SEND—not yet.

Cell in hand, I keep going, turning right and then left and then right again, telling myself I know exactly where I am in the maze even as I will my Alt to absorb the jagged emotion of my wild, unchecked steps. Our reflections fly by in blurs, patches of wavy color that chase us along the mirrors. My gun is in my other hand, drawn but deliberately pointed straight down at the ground, my finger just outside the finger guard. The worst possible thing would be getting caught by surprise and shooting Bryn out of reflex. Reflex for me is aiming to kill.

I pause again and watch my reflections swivel with me as I turn to peek over my shoulder. This time my Alt doesn't slow, and that's how I know it has to happen now.

With my thumb I hit SEND on my phone. A single text to Auden with a simple demand: *Call Bryn now.*

Seconds later, I hear the soft buzz of a ring—not from my cell but hers, a long *trill,* and then a "Damn it!" that is full of rage—and I spin on my feet and start running again so fast my head swims. For a second I wonder if I'm going to do something stupid like pass out from fear, but my ears never lose the sound of that ring from her cell, homing in on it like the drowning to a light on the shore.

She's on my left, behind the mirrored panels that make up the maze's paths, and only feet ahead of me now that I've changed direction. Maybe thirty at the most, and headed my way. We are separated by space that could be measured by hand spans, by material measuring a fraction of that, and she is only here for one thing.

I keep going, the slap of my bare feet on concrete nearly as loud as the ring of Bryn's cell had been. Both of them are only handfuls of decibels, I know that, but I also know they are somehow as loud as thunder.

My Alt chases. She is no more than twenty feet behind me.

In less than fifteen seconds the three of us will pass each other.

Still running, suddenly feeling as though my hand is moving through quicksand and that time no longer has rules, I lift my gun and shoot out the bottoms of the glass panels just ahead of me. The ones on my left—the ones that no longer keep me safe from Bryn or her safe from me as they shatter into thousands of tiny little shards and the path breaks open.

I dive to the ground, sliding along, and I shut my eyes tight as glass bits rain down on me. They land in my hair and on my clothes, silver and sparkling.

When I open my eyes again, Bryn is just up ahead, her run finally coming to a shaky stop. Her eyes are wide and startled. Her face is pale and her gun is drawn.

But not on me.

My Alt rushing from behind doesn't stir the air at all as she blows past me—every strand of my hair remains unmoving, undisturbed, like she wasn't even there. But I see hers move as though it *were* real, her eyes and feet still keeping hard to the same path as before I'd dropped from view, and all of that is just as real to Bryn who in this split second sees my Alt as me.

Bryn shoots at my Alt. The bullet whistles through her chest and lodges itself somewhere in a mirror behind me, shattering more glass.

And then I'm struggling to my feet and running, tiny bits of the broken mirror digging into the soles of my feet and setting them on fire. I jump through my Alt as she dissolves into nothingness and when I fall on top of Bryn, my desperation and her shock are enough to topple her over.

She's taller than me, and bigger—in sheer muscle, she has the advantage. Her clothes against my skin have an odd feel, and I know she's wearing protective clothing to help withstand the slash of a blade, the stab of a knife.

The impact of my falling on her smashes her wrist into the concrete floor, loosening both our grips. Her gun—a Ronin, the kind Level 2 Alts and Operators use—goes spinning; my cell skids along the ground alongside it. My gun is still in my other hand and I swing it over now to point it at her face. I can't shoot, but she doesn't know that. Doesn't know that she still has the advantage here. My finger catches clumsily against the finger guard as it feels for the trigger.

Bryn's left arm slices through the air. So fast. The glint of silver in her hand is thin and sharp.

I lift my empty hand to deflect the blade. Too late.

Her blade cuts through my left palm.

Another slash, catching dangerously close to my wrist this time, and pain on top of pain. *She's cut my marks.*

My finger finally finds the trigger and I pretend to still be able to kill.

"Drop the knife." My words come between pants.

Bryn's eyes go narrow as she glares at me, her expression a battle of emotions. I see hate for me, disbelief at her situation . . . and deep shock and confusion that speaks of something else.

"My cell," she says dazedly. "That call . . ."

Auden's name would have showed on her screen.

"What about it?" I say to her, still out of breath. I need to hear her say it first. I need to be sure that none of this comes from me.

"Auden . . . it was him," Bryn says. "He's alive?"

I say nothing, then finally, "Yes. He is. Now drop the knife."

Her eyes flash fire at me, new suspicions there. "Where is he? Are you holding him somewhere? *I will kill you!*"

"Drop the knife!"

She lets the knife drop to the ground. Too close to her, still—Bryn is no typical Alt, and Auden being alive but not here means I'm still a threat. I lean forward and send the knife scattering with my wrist, because my hand is strangely limp. Useless. Even if I could chance a look at anywhere but Bryn, I wouldn't look at my hand. I don't need to look to know the damage is very, very bad.

The knife spins hard down the open path in front of us and stops.

Abruptly.

It's the space of a heartbeat, or a breath, but the air in the room grows heavy with another presence, and I think even Bryn knows as I tilt my head up to see. I'm hollow with dread, slow with terror.

Like Bryn, Hollis is also wearing combat gear. His gun is in his left hand—left-handed just like his Alt. I stare into the black eye of its muzzle.

He bends to pick up the blade that hit his shoe. The motion is relaxed, and I can almost believe he's simply picking up something he's dropped onto the ground. But it's his sister's blade, stained with my blood.

With his gun still aimed at me, he snaps the knife shut with his other hand and stuffs it into his pocket. Whatever time I might have bought with his surprise—at finding me here, at seeing his sister defeated—is gone.

"Hello, Grayer," Hollis says, dead calm. "You didn't have to rush. We would have come to you."

Shoot! I clench my hand tighter around my gun and am still swinging it from Bryn's face to Hollis's when there's the sound of feet out in the hall, moving fast and growing louder as they head for us. A flicker of alarmed surprise crosses Hollis's face, his mouth going hard at how things are not going the way they're supposed to, though his gun barely wavers.

Mine manages to hold still. Deliberately, I shoot him in the hand.

Hollis drops his gun with a clatter and a muffled yell, and the Ronin bounces and skates to a stop against a mirrored panel. He staggers over, picks up the gun with his good hand, and takes off.

When Auden bursts into sight seconds later, I don't even feel surprised. As he looks at Bryn, emotions flood his face— hope, worry, pain. Too much to not give away what he feels for the Alt who would have killed me if given the chance.

Auden starts to help me up, but I wave him away.

Rolling off Bryn, I'm careful to cradle my bad hand. Doesn't matter—each jostle feels like a punch. Not my dominant hand. There's that, at least. And I'm sweating by the time I get to my feet, which stings with what must be dozens of little cuts on their soles.

"Auden." Bryn's staring at him, stunned. Her voice is a whisper and so choked with feeling that I have no doubts now. She was doing this just as much to avenge Auden's death as to prove her worth. She shakes her head, unable to look away from him. "I don't understand."

"Are you okay, Bryn?" Auden pulls her to her feet, and I

don't miss how his hands linger on hers. "West wasn't going to hurt you."

Her tears come fast, making her eyes go bright, and I understand when her fury breaks through the shock. At him now, not me. "They told us you were—"

He brushes her tears away, murmuring, and I glance away as I tuck my gun under my arm so I can pick up my cell and shove it in my pocket.

I inspect my hand and grimace at the gaping mouth that's open wide across my palm. A shorter, shallower line cuts across my wrist's marks before falling away. The blood seeping from the wound looks . . . metallic. I rub a finger across it. There's a hint of graininess there, like sand.

My tracking chips.

I wipe my finger on my leg, thinking fast.

CHAPTER 17

Such a waste of valuable time, but I need my shoes. I don't know what's next, and I can't risk letting my feet getting even more hurt. And if tracking wet footprints can give me away, then tracking blood must be much worse.

"My shoes," I call out to Auden as I move away, already trying to locate them, peering down one mirrored aisle after the other. "Help me find them, please! This damn maze!"

It's probably less than a minute later that he's pushing them into my hands, but it feels like much longer than that. Hurriedly, I wipe off the bottoms with my socks, and then I'm cramming the shoes onto my feet. I leave the socks. No time.

I shove my gun back underneath my arm so I can use my good hand to dig my cell free. My left hand can't do much for me anymore. Not right now, at least. The pain has ebbed into a slow, low throb—a sign of shock. I tap my cell awake as I start walking, following the same path Hollis took toward the training room. His trail of blood has already petered out, which means he's lucid enough to think of wrapping it up. Not good.

Dire, I need you to track my chips now. I send the text with a fast flurry of fingers. Turn off the buzzer.

"West," Auden calls out to me, trying to stop me from leaving. "Wait, what are you—"

"You know what I have to do." My voice is grim. But not cold, or shaky, just hard. Settling in for this last completion that I have to make sure falls short. "Did Dire let you just walk out?"

"I came here with Innes. She wanted access to the lab."

Freya's notes. "She's in there right now? Auden, are you crazy? They'll—"

"Innes knows how to protect herself, West. Now let me talk to Hollis."

"You can't, Auden," Bryn says, her words fading as I move farther away. "Who do you think came up with this idea? Let this finish here."

Their voices fade; I'm no longer listening. Auden and Bryn don't matter now. Only Hollis matters. The very last.

The door to the training room is already half open, but I slide it over the rest of the way, staying well off to the side until I'm as sure as I can be that Hollis isn't waiting on the other side for me. I make myself count slowly to twenty, listening for breathing not my own, the scent of blood not my own. Finally I step inside.

It's the same room Sabian showed me just days ago, and even though the stations are cloaked in half dark, the only light coming in from the maze room and the open door to the outer hall on the other side, I recognize everything. Slowly, I make my way through the shadows, the wall against my back cold through my clothes as I slide along. My gun is in my hand, held out and ready to fire, but I dread using it. Hard enough to aim for vitals in this dim light.

The door to the hall is open. No way to tell if Hollis simply left it open on his way out—or if he's still waiting somewhere in here. A trap.

The vibration of an incoming text. I can hear Dire's brusque voice in my head as I read his words. *Getting two signals, both in the building. One's weak. Which one?*

Weak, I send back.

Unease uncoils inside my gut, spreading out as I keep moving along. I walk past the oxygen pods, the shooting targets ready to be destroyed, a stand of swords that's been knocked askew.

Buzz. *Less than a hundred feet away from you, toward your right.*

The lobby.

My first thought is *Why?* It's such an open space; there's nowhere he can hide. So why go there? I remember how exposed I felt, walking in there, already at a disadvantage . . . and then I realize he knows it has that effect, too. And wants me to feel it now.

I turn my cell off all the way and shove it back into my pocket. I can't risk another text coming through and distracting me at the worst possible moment. I shift my gun back into my good hand, but as careful as I am, I still jostle my bad hand. The injury burns, is furious again.

Out in the hall, I turn right. The lobby is up ahead, and its windowed walls lift the darkness. It's going to be clear today, cloudless and sunny.

The fresh sweat on my brow drips down my neck. Even to

me it smells of fear. At least I've taken away his shooting hand. Hollis at top strength is terrifying, and I cling to that single weakness now.

I keep making my way down the hall toward the lobby, staying as close to the wall as I can. It's stupid, really, this pitiful countermeasure. He's already expecting me to show. One way or another, I have to face him. It's an ugly and undeniable fact that for this last contract, one in which more than my own life is at stake, I have absolutely no strategy.

When I finally reach the edge of the lobby, I peer into its vast space.

A sniper's field.

The room is bathed by a cool flat gray that's taken on just the slightest tinge of plum. Dawn is less than an hour away. I can see the shapes of the buildings across the street through the windows, windows that are uncovered and already ushering in the day. I think of that first meeting with Sabian, of that bug lying dead on the windowsill, trapped.

I can't remember the last time I wished for more shadow, less light. Because there's no place to hide out there. With my back still against the wall and gun in hand, I slowly round the corner and take my first step out of the hallway and into the lobby.

My pulse races, a crazy staccato beat. I feel a sharp flare of surprise when nothing happens.

There is still no sign of him.

Where are you? I know you're waiting for me!

I take another step to the side and my foot touches something on the ground.

One look down and I see it's Bryn's knife, the one with my

blood and tracking chips on it. Whether Hollis dropped it by mistake, I can't tell. Though one thing is for sure: he is no longer trackable. He could be anywhere. I could be wrong about him leading me out here intentionally.

Except I don't think so. He needs this challenge just as much as I do.

My eyes dart up to the stairways, the ones that cross the lobby overhead, connecting wing to wing. It's darker up there, much easier to hide.

That's where I would go and wait, if I were aiming to kill someone down here. But the elevator didn't sound; I would have heard it. And the knife is *here*—it's not possible that Hollis turned and headed the other way, toward the fire stairs at the end of the wing, the only other way to go up from this position in the building.

Which leaves the ground floor.

He *must* be here.

I look across the floor of the lobby. It opens up to the other wings of the building, dark gaps between teeth. Five of them, not including the one from which I just stepped. Each entryway is shadowed, not yet lit from the thin light starting to stream into the lobby.

He can probably see me right this very second, from whichever one he's waiting in. Maybe he's already aiming his gun at me while I stand here, still and unsure—

Frantic and panicked now, I sweep the whole place again with my eyes. He needs me to cross the lobby—and if I go back the way I came, the only other way out of here, then where would that leave Dess?

Again! Look again! Floor to ceiling, elevator to entrance—

The light on the lock plate of the main door is green, not red. My heart pounds.

It should be red. At this time of day, the door should be locked.

And how silent it was, revolving on its well-greased axle as I walked through the entrance two days ago. No sound to give it away at all.

Hollis's injury. Was it too much pain, even for a Board Alt? *Especially* for a Board Alt, someone who isn't used to having a weakness?

But if he runs—

Then Dess—

I lurch from the wall, flung into action with fear in my mouth, sharp and tinny. My shoes hit the ceramic with a vicious smack and I'm sprinting hard across the lobby.

The impact of my left shoulder as it hits the glass door, getting ready to push it open, should hurt. It should ring along the bones of my arm and make my hand scream, and it probably does, even. But I feel nothing. Only the need to hurry and catch him before he's—

Wait.

A trap. Hollis must be just outside the doors, and whatever weapon he'll be using, injury or not, he won't miss as soon as I'm through.

But it's too late to slow down. My momentum is already starting to push the door open, my gun only starting to lift up from my side even as my eyes are looking for him, squinting against the sudden brightness that hints of morning.

"Stop."

His voice comes from behind me. I wilt against the door.

One low sob breaks from my throat. A lone puff of condensation blooms against the glass.

Trapped.

"Now it's your turn to drop the gun," Hollis says. "Then turn around."

I lower my gun slowly, but I don't drop it. To have only a blade left on me . . .

Footsteps come closer, and a sharp point presses against the back of my neck. *"Now."* Hollis's voice, right in my ear, and it's harder not to cringe from his tone than from the blade that's digging into my skin.

I drop the gun. It falls to the ground with a sad clatter. He kicks it and it spins away, coming to rest close to the elevator, far from my reach. When I feel the knife ease away from my neck, I turn around and face him.

Five inches from my face is the point of a steel sword. I stare down its long silver span. It must be one of the ones from the training room. When I lift my eyes to meet Hollis's, they are narrowed as he watches me. There's no sign of pain in his eyes from having just been shot in the hand. A half-formed thought that I should have remembered to ask Auden about pain-management training for Board Alts.

"I can kill you right now, but I won't," he says. "I want to give you a fighting chance."

I don't drop my gaze. "I made you a complete."

"You had no right to do that."

"So talk to your father."

The tip of the sword drops to the side of my neck and digs in just the slightest. My skin stings with blood and sweat as dawn glints off the blade, winks off the sharp edge.

He gestures with his head toward the entryway of the wing off to the side, the one just behind him. Less than thirty feet away. It's an awkward movement, and then I see how his damaged hand is cradled against his side. It's starting to bleed again now that he's no longer staunching it tightly against himself.

"On the ground over there, just inside the entrance of that wing," he says. "There's another sword."

I hear it in my head—my own voice judging Baer and the time spent on swordplay in class. It sends fresh dread rolling in my gut. When was the last time a sword was used for a completion? I can't recall.

"I thought you wanted to re-create a natural assignment," I say to him, my voice bland. Careful to hide any sign of my dismay that he has somehow selected the one weapon I wouldn't. "Swords aren't typical."

"I don't care about typical. We're far from typical Alts. And I like swords—I'm good with them."

"You don't have your hand."

"Neither do you."

Weakness for weakness, then. As though we truly are each other's Alts. "Back off so I can get it, then," I finally manage.

He follows me the whole way. I don't have to turn to know that his sword is pointed at my back, only inches away.

As he said, the second sword is lying on the ground just inside the entrance. I pick it up. The hilt is neither a perfect fit nor uncomfortable. At slightly less than three feet long, the sword's blade is brushed silver. The edges are honed to a liquid gleam.

It's heavier than I expected.

"Move back into the lobby," he says, and the prod of steel in my back leaves no room for argument. "The center."

Be the one, be worthy.

The letters engraved into the brass plate at our feet glow dully in the low light. I know that saying so well—everyone in Kersh does, like knowing the alphabet or our own names. But it seems hollow now, knowing what I know about the beginnings of this city and its barrier.

It still means the world to Hollis, though.

I look up and face him.

And barely have time to adjust my grip before he's swinging his sword at me.

My breath leaves me in an audible rush as I rear back. My blade swings out, a hand span away from his stomach in an ungainly arc that's not quite ready. I can't have another one of those. Not if I want to get out of this alive.

Hollis says nothing, his sword carefully held so it spans the bottom of his torso to the top of his head, protecting where he's most vulnerable. Whether he's taken aback by my clumsiness, I can't tell. His dark eyes are measuring me, looking for where I'm most weak.

I hiss in a breath and center myself. Pull up my sword and angle it across my front, my own shield. I'm all too aware of my damaged hand, how it's hanging awkwardly at my side. It's worse than useless, the dead weight throwing me off balance. But at least Hollis is dealing with the same problem.

I swing at him, this time the arc of my sword much more true, coming within an inch of his chest.

Hollis dances back. His recovery time is fast, and as I sidestep his next swing, despair floods through me. To have gotten this far only to meet another Alt who might not only be my match, but also better.

Oh, Chord, I'm sorry.

The clang of steel against steel echoes throughout the lobby. It's high-pitched and sharp, mellowed out by the softer shuffle of our feet along the ceramic tiles, the low, ragged breaths torn from us with each swing of our swords.

I'm getting tired. My muscles are screaming, my arm trembling. My hair is damp with sweat. The soles of my feet hurt.

Sweeping his blade away, I feel it vibrate through my entire arm. No time to counter it with a move of my own before I'm dodging his next swing, coming so close to my shoulder that the wind of it cools my skin.

"You're slowing," Hollis says, his breathing not nearly ragged enough for me. "Can't you tell?"

I shake my head as I push away his blade yet again. I bring mine across as I aim for his arm. Not quite. "No," I gasp. "I can't tell. Because I'm perfectly fine."

Fire sizzles along my arm as Hollis's sword skims across it. I match it with a thrust of my own, and finally the tip of my blade pierces the side of his hip. With another slash along his upper leg, I feel silver kiss and burn my shoulder. The glancing blow of his sword off my elbow, the long draw of mine off his other leg. Blood blooms over us and still we can't stop.

When my next thrust goes wider than it should and Hollis's recovery after a swing takes a second too long, I know—that it's time to end it somehow, someway. Thin daylight all around us, another sign that time is very, very short.

Soon . . . now . . . do it.

The sound of our breathing is louder now, raw and chaotic. The smell of blood is a cloud around us, cloying. I force my sword up, lifting his with the motion and throwing him off balance. He adjusts. Again and again I maneuver him with my swings. They're close to wild now, the muscles of my arm trembling in protest and pain and the heat of adrenaline making them burn from the inside out. He shuffles over, inch by agonizing inch until he's finally standing with his back to the elevator—

And facing the huge windows on the opposite side of the lobby.

The sun pops out over the roofline, sharp and laser bright.

It hits Hollis right in the eyes. He squints, just for a second, but it's enough.

I don't hesitate.

I lift my sword again, and it's so incredibly heavy, like lifting the world. I aim high, and the shadow of my arm makes Hollis—still adjusting, caught off guard—instinctively lift his own sword to protect his head.

But I pull short. Abruptly draw my blade back while he's vulnerable down below. I curl my arm over, let it drop, and slash open the side of his lower leg. Where the damage to the tendons will be enough to cripple and not kill.

Hollis falls to his knees with an agonized yell, his leg splintering beneath his weight. The tip of his sword scrapes across the ceramic. I stand over him, my sword still held out and ready, not quite able to believe it might actually be done. It feels like I've been fighting forever, and it's hard to turn back now. My body hurts all over, from my arm that shakes from exertion to my bad hand that pounds with each rush of my heart. My skin feels raw, torn open in countless places, my price for not dying.

Hollis's eyes are wide and stunned as he looks up at me.

"So is this it, then?" I say to him, my voice a rasp. I let my sword drop to my side. Too heavy to lift again. "Is this good enough for you?"

But defeat does not come easy. It has to work its way through rage and denial, and it's these two that darken his face as he gathers his sword again. Swings. Upward. Toward my neck.

Only the most basic of instincts has me ducking, hitting the cold floor in a tumble as the sword drops from my hand. So fast it's not even a full thought, just a flash of understanding, of self-preservation. What all people of Kersh are taught and never quite forget.

FDFO. Fall Down and Fade Out.

Chord's suddenly in the lobby and next to me. One hand holding me low to the ground while the other is pointing a gun at Hollis. His voice is frightening in its controlled softness as he says to Hollis, *"Put it down."*

The same words, said in that exact same tone, came from his lips when he fought his Alt and Luc died. An ache ripples through my chest at hearing them, and I shudder. Because Chord had gone on to kill his Alt, hadn't he? But Hollis dead will undo everything.

"Chord." My good hand is frantic on his, trying to pull the gun down. "I'm okay. It's fine," I say to him. It's hard to force the words past the lump in my throat. "Don't."

Seconds of distrust and hatred stretch out between Chord and Hollis. Only when Hollis flings the sword far to the side does Chord finally lower the gun—just enough.

He looks down at me. Takes in all the damage and swears loudly. His arm is both gentle and hurried as he pulls me closer to him. "West, where are you hurt? How bad?"

I shake my head, struggling to sit up with his help. "I'm fine. They're just—" I glance down at my bad hand, the one that isn't fine. It's cradled in my lap. I look away. "They're just cuts."

His gaze falls to my hand. "That's not just a cut," he says, his voice hoarse.

I hunch over it, not sure why I'm trying to hide it from him. Maybe because it's a sign of how close it all was, of what I was willing to risk losing. I reach over without thought and pick up my gun from the floor, now within reach again from when Hollis kicked it over. "It's not my right hand," I say dully. "It'll be okay."

"Do you know how hard it was to stay away?" he asks, both a plea and a curse in his voice.

I nod, then shake my head. Unsure of what I mean, only that I'm so happy that he's here. My good hand against his jaw, sliding into his hair so I can bring him even closer. "I'm sorry."

"Good." The word fills my mouth as he kisses me. "You'll be okay."

The whirr of the elevator doors as they open and Baer and Sabian step out. Baer's gun is pointed at Sabian, whose expression is as set as stone. No sign of warmth now. His hazel eyes are careful even as they take in the scene: his son's defeat at the hands of the person who also saved him.

Where is Dess?

Fresh fury has me lifting my gun. I point it straight at Sabian, my muscles made steady and willed on by hate. "Dess. Where is he?"

The briefest flicker of bland disdain and his smile is like ice. "Well, where is Auden?"

I swing my gun until it's pointed at Hollis. Only vaguely

aware of Chord's hand on my back, steadying me. He understands, as always, and his own gun moves toward Sabian. Covering for me.

"It's over," I say to Sabian, my voice choked and thick. "You're not getting Auden. And if you don't want me shooting your son, then I want Dess back."

"Tell her, Sabian," Baer says coldly. "It's not too late to set things right."

A half-truth, we all know. Sabian will have the Board to answer to, but it's Hollis and Bryn who are going to be the hardest to deal with.

"The old conference room," Sabian finally says.

"I'll get him." Baer disappears down one of the wings, his footsteps breaking through my haze of red, and I wonder what he feels being back here. This place where he grew up, thinking it was going to be his future.

Sabian laughs softly, and in the vast space of the lobby, it fills the silence. Worms into my ear and leaves me chilled. "One last Alt, Grayer, and you could have had everything," he says to me.

I keep my gun on Hollis. Neither he nor Sabian need to know I have no intention of shooting. "I know Auden isn't a Level One idle. Why the lie? Why did you want me to kill him?"

"He isn't quite worthy of being a Level Alt. Too soft, just like his father. I should have taken care of Meyer long ago. Auden finding those old notes simply reminded me of that."

Freya's notes. "That's not it, I know it. What else is the Board hiding with those notes? How did you even know Auden found them?"

"From his father. Meyer always did talk too much. And he

never learned that all information has value, no matter how innocent it seems."

"But Auden was already a complete," Hollis says from where he's still lying on the ground, sounding dazed as he looks up at his father. "It shouldn't matter that he didn't care about his position in the Board."

"By a PK." Sabian's words are bullets. "He was a Peripheral Kill, and a complete through unnatural means does not measure up to a complete from skill."

I can feel Chord go still next to me. He's a complete by PK, too, and under the ugliest of circumstances.

"How are your kids any different from Auden now?" I ask Sabian. "By having me assassinate their Alts, you made your kids unnatural completes, too."

Seething resentment at my revealing his weakness—that he hired me as a parent worried about his children—slides across his face. And it's this rage he now turns on me. I'm the source of everything that went wrong for him, after all. The one who screwed it all up.

"It was a simple trade, Grayer, despite all your doubts and your questions," he says. "It should have been enough for you."

"I let your kids live," I say evenly. "Shouldn't getting your son and daughter back alive, and completes, be enough for *you*?"

Sabian's control finally snaps. I see his hazel eyes glisten with tears, his face crumble and go lax. He falls to his knees over Hollis and the sight of such a powerful man broken and defeated leaves me stunned.

"I'm sorry, Hollis," he says quietly. "It's too late to change anything now. But it really is all for the best." And Sabian yanks the Ronin from Hollis's pocket and aims it right at me.

I'm frozen. And only dimly aware of Chord shouting, his hand starting to shove me down low as his body moves to cover mine. But too late, I know. A Ronin in the hand of an Operator does not miss.

A shot rings through the air . . . but it's not from Sabian . . . and it's not for me.

A small puff of black opens up on Sabian's chest. Immediately runs red. And he falls.

I hear Hollis's anguished *"Dad!"* but it sounds like it's coming from somewhere far away. Over Chord's shoulders I see someone stepping into the lobby. I blink away the image of Luc, helping me with my aim and stance when we were kids, to see Auden, Ronin in hand. There is no remorse on his face as he looks over at Sabian on the ground. Only thoughts of his dead father, and maybe that in saving me, he was saving the person who let him live . . . and the sister of a dead Alt who made him a complete.

The low gurgle of a breath from Sabian's form, the frantic flap of one hand trying to go to his wound. He's not dead . . . yet. There's too much blood pooling around him, though; it's just a matter of time. I've seen others die this way before.

Coming from behind Auden, Bryn races over to her father, falling to her knees beside a gray-faced Hollis. Only then does Auden's expression falter, become softer. He moves to her side, and Bryn leans into him. Whether it's her accepting him or him accepting her, I can't say. But they're folded up into each other, and I know they'll have their own hurts to work through.

Chord lifts me from the floor and crushes me against his

chest. Too hard—he's forgotten about my broken hand, my shredded skin—but I hold on to him just as tightly.

"Sabian." Innes's voice cuts through the room as she enters from the training wing. In her hand is a cell—Auden's, with all its access codes to this main building and to the bio lab in one of the satellite buildings outside. She approaches us, and her expression is a curious blend of vague sympathy and stunned disbelief as she peers down at Sabian.

His skin is pale where it's not splattered with blood, and no one misses the shock that crosses his face as Innes stands over him. "You . . . ," he whispers. "What . . ."

"Freya and her notes . . . that miscoded file. It wasn't all miscoded like you said—some of it really *was* a lab project." Innes is pale herself, and a chill rolls through me. I realize now that Sabian never answered my earlier question: *What else is the Board hiding with those notes?*

"No, shut . . . up," Sabian says, and it's not just pain but also sudden panic that's making his eyes flicker bright. Innes has discovered something else about Kersh. Something that goes beyond it once being a prison, what it still is today, in many ways. The room is electric with expectation. *"Don't."*

"The Board making Alts," she continues. "You could have stopped a long time ago."

"For the barrier," he chokes out, and his eyes start to dull. Blood, everywhere. I'm watching Sabian die. "To keep it *safe*."

Innes slowly shakes her head. "That's not what I mean, and you know it. What I mean is that the Board could have stopped making Alts a long time ago. Fifty-five years ago, to be exact. Because that's when the Board discovered the cure for our sterility. And buried it."

CHAPTER 18

It's the same meeting room as before, but I'm not scared this time. Not left alone to wait—and Sabian's gone.

Dire thumps his knuckles against the window. Turns to Baer and me. "This glass—I'd forgotten how much better it is than the kind we get in Jethro. You can see clear across the whole ward out there."

"One of the easier things to forget," Baer says as he continues to look at the view, seeing something that's probably not outside that window. He's sitting in the chair next to me, and the expression on his face says it all. He doesn't want to be here any more than I do. Like waiting to be handed our punishment for misbehaving. Board Operators getting shot by one of their own and left to die in the middle of their grounds means questions will need to be answered.

But Dess didn't need to be any more involved than he already was, and only after I begged him to let Innes take him home did he give in. It was guilt that made him want to stay, I know—for seeing me hurt the way I was, for endangering so many people with one misstep. Dess didn't say, but I think Sabian made no secret of his eventual plans for me, even if I did end up killing Auden for him. I simply knew too much.

"Can you text Dire for me, please?" Baer had asked Innes as she headed for the lobby door.

"And tell him?"

"Just tell him the Board will want to talk with West."

"All right. It shouldn't take him long to get here."

Clearing came quickly for Sabian's body after Auden notified them, as though it were no more than another incomplete. Level 1 Operators arrived just as swiftly, dressed in gray and speaking in low, clipped tones. Auden and Bryn were led to a room for questioning, Baer and Chord to another, and it was the med unit and oxygen pods for Hollis and me.

And the whole time that was happening—while the med techs were busy cleaning and gluing my slashed skin, while they helped me slide into an oxygen pod for a quick hour blast to help everything heal—I couldn't stop thinking about what Innes said.

The Board could have stopped making Alts a long time ago. Fifty-five years ago, to be exact. Because that's when the Board discovered the cure for our sterility. And buried it.

Before calling Clearing, Baer and Dire decided that the safest thing to do was for us to keep quiet about Freya's notes and the file. That included Hollis and Bryn not talking, too. But both of them were still in shock from Sabian's death, and I couldn't be sure they even knew what they were being warned about. The shared look between Baer and Dire and Auden said it all—that Hollis and Bryn might not be any safer than any non-Board Alt would be with such information.

We had to pretend to know nothing . . . for now.

How different things would have been if the Board's most powerful hadn't decided to cover up that lab side project and hide away the cure for sterility that came from it. If they hadn't argued that without Alts to test each other, we'd have to rely on weak and inferior soldiers to protect everyone.

But what if the Surround wasn't as they said it was?

Who would I have been, without an altered gene code, without an Alt? Would my family have been my family, Chord my Chord?

And one more thought, maybe the biggest one of all: No one would have to kill to live.

I fell asleep in my oxygen pod thinking about it all. After everything that had happened, I assumed I would dream like mad. I could almost hear Julis's voice in my head: *Write it down, West, write it down. It'll make more sense.* But my sleep was thick and dreamless. And when the med techs came to get me, my body nearly completely healed—except my hand, which would never be quite the same again—I woke up lost, disoriented, not sure where I was.

Well, things *are* different now, I tell myself as I sit and wait in the meeting room with Baer and Dire. I can never think of Kersh in the same way. Even my body feels different—more vulnerable, softer, even with the fast healing. We're made for more than just war.

And my mind goes to Chord.

He's no longer at headquarters. While I was healing, Dire arrived and told Chord he should go. The Board had no questions for him that couldn't be answered by Dire, Baer, or me.

"I doubt that excuse worked," I mutter to Dire when I find out Chord is gone.

"It didn't. So I told him you'd be too busy worrying about him instead of focusing on the Ops when they talk to us."

I nod. "Thank you. For thinking about him. I know you know what he thinks about strikers."

"Doesn't matter what he thinks of me, West. Seems like a good kid."

I nod again. It's strange talking about Chord with Dire. I'd kept them separate for so long, two different lives.

"Did you really want him here, getting questioned by the bots in gray?" Dire asks, and the frown on his face reveals fresh doubt about his stepping in.

I shake my head. "No, I just . . ." I feel my face flush. "I wanted to make sure he was okay," I finish lamely.

"I told him to go home and wait for you there. Means he's probably just outside the main entrance, nose pressed to the glass."

At this, Baer coughs, the sound suspiciously close to a laugh, before returning to staring out the window.

The door to the meeting room slides open, and a woman steps in, a tablet in her hand. Hair as black as ink, worn iron straight and hanging down to her waist, eyes the same color. She's dressed in a suit the same shade of gray all Board Operators wear, and the cold silver handkerchief in her chest pocket leaves no doubt she's a Level 1. So she worked directly with Sabian. Every day, for however many years. But there are no signs of grief on her face—whether this is because she's been trained to show nothing or because she's not mourning him, I can't tell.

I wonder if she's one of the very few who knows about

Kersh's beginnings. Or if she knows about us being forced to have Alts when we didn't even know it was a choice.

Her eyes fall on each of us in turn—Baer, me, then Dire—before she pulls out a chair on the opposite side of the table. She puts the tablet on the table and sits down, her motions measured and precise.

"This is a meeting with West Grayer," she begins, "and only with West Grayer." She looks at Baer and then at Dire. "You've both made it clear that you intend to stay while we question her, but let me take this opportunity to encourage you to wait in anoth—"

"Do you know who we are?" Baer asks abruptly.

The Operator doesn't flinch, as though she was expecting the interruption. She keeps her eyes on Baer as she speaks. "Baer Tellyson, former Level Three Operator, desertion of post fourteen years ago. Currently a weaponry teacher within the Alt Skills program, Torth High School, Jethro Ward." She turns to Dire. "Dire Latimer, former Level Three Operator, desertion of post fourteen years ago. Currently the recruiter of strikers of active Alternates at your place of business, licensed under the name of Dire Nation, Jethro Ward." Her eyes scan both of them. "Tell me, did I miss anything?"

Dire utters a short laugh. "No. You guys covered all the bases."

"I'm afraid we're going to have to stay," Baer says, his voice just as calm as hers. "Considering what we know about Sabian and other . . . aspects of the Board, I think it's in your best interest to not fight us on this."

"You chose to leave the Board of your own accord. That does not mean you are given the same freedom to return."

"We don't want to come back," Dire says flatly. "As soon as you're done with Grayer, we're gone."

The tiniest flicker of annoyance crosses her features. "Have you ever asked yourself why the Board has tolerated what you do for so long?" she asks him.

"Don't need to. Though I'm sure Innes wouldn't mind coming in to hear you out."

"Our tolerance is not a given."

"I'm not worried." Dire shrugs, but his blue eyes are cold and hard and impossible to read, and for a second I see how he would look if he were an Operator today. "The dirt we have on you guys *is* a given. So say what you need to say to Grayer and then we'll leave. Simple."

The Operator smoothly turns away from Dire and faces me. She taps the tablet awake and slides it over so it's between us on the table. Sets it to record.

"Please start from the beginning," she says.

"I . . . you mean just start talking?" I ask, feeling incredibly self-conscious. To have to say everything out loud . . .

"Yes. Start now."

"Sabian hired me to kill three Alts of three Board kids. In exchange for that, he was going to erase my striker marks." My urge to hide my exposed marks is ridiculous. The med techs already saw them, and this Operator must already know. "He also said that when I . . . have children, he'd guarantee they'd be born without an Alt." The tips of my ears are hot—how awkward to be talking about something so private and have it officially recorded. Talking to Julis is almost fun compared to this.

"Did he say how he planned to do that?" The Board Operator's voice is brisk.

"He said that he was going to sneak into the lab and doctor the gene maps so it would look like an Alt was already made. Later, I would get a notice that that Alt was a PK."

"All right. Continue."

"But the last Alt I was contracted for turned out to be Auden, my brother's Alt, and already a complete. I couldn't kill him—"

"Did you fulfill the two contracts prior to Auden?"

Yes and no. "Sabian's kids are now completes, yes."

"Continue."

How to pick and choose what to say? I can feel the weight of Baer and Dire's caution, and their support helps me slow down, be more careful in speaking.

"I was trying to figure out why Sabian would want a complete dead when he released that news file that I'd assassinated Auden and Meyer. So I had to go into hiding, and that was when Bryn and Hollis challenged me to fight them. They felt cheated that I made them completes. And so I did, and now we're here."

The Operator looks at me. "A Level One Board Operator is now dead."

"Auden shot Sabian to stop him from shooting me."

"And for revenge, since he believed Sabian killed his father? You are still on record for killing Meyer Parrish."

"We all know who really killed Meyer," Dire grunts. "Let's not kid ourselves here."

The Operator flicks her gaze over to Dire. "The info entered into our system—"

"Was done by Sabian. Bet you can't tell me I'm wrong."

She remains silent.

Dire nods, cold. "Which then led to a black contract being issued for Grayer. Not as splashy as setting up a gas leak or anything, but he was probably short on time."

Baer sighs.

"Sabian was angry you didn't finish the final contract?" the Operator asks me.

"Yes."

"Why would he want a Board Alt, one who was already a complete, dead?"

"He told me it was because Auden wasn't worthy and that the Board didn't want to chance him advancing through the Levels." Not the full truth, but I can't risk bringing up Freya's notes. "Same as how he always felt Auden's dad being a Level Operator wasn't right."

"You understand that Sabian was acting on his own?" the Operator asks me. "None of his actions were condoned by the rest of the Board."

Do you know about Kersh once being a prison, though? Or about us being forced to be sterile? "Yes, when I found out Bryn and Hollis were his kids, and no other parents of the Board were involved," I say. "Also, Auden already being a complete kind of made it obvious Sabian had something else going on."

"He made promises to you that the Board cannot keep. The Alt system has never been open—or will ever be open—to exceptions. Each child born in Kersh is born with an Alt, and this will be so as long as the city stands."

Not true. And it's impossible to tell if this Operator simply doesn't know or if she really is that good of a liar. For a second I want to confront her with Innes's discovery, the words forming on my lips against my will—

"West." Baer's low, mild warning makes me look at him. And Dire's more obvious glare from his seat: *Grayer, shut up!*

"I understand," I say to the Operator.

"We have also chosen to not remove your striker marks. The fact that you have voluntarily worked as a striker is a fact that cannot be changed."

I nod. The truth of it is, I think even if the Board was willing to erase my marks, I would have said no. Not being able to see them anymore wouldn't change what I've done.

"However, we will immediately release a news file clearing you of Meyer's and Auden's deaths."

"Make it clear that Grayer's death is no longer worth anything," Dire says. "And admit it was Sabian who killed Meyer."

The Operator's eyes narrow a fraction, but she sounds calm when she says, "Of course." She pulls the tablet on the table toward her, taps something on the screen, and then slides it over to me again. "Please sign off on your report with a fingerprint."

I look at the screen, see how the audio recording of my voice was transcribed into words. I read through the pages once and then press my thumb on the pad.

"We're done here, then?" Dire says as soon as I'm done signing. His eagerness to leave is obvious. Memories are haunting these walls.

"There is one more thing," the Operator says, taking the tablet and sliding it to sleep.

The words are more ominous than they should be. But I'm

here, deep in headquarters, and for a second it's just me and Sabian and an idea about to go wrong.

"And that is?" Baer asks, filling in for the silence of my nonresponse.

"The Board acknowledges the wrongness of Sabian's actions, as well as the magnitude of your skills to have survived them," she says to me. "As we understand it, you became a striker to learn the skills to complete your assignment. Is this true?"

Beside me, both Baer and Dire go very still. All three of us, wondering just how far the Board's reach must go to have picked up on that.

I can only nod. Wait for the rest. Hoping that not all parts of me have been examined, sifted through, judged. No Operator needs to know that my becoming a striker was also a means of escape—that focusing on a kill helped numb the memory of those I had already lost.

"Was this a decision made because you weren't able to afford training outside of the Alt Skills program?"

"Yes."

"What we can offer is this: for any children you choose to have in the future, they will be given elite training here at headquarters until their dates of activation."

That training room with its stacked odds, the maze room that lets Alts meet again and again. It's nothing like the kind of training I knew as a kid, slick and polished rather than desperate and gritty.

But it's the Board. Who knows what other secrets are here? This is an offer that takes as much as it gives.

"Is it an offer, or an order?" I ask her. *You're asking me to tie myself to the Board again.*

"An offer, of course. Though why you would turn this down—"

"I'm not turning it down, but it's not a decision for me to make alone, either."

"Do you mean the potential father of these children?"

"I mean our kids themselves."

She's watching me closely, and there's a hint of curiosity on her face. "Leaving such a decision up to mere idles would be risking their lives, no?"

"I just don't know if there's any one right way anymore," I say slowly.

"The offer will continue to stand, then."

"Thank you."

Everything's changed, knowing that we might not have to be sterile anymore and are capable of more than just killing. It's no longer so crazy, this idea that the world doesn't have to end at the barrier, this idea of sons and daughters who might not die incompletes.

Sitting in Julis's office the next week, it feels weird to be talking about my nightmare again. Like another lifetime, or talking about someone else. In this life, there are much more frightening things to be chased by than the ghost of a dead Alt.

I can't tell Julis anything about what happened. Not about Sabian or Auden or the idles I left alive, mistakenly or not. And especially not about Kersh's origins or the Board keeping everyone sterile. There's that confidentiality clause between us, but I'm assuming it only goes so far—discovering that our whole reason for being is a lie probably isn't covered. And it also feels disloyal, talking about it so quickly afterward to anyone who wasn't there—as though everything Baer and Dire and Innes did to save me was no big deal.

"West?"

I startle in my seat at the sound of my name. The tablet is in my hand, and the screen is still blank.

"The nightmare that bad or that boring?" Julis asks. She has her own tablet on her lap, synced with mine so my words will show up on both. Her light tone doesn't hide the concern I see in her eyes, watchful behind the scrutiny.

"Sorry, it's neither, really," I tell her. "I'm just distracted today."

"*Have* you had the nightmare again since we last talked?"

I shake my head. "No." That's not a lie, at least—bits of bad dreams that first night after talking to Sabian, then a fitful night spent in that motel room in Calden. And for the nights since, I haven't slept alone.

"Julis, I should probably tell you that Chord's staying at my place now." I say the words carefully, enjoying how they sound put together like that. I suppose I should feel bad that we're basically ignoring Julis's advice. But I don't. And I know Chord doesn't, either.

She snaps her gum, lifts an eyebrow. "A new development since our last session, or have you been keeping things quiet just in case I decide to lecture you again?"

"It's new. I . . . well, I guess it just felt right. The timing and everything. We were always over at each other's place, anyway."

"Can I ask if something happened to lead to this decision?"

I became a striker again, for what I thought were the right reasons, but they weren't, not really. I almost lost Chord because of that, and it would have been my fault. I couldn't not be with him anymore.

"I did some pretty stupid things over the last few days" is what I say to Julis. "And Chord didn't leave, even though I wouldn't have blamed him."

"Was he threatening to leave if you *didn't* move in together?" she asks mildly.

"Julis, no. Give us some credit here, will you?"

"Had to be asked. Anyway, go on."

"So you said we should wait because we each needed to establish our own spaces first, right? That a shared space is only as good as the personal spaces it's built on, and because of my nightmares, I still had some stuff to work through."

"Sounds familiar."

I rub at my jeans with my good hand, feeling a bit awkward, but more importantly, secure. "I decided that being with Chord doesn't mean I'm using him to feel strong or that I need him to get better. It just means he's going to be around to know those parts of me that I might not want him to know otherwise."

"Such as?"

"Like with my nightmares. I never wanted him to see me whenever I woke up from them because I felt dumb for being so afraid. So even though I did want us to live together, a part of me was also happy that you said we should wait."

"Hmm. And?"

"I mean, us living together means I'm okay with Chord being around for all the bad times, too. That's a good sign, that I'm not afraid of him seeing me like that." I look at Julis. "Don't you think?"

"I think all of this is a good sign, West," she says, smiling.

"So you're not mad?"

"It was never about me being mad; it was always about what was right for you."

I smile back. "Chord's right for me."

My left hand is the last lingering injury from that terrible night in Leyton. It hasn't healed nearly as well as my other slashes—too deep. Even coming out of the oxygen pod, still half groggy from having fallen sleep, I could feel the stubborn soreness of it, the continuous burn of damaged tissue.

It's this burn that wakes me up the next morning.

I crack my eyes open, and by the way the light falls into my bedroom, I know it's too early to be awake.

But the Board's doctors' parting reminders to change my bandages regularly won't let me fall back to sleep.

I'm sitting up in bed, slowly working off the bandages, when Chord stirs beside me. His eyes are dark as ink in the early light, his wavy hair thick and messy.

Still lying down, he slides his arm around my waist. "West, you okay?" he asks quietly. "A nightmare?"

"No," I say. "My hand is hurting, so I'm just going to fix it up and then go back to sleep. Sorry for waking you."

Chord looks over at my work, the messy roll of bandages pooled in my lap, and sits up all the way. It's warm in the room. His wide shoulders are bare. "Here, let me help. It's hard to do it with just one hand."

He leans his back against the headboard and adjusts me until I'm sitting in front of him, both of us facing the room. With his arms coming from behind to circle me, he unwinds the rest of the bandage from my hand. I watch his fingers move. They are careful and efficient, not clumsy the way mine are with gauze and tape.

"Chord?"

"Yeah?" He's holding out my hand, taking a closer look at the wound. His jaw is tight as he reaches over to my bedside table for the tube of binder agent Innes gave me. It's meant to speed along the healing, but we both know it's unlikely I'll ever make a proper fist again.

"What if I can't do it anymore?" I ask him.

"Do what?"

"Weaponry."

"Why couldn't you?"

My throat is tight. "Only one hand now, right?"

Chord presses his lips to my temple, dissolving my worries with his kiss. "You beat Hollis with one hand, didn't you?"

I lean back against him. His fingers are warm on my skin as he starts to wrap my hand. "How's your place looking, by the way?" I ask, seeing his clothes on my floor now. How the sun peeping in through the blinds touches on our things strewn next to each other on my desk—my art supplies, his half-finished tech projects. "Do you have a lot of stuff left to bring over?"

"My room is pretty much cleared. I just threw things in boxes and carried them over. Don't look in Aave's bedroom."

"Does it look the same way your room used to?"

"Yes. Probably worse."

"Not possible."

"Just remember I warned you." I can feel his smile in my hair.

"Chord?"

"Yeah?"

"The other day, when you told me about what you found during your tour. The key-code disrupter and the temporary break in the barrier . . ."

"What about it?"

I bring my free hand around so it's touching the side of his face. "I was wondering why you decided to tell me what you did, when you never talked about your tour before. Not anything so specific, anyway."

His hands go still on mine for a fraction of a second before slowly continuing to wrap my injury. "You had this look on your face, West," he says quietly. "I've seen you scared before, but something about that fear was different. It caught me off guard."

I *was* scared, I know. The fear I felt at headquarters followed me all the way home, a persistent finger of ice that wouldn't lift from my chest.

"I had just gotten back from talking to Sabian," I tell Chord. "I was thinking about what he said. About how even if I didn't agree to the contracts, if he ever found out that I leaked info about it, he'd find me. I mean, all strikers are terrified when they hear that long buzz for a news file. So when we got that one about the Alt who got caught digging beneath the barrier, I was picturing myself back in that room, listening to Sabian lay out a trap for me and call it an offer."

Chord finishes tying the bandage, but his hands stay on mine, slowly playing with my fingers as he speaks. "To be honest, West, I don't know how much I meant to tell you. I just started talking because it scared *me* to see you so scared. But once I started, it wasn't as hard as I thought it was going to be. It *wasn't* like reliving all those hours spent walking alongside the barrier, constantly waiting for someone to attack and being terrified I'd fail to stop them. Or imagining all the different ways I *would* kill an attacker, if I had to do it."

My hand curls around the back of his neck, into his hair, and I press my face against his skin.

"I was worried I'd feel myself accidentally stumble over the bodies again, the ones I never noticed until it was too late to avoid because it was dark. Clearing's always slowest to get the ones that far out, you know?" Chord clears his throat. "And those times there was movement in the Belt, just outside the barrier . . . I told myself it was simply wild animals. The bot scouts I sent out always came back with negative readings. But I couldn't stop thinking that it was someone from the Surround out on *their* tour, watching *me*."

"But knowing what we know now, about us being here against our will," I say, "maybe that person watching you was actually someone from Kersh."

Chord's arms tighten around my waist. "Sent by the Board to make sure I wouldn't get any ideas about trying to leave?"

"I know Dire said my not killing those idles was worse than just making them incompletes outright, but that was before he found out about the Board forcing us to be Alts. So what he believes the Surround to be like . . . maybe that's not true anymore, either."

"I can't imagine it being *good,* though, West. Otherwise the Board would have to admit that the Alt system simply isn't the better of two bad choices."

"Or maybe they just like being in power."

"Well, yeah. There's that, too."

"And something else, Chord."

"Hmm?" He's kissing more than just my temple now, and his hands . . .

"What if the Surround's already figured out their own cure for sterility and they are actually using it?"

"Maybe they have . . . maybe not . . . I don't know . . ."

"Auden told me he and Innes are going to secretly work on piecing together the rest of that coded file. To try to re-create the cure the Board hid away all those years ago so they can fix everyone—fix *us,* if we wanted . . ."

"Okay. But, West, just . . . stop talking. . . ."

He nudges me until we're both lying down again, our limbs all wound up together. Aware of my injuries as always, he gently holds my wrist down with one of his hands. His other goes for the rest of me. His mouth all over, making me forget the deep ache in my palm, ignore it entirely so that touching him is as easy as it ever was.

Later, it takes us a few minutes to untangle ourselves from my bandages that came loose.

Chord's voice is husky as he murmurs an apology, retying the gauze around my hand. I don't miss the quiet laugh there, even though I'm sleepy again and watching him with eyes that are already half shut.

He sits up, leans over, and takes something from one of the

desk drawers. And it's only when he places it in front of me on the bed that I'm suddenly wide awake, my heart thumping wildly again.

It's nearly identical to mine, the one he once made for me, but not quite. This one serves another purpose, so Chord had to use different pieces.

But I have no doubt what it is.

A key-code disrupter.

And a choice.

ACKNOWLEDGMENTS

My agent, Steven Chudney, for his continuous guidance, encouragement, and hard work. Thank you so much for making all the things happen. None of this would be possible without you.

My editor, Chelsea Eberly, because she never fails to amaze me with her wisdom, generosity, and insightfulness. Thank you, always, for making everything I write better. You are truly wonderful.

The fantastic people at Random House Children's Books for helping bring *Divided* to life: Mallory Loehr; Alison Kolani and her copyediting team; Lauren Donovan, my publicist; graphic artist Michael Heath, designer Nicole de las Heras, and Barbara Cho in production for creating *Divided*'s beautiful cover; John Adamo and the marketing department; and Joan Demayo and her sales team. Thank you all so very much.

Ellen Oh, thank you for being such a brilliant and incredible friend while we continue to navigate this publishing thing together. We need to meet up and eat donuts. Please keep writing fabulous books.

Andrew Fukuda, Elana Johnson, Mindy McGinnis, and Kasie West: You guys absolutely rock. Thank you so much for all the support. All of your books look awesome on my bookshelves, by the way. I need more of them.

Emma Pass, my lovely and talented author friend, for you: SMOTE. In caps, of course.

The Lucky 13s and Friday the Thirteeners, because where would I be without all of you?

Ash Guevarra, Elizabeth Salas, and Netchanok Phungsuk, thank you for keeping me laughing while I work, for all the enthusiasm and kindness.

Thank you, ONE OK ROCK, for making the music that you do. I wrote and edited much of *Divided* while listening to all of your albums. You make each and every one of my writing days awesome.

My tumblr and OORer buds. There are way too many of you to write here, but you guys are the best. You really, truly are.

Wendy Wong, my sis. Because we are both ridiculous together and know it. Let's keep going to concerts all over the world.

And much love, always, to Bak and Hing, Ray and Peggy, Heather and Terry, Ashley and Dallas. THANK YOU.

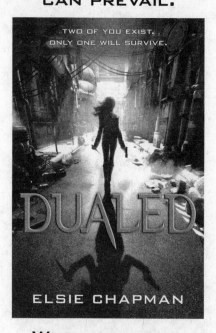

FROM DUALED

The doorbell rings. I barely hear it over the sound of running water.

Who could it be? Not Chord; I told him weeks ago I wanted to walk to school from now on. By myself.

He went quiet, and from the look in his eye I knew he was as upset as he was angry. But he didn't argue. As much as he understood that it was hard for me to see him because of what happened to Luc, he was also still struggling with the fact that I was a striker. That right or wrong, whatever I needed couldn't be found with him. Which made it hard for him to see me, too.

My eyes dart over to the clock above the stove. Nearly nine. I finish washing the specks of blood from my hands and turn off the water. Glance at the switchblade on the counter I was in the middle of cleaning.

It must be something important. I don't think Chord would come by otherwise. Not after how we left each other last time, when I refused to get into his car for school.

I kick my open bag out of the way as I run from the kitchen, reminding myself that I still need to throw something in there for lunch. At the same time, I yank my sleeves down over my wrists, poking my thumbs through the holes I've cut out. The motion is almost second nature now. At school, and around Chord especially, I'm always sure to hide my marks.

Doorbell again.

And when I open the door, it's not Chord standing there after all, but an Operator from the Board.

The way he's dressed tells me instantly he's a Level 3—standard assignment policy. Still rising in the ranks, they're the ones sent out to deliver the news to idles that they're now actives. Clad in dark gray from head to toe, from the cuffs of his trousers to the tweed epaulets on the shoulders of his jacket. A slip of silk in the left front chest pocket is the lone splash of color. The bright red of poppies and pomegranates and fresh blood, it's the signature color of this particular Level within the Board.

So numb. Still, I take in every detail.

The morning sun hits his scalp, bare from the required daily shave. Nails trimmed to the very quick and buffed to a mild shine. No jewelry of any kind, of course—that would speak of some individuality. And his eyes are intentionally and carefully blank, just as they have been trained to be.

The tips of his gray shoes are slightly scuffed.

How is it possible the Board missed that when they sent him out? I wonder dazedly. Even for a Level 3, it's important to maintain the uniform to the most exacting, demanding degree. It has to be all the legwork, I tell myself. As early as it is, I'm probably not the first assignment he's had to deliver today.

"West Grayer?" the Operator asks. His voice is bland, stuck in neutral, without an inkling of personality.

I've been told that when it finally happens, it's like watching the whole world go dim, all lights extinguished with one swift snuff. That suddenly I won't be able to breathe, as though I am already dying. That most of me will freeze up, not wanting to deal—neither charging nor hiding but just trying to make the inevitable go away.

That's what they said it would be like. But they were wrong.

It's Chord's face in my mind. A horrible, bone-deep surety that I will never get to know more of him than what I already know. And it's far from enough.

It's anguish over my lost family, cutting through me like a blade. So unfair, that they all died first. What could I have done to have it be so unfair?

It's the face of my Alt staring back at me. My own face.

I am going to die.

"West Grayer?"

I jerk my head in a nod. Blink myself back and stare at him. "Yes. I'm her. I'm West."

He holds his cell to my face at eye level, and a flash of light blinds me for a few seconds, followed by a searing flash of heat across my pupils. Then activation software in the device beeps to signal that my assignment number has been properly triggered.

My eyes, now spiraled with a sequence of numbers that I share with my Alt. Wherever she is at this moment, I know her own Level 3 Operator is right there with her.

"Cell, please," the Operator says.

My hand slowly pulls my cell from my pocket and passes it over. I can see the blood still staining the beds of my fingernails, crescents of evidence of last night's strike. I ended up having to use one of my blades—up close, not over a distance, the idea of throwing still too raw for me to try again—which always leaves more of a mess than the gun does. Getting home super-late meant having to clean up this morning. I put away the gun and the two blades I didn't use last night.

He holds my cell up to his own so it can receive my assignment details. "You'll find everything you need in the file," he says. Another beep. Passes my cell back to me. "As per Board rules, please be sure to read it in full."

Somehow I make myself nod.

The Operator punches something into his cell to close the document and relay to the Board a successful assignment delivery. He neatly tucks his cell away.

"West Grayer, as of this moment, you have exactly thirty-one days to complete your assignment. If at thirty-two days it has not been completed by either you or your Alt, your Alternate code will self-detonate."

I nod again. All I can do.

"Be the one, be worthy."

With that, he's gone, a gray phantom. Only the one dab of blood over his heart remains vivid enough in my mind for me to know he was real.

So that's it. I have my assignment. It's the last thing I would imagine to be possible: that at fifteen, I'd be both an active Alt and a striker.

Though only one is by choice.

I stumble away from the door, heading somewhere else, anywhere else. My eyes dully take in the sight of my bag, still in the middle of the floor, still waiting for a lunch, on a day that is not going to happen as planned.

Get moving, West. You know you have to leave if you want a chance. It's my voice in my head . . . except there are traces of Luc, too . . . all my family, Baer . . . Chord.

I know all the stats, the numbers, the odds. As a striker,

especially. But I'm suffocating now, and none of that seems so important anymore. Safety was being in an assassin's world, staying in the dark, memories gone mute, when it was never me but some other Alt about to die.

I return to the kitchen, study the switchblade I was cleaning just before. There's still blood where the blade meets the handle, deep in the joint. I wonder if I can scrub it away if I try hard enough, long enough. Try to make it disappear before it seeps too far inward.

I turn the water back on, hold the switchblade beneath the flow.

There's a loud banging at the front door before it crashes open. Chord's rushing toward me, his dark eyes meeting mine, and I know what he sees. As good as I might be at denial, it's impossible in the face of his reaction.

"You shouldn't be here, West," he whispers roughly. "Why are you still here?"

I shudder at the sound of his voice. If feelings alone could save a life, neither of us would ever be in danger.

"West, what are you doing?" He takes in the running water, the sink, the blade. "I just saw an Operator leaving your house!" He turns the tap off with a hard twist of his hand.

I breathe out and dry the switchblade with the tail of my shirt before folding it up and tucking it into the front pocket of my jeans. There it is again—that same mix of pain and pleasure at having him so close. "You're going to be late for school, Chord," I say to him.

"Don't mess around, West!" he says, nearly yelling. "What's wrong with you?"

"Nothing." There is no real thought behind my answer. Just rote movements of lips, tongue, air. His hair is wild, his mouth a harsh, savage line. "I'll be fine."

He walks over to my bag and upends it onto the floor.

My mouth drops open. "Hey, Chord, wait. . . ."

But he's already halfway up the stairs, empty bag in hand. The last time he was here, he demanded I shoot for him before he would leave. What does he want from me this time before he's safe and free of me?

Chord is still moving, and as I scuttle after him I pass my parents' bedroom. An image of the remainder of my father's sleeping pills, the bottle still in the medicine cabinet, flashes in my mind. The pills he intentionally took all the way to his death, already more than halfway there after my mother died as a PK. For her to survive to be a complete, only to be killed anyway, was too much for him to wrap his head around.

But then Chord's in my bedroom, and all thoughts of the pills dissipate.

I walk in to see that he's tossed the bag on top of my bed before ripping open the door to my closet. I close my eyes at the clink of cheap wire hangers being moved around, the shuffle of stuff falling off the shelves and hitting the floor. Each sound is a testament to Chord's frustration, his fear.

Sweaters, jackets, jeans, all landing on my bed to create a small mountain. He throws a pair of shoes across the room. Another pair lands on my desk, sending a pile of sketch pads flying. They tip over one of the pails I use to hold pens and brushes and tubes of paint. More than a few of these roll off and hit the ground.

"What are you doing?" I say to his back. Though I know exactly what he's doing. It's what I should have already done.

He turns around and glares at me. "What do you think I'm doing?"

"Get out of my closet, Chord," I say, my voice mechanical even to my own ears. "Stop messing around with my stuff."

"I can't even look at you right now," he says, his disgust too great to hide. "Here." He pushes the bag at me. "Pack it. Take what you think you'll need. I'll give you as much cash as I have with me, to buy whatever else later. Just pack it and get away from here." I crush the bag with my hands before letting it fall to my feet.

"I don't need your money," I tell him through numb lips. "I've been working, remember?"

The reminder of my striker status only upsets him further. "I know you're too smart to touch whatever you've got, if you've been putting it away. Not unless you want it to show up on the Alt log."

He's right, of course. The Alt log is the Board's database for an active's movements. Once an assignment goes live in the system, all transactions require an Alt's eyes to be scanned. The information—assignment number, location, time—gets fed right into the Alt log. Active Alts can then access this data from the terminal station, Kersh's checkpoint during assignments.

I'm live as of this morning. Bank transactions of any kind will need an eye scan now. And that would give my Alt her first clue . . . to where I've been, where I'm going, where I might be.

I can be Dire's highest-paid striker, and it won't make a bit of difference. Apart from the handful of bills I stashed in my dresser after last night's strike, I'm cleaned out. So wrong and stupid to think I was even *close* to being ready—

Chord grabs the bag from where it's still lying at my feet.

He starts shoving in fistfuls of clothes. "West, *move*! What are you waiting for? *Her?* You want a personal introduction or something?"

I can only shake my head. My own anger is starting to simmer, kindled by Chord's rage. "No, I—"

"I have no idea what's going on, why you're still here. Why we're even discussing this. But you're running out of time. Did you even bother to read the assignment details on your cell?"

"Yes." The weight of the cell in my pocket seems to double, heavy with the lie.

Chord's eyes narrow, and he grimaces. "You haven't, have you? You don't know how far away she is—or how close. For all you know, she could be here any minute, if she's managed to do what you haven't."

"You know they never decide that fast. They always—"

"*We* did, West. Remember? We decided right away to find my Alt."

And Luc died, didn't he?

"What we did wasn't typical," I insist, pushing away the memory of that day, that room. "Most new actives take a while to decide—"

"West, you really want to talk numbers now?" Chord looks down, sees the slim bulk of my cell in my jeans pocket. He drops the half-filled bag, holds out his hand. "Let me read it, if you won't," he says roughly. "You can't wait any longer."

I don't move. My nerves sing and thrum, beating back more panic. A flashback to us in that restaurant in the Grid, me reading his assignment, me forcing him to bend, me being the one who let his Alt get the first shot.

"West, pass me your cell," he says, his voice grim. "Don't make me beg."

"If you leave, I'll do it, I promise," I say to him. I don't let myself think about whether I mean it. Anything to get him away from me . . . from her.

His face darkens, goes tight. Quick as I've ever seen him move, he reaches for me.

"Chord, don't!" I shove him away, his determination to help me.

He steps back, runs his hands through his hair. Black fire in his eyes. "None of it is going to mean anything if she gets here first. So move!"

"I said I'll do it!" I yell back at him.

He grabs me by the arm, harder than he probably knows, swearing under his breath. "I was beyond scared the day I got mine. I started thinking that it maybe *wasn't* supposed to be me, that I wasn't meant to win. And it was you who made us go down there to find my Alt. Not me, not Luc—*you*, West. I miss that person." He drops his hand, and it squeezes into a fist at his side. "That's who you have to be again."

Chord's words cut through me, an echo of what I already know. But in whatever way I might have saved his life, I also ended Luc's.

"It's okay, Chord," I say to him, calm again. "I'll do it on my own . . . when I'm ready. I told you, I don't want you here, remember? I don't need you." *Hurt him so he'll want to leave.*

"West—"

I push him. *"Go!"* My voice breaks, and I can't say anything else.

Silence in the room, thick with our breathing. Then he's gone.

I stand there, frozen by the need to keep time from moving forward. To stop the beginning of the end. But I can feel it anyway. I'm being drawn closer to my Alt and her to me. Only three outcomes possible: my end, or hers—or both.

A shiver racks me, even with the light shining in. The morning sun is much higher now, the day crawling closer toward afternoon. Then it'll be evening, then night, and it'll start all over again, thirty more times.

I can no more stop what has to happen than I can keep the earth from spinning.

And I have less than seven hours before it's dark.

I dump the freshly packed contents of my bag back onto the bed.

Chord has picked all the wrong things, of course. He never feels the cold like I do. I need layers, not bulk. The test comes in a few weeks, closer to winter, when the temperatures drop steeply at night.

If I make it that long.

I stuff thermals into my bag. A thicker fleece pullover to double as a jacket. A lightweight shell for rain. A pair of jeans, because although denim's heavy, it's also warm and sturdy. Socks and underwear, enough to last me for a few days, so I won't have to wash or steal more right away.

I bend over, pick up the pens and brushes and tubes of paint that fell from my desk, and tuck them back into the pail I set upright. Pile up my sketch pads again.

Then I get down on my hands and knees, and from underneath the bed I pull out my old jewelry box. Ehm gleefully claimed it as her own years ago, but after she died, I took it back, a part of her mine again.

Carefully, I lift the lid and move aside the old shirt I tossed in there to hide the real treasure.

Inside is Luc's gun—*my* gun—cleaned and ready for the next job. Beside it is Aave's old knife roll, what I now use to hold my own collection of blades. They're nothing fancy, but more than adequate.

I'm still not as good with a blade as they were—Aave, especially, who was at the top of his class. But I'm getting better, stronger. No longer does my blade catch when slashing. No longer does my wrist seize up with the quick motion. Years of training with my brothers, coupled with my work as a striker, all to prepare for something that will last no more than seconds.

Only with my aim am I less than I should be. My weak spot, what nature's decided to make me work for, forcing me to go against the tide just to keep up.

The knife roll—minus the one blade still in my jeans pocket and the other that I slip into my jacket pocket—goes into my bag. The gun I put into my jacket's other pocket. Together, they'll be what keeps me alive. Not food, not clothes, not money. What will any of that amount to when I finally see her? When she sees me?

It's habit that has me going through the rest of the house, turning off lights, pulling down blinds, and locking all the windows and the back door. In the garage I drape drop cloths over the largest of my father's factory belt servicing tools, his off-site building components, his programming tablet. After securing the heavy metal door to the driveway, I return to the kitchen and wipe out the sink and throw away the milk I find in the back of the fridge. Little things like that. Normal things.

And that's it. I'm done saying good-bye to my home . . . and it didn't break me. I guess it really is just a house now. A case made of concrete and wood and drywall. I've been living here, but it's been long empty in every way that counts. From Aave's death onward, life has seeped from the walls like blood from a wound, refusing to stop until there's no more blood to bleed. It's finally dry. *I'm* dry.

I open the front door and step outside. Lock the door behind me by punching in the key code.

He's sitting on the bottom step, and I've been moving without really seeing for so long that I nearly fall over him. At the sight of him an ache shoots through me from head to toe. Maybe it's because I truly thought he'd left, but the depth of it catches me off guard, leaves me winded.

"Chord." I go down the stairs to stand next to him, my eyes locked on his face. "What are you still doing here?"

He gets to his feet. "Thought I'd stay until I knew you were ready to go. Safe."

I shift the shoulder straps of the bag. Already it feels too heavy on my back. I packed too much. "What made you think I was going to leave anytime soon? I never said I was ready. You might have ended up waiting all day."

A quick flash of a grin that's loving and bleak and desperately unhappy, and I know the sight of it is going to haunt me for a long time. "You've always been ready for this, West," he says. "You just forgot for a bit there, that's all."

I can't think of anything to say, but somehow it's okay. The silence between us isn't awkward or tense, but almost trembling and fragile, a haunting kind of vulnerability where we're just happy to be together and not wanting to think about anything else.

A few seconds, and then it has to be over. "Chord, I have to go—"

"Take this," he says abruptly. He holds out his hand. I can see a bunch of bills there, a cell. And a flimsy black strip I don't recognize, about the length of my hand.

"I don't need your money," I tell him, shaking my head.

"You will. C'mon, don't be stupid. Take what you can get. Being stubborn's not going to help you anymore."

"You should keep it, Chord. You don't know what you might need it for."

"I need it for this. Will you quit finding reasons to argue with me and just take it?" He lifts my hand and forces the money, cell, and strip into my palm. He says nothing about the sleeve I've got pulled over it, even though he knows what it's hiding.

"What's with the cell?" I ask him. "It's not yours."

"No, it's just an extra one I had lying around. I was just . . . messing with it. You know how you always bug me about having all that tech stuff in the house."

"Well, your room *does* look like a parts shop."

He smiles. "Anyway, keep it on you as a backup, in case something happens to yours. It's bare bones, but it should work well enough for texting and calling."

I hold up the black strip. The material is more mesh than solid, a fine web of the thinnest black wire I've ever seen. "And this?"

"It's a key code disrupter."

"That doesn't really tell me much, Chord."

"It's for bypassing locks," he says. "For when you need to get inside somewhere. Or if you just need to get out of sight . . . hide."

"How does it—"

"Hold it between your wrist and the lock faceplate. It'll read the chips in your marks, scramble them, and temporarily mess up the lock's key code. The broken signals will unlock the door. Quieter and faster than having to force your way in."

"Oh. Thanks for thinking of that."

"I didn't really have a choice."

I don't know how else to ease his worry, so I carefully zip it into one of the outer pockets on the side of my bag for easy access. I tuck the cell into the main compartment, the money into my jeans pocket. Just by feel I can tell it's too much, but still not enough.

Suddenly I'm unable to look away from him. When will I see him next? Whenever it is, it will be too soon. I don't want him near me at all. Not while I'm a walking target.

"So let's go, then," he says.

I go cold all over. "What are you talking about?"

His eyes are hard now. Gleaming against the sunlight as they scan my face. "I'm going with you."

I laugh, though there's no humor in it at all. "No way."

"Why wouldn't I? There's no reason for me to stay here."

"School." I'm scrambling, grasping. "They would notice if you just stopped showing up."

Chord shrugs. "I'm over fifteen," he says simply. "I can just tell admin I'm opting out to work somewhere." He takes a deep breath. "And Luc would have wanted—"

"Luc again? Chord, I told you, you don't need to do this for him. *I* don't need you to do this." Even as the words leave my mouth, Luc's request echoes in my head. How he wanted me to promise him I wouldn't keep Chord in the dark, that I wouldn't shut myself off from him.

I press a hand to my chest. There's a pain that comes with the memory of his voice. And, worse, with the realization that I'm not going to be able to keep my promise to him, after all.

I'm sorry, Luc. But you're already gone, and Chord's not.

"He wouldn't have wanted you to go it alone," Chord says. "Not if you didn't have to. And, West . . . I told him, you know?" His voice is husky, full of the same memory that's in my head, full of purpose. "As he was dying, I told him I would. How can I fail him now? I can't screw up again. So I'm coming with you."

I know that voice . . . and I know I have to hurt him some more. Because as hardheaded as Chord is, his stubbornness is nothing compared to mine. And I've become a very good liar these past few months.

"Fine." I make sure to sound ungrateful about it. It's what he would expect, and I can't afford to have him thinking any-thing else is up. "Keep an eye out while I run in and grab a bag for you. No way you're making me carry all this by myself if you're coming with me."

"Time." Chord's watch instantly processes his order, spits out the numbers in a modulated burst. Nearly eleven in the morning. I think of Luc's watch, carefully strapped around my own wrist.

He frowns, knowing I've already lost a couple of hours, and says to me, "Okay, but be quick, all right? We want to get a good head start."

I don't let myself look at him, as much as I want to. It would be written all over my face. What he doesn't know, what he can't know—that for me, this has to be good-bye.

I run back into the house and keep going straight through

until I'm leaving again, this time out the back door at the other end. If I stop for even a second, I will go back, hold on to Chord, and not let go until someone is dead: my Alt, me, or Chord, somehow caught in the middle.

I step out onto the porch, lock the door behind me, and silently cross the length of the yard until I'm at the back fence.

Three boards over from the left. I can hardly dare to believe that I still remember.

I count them with my fingers. One, two, three. The third cedar slat wiggles slightly; it has more give than the others, just as it always has. I slide it over until there's a gap in the fence. It's no more than a foot and a half wide, but I know I can squeeze through. There is no choice but to squeeze through.

For one horrible second, I'm stuck, the sheer bulk of my bag catching on the sides. But I work it free and replace the loose board so the fence looks whole again.

I'm moving fast across the neighbor's yard now—past the large sugar maple cradling the old tree house in the back, along the side of the main house, through the tangle of bushes at the front—to come out on another street altogether. Chord's in a hurry. He'll be heading inside any second to see what's taking me so long. And I can't risk his seeing me.

My eyes burn as I run down the street, and soon I'm blinded with tears. Throat on fire from a withheld scream, chest tight with agony.

I'm sorry, Chord. Stay safe. Stay away from me.

31901059441198